House of Fate

House of Fate

∞

Richard Leighland

Wagoner Oklahoma

Cover art and design by AZ Designs
image elements courtesy of:
evilico-inc, Shahin Khalaji, and Oleksandr Akulenko

ISBN: 978-1-947035-57-7

Published by AZ Literary Press
an imprint of AZ Entertainment Group, LLC

For inquiries, including bulk orders, please contact:
AZ Entertainment Group LLC
PO BOX 854
Wagoner, OK 74477-0854

Email: info@az-entertainmentllc.com
Website: www.az-entertainmentllc.com

Second Edition

Printed in the United States of America

To my favorite person

Preface to the Second Edition

I finished *House of Fate* back in 2016, and a small independent publisher, Winding Hall Publishers, released it in 2018. They were great and were a joy to work with, but they eventually went out of business and, subsequently, the book went out of print. Now, thanks to AZ Literary Press, it's back, and I think it's better than ever in this second edition.

This isn't just a straight reprint. The team at AZ Literary Press put a lot of time and effort into making the book better. They took care of some small errors, tightened it up a bit, and a couple of scenes have been restored to my original intent. Since the first edition was published, I feel I now write gooder—so this book *is* gooder!

The story itself hasn't changed. Yeah, okay, it's labeled horror, but it's much more. It's a story of love, friendship, fate, and the human struggle: living our lives, looking for where we fit in, finding love, meaningful relationships, and just feeling like we matter in the grand scheme of things. Harry isn't an expert in anything. He's just a normal, everyday guy who happens to find himself in a strange (and scary) situation. Aside from the house, he's just like us.

There's a point in the novel where Harry happens upon a bottle of *Sa-Tan-Ic Laxatives*. This is real. It was the flagship product of the Sa-Tan-Ic Medicine and Manufacturing Company, based in Wichita, Kansas, which trademarked its brand in 1915. If you happen to come across a bottle—or anything—*I want it. Bad.* Feel free to send it in care of my publisher. I'd appreciate it. And if there's anything in it, my bowels might appreciate it too.

Thanks for giving this story another look. I've enjoyed the ride so far, and I'd be happy to have you along on this leg of the tour.

Enjoy!

—Richard Leighland

Epigraph

Places have a life of their own. All kinds of places: forests, rivers, deserts. Houses and buildings have lives of their own as well. They have their own personalities, their own quirks and individual stories to tell, exactly like people do.

Modern places don't really have that kind of life anymore. In the past, houses seemed to reflect the individuality of their builders and owners. Now, material conformity has drained that personality. Today's places feel as plain and dull as possible; lifeless and unoffensive. Perhaps a reflection of their modern creators.

You know it when you come across a place with a story. You can feel her spirit. It's like an old whore, worn out and used up, but oh, the stories she can tell. They're tales for everyone and no one at the same time.

You've heard the adage, if these walls could talk? I'm here to tell you they most certainly can. All you need is to be still and listen.

Chapter 1

I can't pinpoint the very first moment I was called to Her, nor can I tell how it all started. It could have been subliminal; heard offhand in someone's conversation, a glimpse of Her in a dream, or whatever. What I can say is I was drawn to Her the first moment I became aware. It wasn't Her beauty that drew me, no, though you could see a hint of it, somewhere in the long ago.

I'm no architect, or even a carpenter, but I could tell She must have been built sometime in the nineteenth century. Her walls were crumbled with age and rot; windows shattered. Her front door, once heavy and regal, hung off the hinges and served as a buffet for termites. She was big, larger than anything I had seen before, outside of pictures. Even in the ruin, it was obvious someone had loved Her, once. Had taken care in building the gables and walls, now only a dark shadow of Her past. There was a fragility to Her, as if She would crumble into dust and disappear if I merely brushed against Her.

Even in Her present condition, She stood tall and proud amongst the ancient oaks and wildflowers growing around Her and they lent Her some semblance of life. Birds and butterflies were Her only neighbors, and gave Her movement and song, a peaceful co-existence. It was easy to imagine Her in Her previous glory.

My curiosity was piqued and ran wild as I felt Her beckon me to draw near. Her pull was irresistible. I succumbed and pushed aside my fear of confronting the unknown.

Part of me whispered, "You don't know what's in there," but I ignored it and slowly climbed the front steps toward the arched doorway.

At the threshold, I shivered in the autumn air. "Here goes," I said and took a breath, held it and plunged through, as though I were diving off a cliff into the sea.

A warmth enveloped me as I crossed. It felt like the embrace of a lover. Dust motes danced around me in shafts of fading light as if awakened from a long slumber. Ahead of me stood a wide staircase with carved oak banisters. At its apex was a broken stained glass window, the frame toothed with jagged shards of glass, tipped with red. I wondered what it might have depicted.

I hesitated as I put my foot on the bottom stair. The carpeting was moth eaten and worn through in places. It telegraphed omi- nous warnings the wooden steps beneath might be weak and rot- ted. Under normal circumstances, when presented with a stair- case, I get an impulse to run up to the top and slide down the rail like an eight-year-old, but not today. This time, the impulse was overcome by a strong sense of self-preservation. I excused it by saying the rooms were probably personal and not places I ought to be nosing around in. It looked like there was plenty to explore downstairs anyway.

The foyer was large and had been built to impress. The air was musty, infused with the strangely pleasant smell of old wood. Around me, heavy doors closed off the other rooms, as if they hid secrets. The floors were made of thick planks which creaked beneath my feet despite the tattered rugs covering them. Along the walls, broken furniture rested between the doors, and thick drapes, faded by sun and time, covered tall windows on either side of the front door while sunlight punched through holes in the fabric. Columns stood on both sides of the staircase like sentinels and supported the floor above. The space on the left was cavernous, inexplicably darker than the rest of the room. And, just as inexplicably, I walked into it.

My foot caught a small object and sent it skittering across the floor until it pinged against a brass umbrella holder. I stopped and glanced toward the sound. An old-fashioned key caught a glint of sunlight, and I bent to pick it up. It bore a polished shine, as if it had just fallen out of someone's pocket. I stupidly looked around to see who might have dropped it, but of course, I was alone.

I gazed at the key in my hand. It almost felt like an invitation.

I'm not sure I have the words to describe what I felt. Something was calling to me. Not in words, but from deep inside my core. It was almost like a compulsion. Whether it originated within myself, or was planted by someone—something—else, I couldn't say.

Whatever it was, it was telling me to seek. To seek within this house.

So I did.

Chapter 2

What was I supposed to be looking for? I had no plan, no system, and why should I? I had no idea if finding anything would put me at risk. I realized I was inviting chaos to waltz right in and jerk me around like a puppet. But it didn't matter. The compulsion to search the house was too strong.

I slipped the key into my pocket and went to the double door near the end of the foyer. The knob turned easily and the door opened without a sound. I entered, and left it open.

The dining room stretched long and narrow. Eight place settings sat atop a lace cloth, yellowed with age. China cabinets lined the walls, alongside a Victorian sideboard topped with crystal decanters and fruit bowls, untouched for untold years. A fireplace was set into a wall, cold and empty. Dusty oil paintings of fruit and gardens hung on peeling, water-stained wallpaper. A chandelier hung over the table, its crystal teardrops, once sparkling, now festooned with cobwebs.

Beneath the layers of dust were the remnants of an elegant life; the moment before dinner would be served.

I walked around and ran my fingers through the dust on the sideboard. Long, clean trails exposed the dark wood beneath. I felt like an intruder in a life I didn't belong.

I heard a piece of metal clatter onto wood behind the swinging door at the end of the room.

"What the hell?" I said.

Only half-convinced my imagination was running amok, I carefully approached the door and pushed through.

I was in a kitchen. An iron cauldron hung inside a large stone fireplace, above the ashes of a long-dead fire. A pot lay on the wooden floor. It looked heavy. Had it really just fallen?

Through a dusty window, a crumbling smokehouse and icehouse stood before a background of thick woods.

Beneath the window, I saw her. A woman in a threadbare, dirty dress huddled against the sinks. The dress seemed to swallow her. Her dark hair covered her face, so I couldn't see her expression, but her shoulders trembled in silence.

"Hello?" I asked, hesitant to get closer. Could she even hear me? Was she just a figment of my imagination?

She didn't respond, so I tried again. I didn't know who she might be, a servant, or a member of the household, but I couldn't leave her like that, bent with misery weighing on her.

I approached, knelt down, and laid my hand on her shoulder. The warmth of the kitchen contrasted sharply with her icy skin. I fought the instinct to pull away.

"Are you okay?" I said again.

She raised her head. Impulsively, I brushed her thick hair from her face. I braced myself for something malformed, something ugly. I didn't know what to expect.

It surprised me she was beautiful, even with sorrow twisting her features. She looked young—seventeen, maybe twenty at most, though grief could have aged her a few years.

She looked at me without fear. Her eyes, large and moist, showed only a deep sadness. Her mouth moved in a silent language I could not hear.

"I...I don't understand," I said as she persisted in silence.

She glanced past me, toward the door. A subtle fear crept into her eyes before they met mine with a plea I couldn't interpret.

"I don't know what you're telling me," I said.

Frustration clouded her face. She didn't offer any vocalized affirmations, so I remained confused.

"I wish I could understand you," I said sadly. "I want to help."

I had no clue what I could do, or what she was trying to tell me, but my words seemed to satisfy her somewhat. Her hair fell back over her eyes as she bowed her head and silently sobbed again.

I stood and watched her. Who was she? What had made her so sad?

"What am I doing here?" I asked as I closed my eyes and grasped the sink. I wished there was someone, or something, to tell me what to do.

I sighed and opened my eyes. With a sharp gasp, I stumbled back and caught myself on the table behind me. I looked at the sink warily, not sure what I had seen. I crept back to the sink and reluctantly looked inside.

I could have sworn I saw the severed head of a gray-bearded man, but it was only the bottom of a pot half-submerged in brown, rancid water. My mind refused to let go of the image—glazed-over eyes, a swollen, lolling tongue.

I searched for the girl, afraid I might have kicked her when I lurched back, but she wasn't there. Yet I still saw her in my mind, huddled, miserable, alone. My heart twisted at the thought. I had no idea what I could do, only I had to help her. Maybe the house held answers.

I pushed through the door back into the dining room, paused and glanced back.

She was gone.

I sensed something different in the dining room, but couldn't discern what. I looked around to find the source of my unease.

Then it struck me.

The table was clean. Not a speck of dust or anything. It was just the table, everything else was dingy and dusty, just like before. Maybe it was my mind playing tricks on me, but no. It was definitely there.

Explain *that,* I thought. Explain a girl who vanished, just like the severed head that appeared for an instant in the sink.

Shit. I might be having the worst flashback of my life, except it wasn't my life.

I re-entered the foyer. Nothing had changed. The exquisitely carved grandfather clock still stood by the staircase, with a handsome roll-top desk beside it. I inspected the clock and admired the craftsmanship, pleased it was still working. Its mechanism emitted a clear, mesmerizing tick-tock. I checked my watch and found they were synced as the clock struck the hour with a deep, resonant gong.

I ran my fingers over the wood of the dusty desk, over the textured slats. There was a key set in the lock. Curious as always, I turned it and rolled the door back.

The desk looked ready for use with an inkpot and pens resting on a blotter; a stack of paper nearby. The drawers slid open smoothly, as if freshly oiled. There were some ledgers and documents that didn't hold my interest, so I closed it, and slipped the key in my pocket. Did it make me a thief? Who exactly would miss it?

To my left was a door. "Blast, locked" I muttered as the doorknob refused to yield. I gave it another try, but it just rattled uselessly under my grip. Disappointment washed over me. I was about to give up when I remembered the key I found earlier. I dug it out of my pocket and slid it into the lock. To my relief, it turned and the bolt clicked open.

The room was cloaked in darkness. Heavy velvet drapes blocked all traces of light. I left the door open and, as I waited for my eyes to adjust, searched for a lamp or candle. I was about to give up when a dim blue glow flickered at the corner of my eye.

I turned toward the source. I expected it to vanish, but it lingered, like a ghost, in front of a large bookshelf. I cursed myself for not having a small flashlight clipped to my keychain. However, my old silver Zippo, my constant companion, nestled in my pocket.

I pulled it from my pocket and flicked my thumb across the wheel. The familiar click sounded, and the flame jumped from the wick on the first turn. It had lived up to its promise, a light in the darkness, just as my grandfather had intended when he gifted it to me. Its glow revealed a previously unseen oil lamp on a side table. I removed the glass cover, lighted the wick, and returned the lighter to my pocket, its metal casing still warm against my palm.

The blue light continued to glow, undiminished by the new source of illumination.

A quick survey of the room confirmed it was a study. An imposing mahogany desk stood near the east wall, backed by a pair of bookcases, one of which still held most of its glass panels. Opposite it, a long leather couch stretched along the wall, accompanied by a sturdy chair and a side table with a notebook resting on its surface. A pair of brass gas lamps clung to the walls, their fixtures dulled with age, long unused. Against the north wall, a modest fireplace stood cold, its grate filled with the remnants of long-cooled ash.

The space was masculine, paneled in dark wood, with a worn rug covering the floor. Though dust lay thick on every surface, the room retained an air of quiet dignity—weathered, but not yet surrendered to decay.

I approached the desk, set the lamp down, and eased into the squeaky chair. The leather blotter was worn, its edges curled with age. Two notebooks rested atop it. One lay open, its pages spattered with thick ink, the writing long lost beneath the stains.

A pipe rack sat in the corner. It held half a dozen well-crafted pipes beside a tobacco container. I lifted the lid and caught the sharp scent of molded tobacco, stale and untouched for ages.

Among the pipes, one stood out. A large-bowled meerschaum carved into the horned visage of Pan. Temptation struck. I enjoyed a fine pipe packed with good tobacco, and I had a fondness for the fun-loving satyr. But I resisted. There was no telling where these things had come from, or what fate awaited anyone foolish enough to disturb them.

Especially someone who had already stolen a couple of keys.

I took the unopened notebook from beneath the ink-stained one and flipped it open at random. The handwriting was large and slanted. Methodical, but uneven. In the lamplight, the words stood out clearly. The passage I landed on was undated, but didn't stop me from reading.

> *"James argues psychologists must concern themselves with the functions of thought. I wonder —how does guilt function? Guilt over what, I am unsure. Perhaps Richard's death has stirred it, but that explains only a fraction of the puzzle. There is more, I am certain. The theory warrants exploration. More than one is affected."*

I closed the notebook and frowned. Who was James? Who was Richard? The passage wasn't offering any answers, only questions. The way it was written was deliberate, as if searching. It made me wonder if the author had been a psychologist, someone trying to make sense of things. But of what, exactly?

I didn't dwell on it. There were already too many unanswered questions in this house.

I turned my attention to the desk drawers. The top one held pens and various odds and ends. There was nothing of interest, except another key. I slipped it into my pocket without hesitation.

The bottom drawers contained papers, a few more journals, and a crystal decanter tucked toward the back. The amber liquid inside sat just a quarter full, dark and undisturbed. If it was scotch, it had been sitting there for years. I didn't bother opening it to find out. Instead, I picked up some of the papers and journals and leaned back in the chair and skimmed the pages.

The writer was named Henry Pierce. He was a medical doctor, though his writings suggested a deep fascination with psychology, which he practiced on the side. He was particularly interested in how disease, medication, and drugs affected the mind, along with thought processes and the impact of events on a person. He mentioned a wife and children, but never named them.

Compared to the kitchen incident and the eerie blue light, the journals felt almost dull. I set them on the desk and turned my attention to the shelves. More journals, but also an eclectic mix— medical texts, philosophical treatises, and novels.

A couple of Dickens volumes caught my eye, along with a first edition of *Sister Carrie*—worth a small fortune if I were to sell it. Tempting, but I wasn't ballsy enough to try it.

On the bottom shelf, a book lay flat. I picked it up. *Principles of Psychology*, by William James.

Maybe it was the James mentioned in the journal.

I brushed my fingers over the book spines in hopes I might find something useful, something to tell me more about this place and maybe a clue as to what I was doing here. I started to pull out a volume when a rat skittered over my foot. The book dropped out of my hand as I jumped.

I considered staying longer, but the rat was a dealbreaker. I'm not fond of the dark, but with the light, minimal as it was, I could handle it. But rats? I'm less fond of those.

I told myself I could return later to explore some more. Per - haps the light would be a bit friendlier, and the rat would have found another place to hang out.

I took a deep breath, extinguished the lamp, and shut the study door behind me.

Back in the foyer, I stood at the foot of the stairs, my gaze drawn to the remnants of the stained-glass window above. Through the fractured glass, I could see the restless movement outside. The clouds raced past in the darkness and obscured the stars beyond. Night had settled while I was in Dr. Pierce's study, though it felt like only minutes had passed. My knees ached, and the scent of rain thickened in the air. A storm was closing in.

I didn't know where I was, how I'd ended up here, or even which way home might be. I knew I didn't want to figure it out in the rain. And yet, something about this place made me pause. It wasn't exactly welcoming, but I wasn't sure it was hostile, either. The silence pressed in, neither threatening nor comforting, just... waiting.

I had the uneasy sense that if I stayed, I might uncover something I wasn't ready for, something I would regret knowing.

An eerie tingle ran through me. The thought slipped into my mind, carried by the heavy air. She wanted me to stay.

I could almost hear it in the creak of Her joints, "stay..."

My free will felt under siege. Something—someone—held me back. There were dark secrets hidden in the recesses of the house, and I felt compelled to uncover them all.

I needed to know who the girl was. I needed to understand how to help her. And maybe help myself.

The answers were here. Somewhere.

I looked around the foyer. It felt odd. Every room was closed off with a tightly-shut door and nothing welcomed a visitor. Yet, there was a lure, a haunted, lived-in feeling which emanated from them. Perhaps there weren't supposed to be any surprises. Just ordinary wood and fabrics that had nothing to hide. But it didn't feel like it.

I closed my eyes, hoping to picture the house as it had been—fresh paint, laughter. Life in the rooms.

Nothing came.

I squeezed my eyes tighter and listened. I heard distant thunder with a piano's soulful melody beneath it as it drifted through the air. So faint, it might have been imagined.

With the darkened sky, the bluish tint from the study had grown brighter, imparting a confused feeling of both warmth and detachment. I turned to the wall behind me, where two old portraits hung, veiled with dust. One was of a woman, more handsome than glamorous. Her clothing was dated, and she stood rigidly straight, her hands folded on top of an ornately carved and empty high-backed chair. Her unsmiling eyes drilled into me. It was hard to tell if she was angry, unhappy, or perhaps only jaded. I shivered with an uncomfortable sense the woman was alive inside the painting and disapproved of my presence in her home. Even with the discomfort I felt, I found it hard to break my gaze.

The other portrait depicted two young children, a boy and a girl, no more than a year or two apart in age. It was my impression the children may have belonged to the woman in the other portrait, for they seemed to share similar features. The biggest difference was the children's eyes laughed and danced in innocent abandon; quite a contrast from the woman's cold stare. I wondered if the woman was their mother and if so, why they weren't painted together. Was the father's likeness hanging somewhere else? Perhaps this was the wife and children Dr. Pierce mentioned in the journals.

Throughout my exploration of the downstairs, it never occurred to me to wonder why the house had allowed me to enter, or by what means I had arrived there. Perhaps it was all just a dream.

A strange, interesting dream, but a dream nonetheless.

Perhaps it was not.

I had a sudden, pressing desire to escape; to run away as fast as I could without looking back. It wasn't the approaching storm, tinged with the odor of ozone. No, there was another, unknown reason. I moved quickly toward the front door. I stopped at the threshold and wondered if I would ever be able to find Her again. If this were truly a dream, maybe my unconscious could bring me back, and She would speak to me still. Otherwise, I wouldn't know how to return. Mostly I wondered about the crying girl, the cause of her sadness, and what I could do to relieve her suffering. I assured myself, dream or no, I would help her.

As thunder rolled above the surrounding woodland and wind began to blow a deluge of rain onto the porch where I stood, I remembered I had no idea where I was or how to get home.

Chapter 3

I closed my eyes against a dazzling bolt of lightning. When I opened them, I found myself standing on a sidewalk in downtown Carson, facing a row of businesses and storefronts. It was far from the empty, weedy plot on which the enigmatic house had stood. I was bone dry, even though I had just felt the raindrops hit my face and soak my clothes. I felt lost. I turned around only to come face to face with a blank wall standing between two plate glass windows. Sure, I knew where I was, but it did nothing to quell the feeling. I couldn't explain how I came to be here, at least not without sounding *non compos mentis*.

I was overcome with sadness and regret. She was gone, and I still had no idea how I had gotten there, nor did I know if it were possible for me to go back again. It would have been easy to say it was only a dream, but if it were I would have awakened in my own bed. The only other explanation was that I had taken a stroll in my sleep all the way here from my place, and I didn't care much for the idea. I could have been naked!

I turned back and saw my reflection across the street between the posters of cruise ships and exotic locations in the windows of the travel agency. I looked as tired and as terrible as I felt, but more important, I had all my clothes on. I hoped it was the distance that made me not look so good, but I was sure that closer, where there was more detail to be seen, I probably looked worse.

As I stood on the downtown street, I wondered what I was doing still there instead of going home to wonder in comfort. I caught sight of leather and chrome in the corner of my eye and turned toward it.

It wasn't the motorcycle so much as the rider. I know it's rude to stare, but I honestly couldn't help it. She had started to put on her helmet, but must have sensed me staring at her.

"What, you like the bike, or is it you've never seen a girl ride one before?" she asked.

"I...well, I..." Holy hell. Now what? Got caught staring and now I couldn't get more than two words out of my mouth. "Sorry," I managed feebly.

"Don't be." Her lip curled into a half smile. At least she appeared amused.

I dropped my face. "I wasn't meaning to stare, I really wasn't."

"No?"

I started to look up, but wasn't able to manage. "It's just... you look like someone."

"Like someone you know, maybe?" she asked with humor.

"Yes. No. Not exactly." Damn if I wasn't making an outright fool of myself. "It's not like that."

Although it was true, I couldn't rightly claim any knowledge of "someone." It was just that this girl had an uncanny resemblance to the girl I had seen in the kitchen, sans the tears and oversized dress.

She held her smile. "So, what's your name?

"My name?"

She nodded. "I like to find out the names of people who ogle me."

"But I wasn't!" I was mortified she thought so.

"Oh, sure you were, but it's all right," she said with a dismissive wave of her hand. "So, what's your name?"

"My name?" I repeated. I was totally embarrassed, but couldn't see a way out of it.

"No, the guy standing behind you. His name."

"Oh, I..." I said, as I turned stupidly to see who was standing behind me.

She laughed. "Of course, I'm asking yours.

"Uh, well, my name's Harry. Harry Harrison," I finally blurted out. "What's yours?"

"Jenny Jennings," she said.

"Really?" I asked, like an idiot.

She laughed again, and I foolishly hoped it wasn't at my expense.

"No, not really. Is Harry Harrison your real name?"

"Of course, it's my real name," I said. I know I shouldn't have felt offended, but I did.

"I'm Gwendolyn. Everybody just calls me Gwen," she said with a shrug.

"I like Gwendolyn." I still felt like a dolt, but at least she was still talking to me.

"Yeah?"

I nodded affirmatively as I studied the curb.

"So, do you need a ride somewhere?"

"Oh no, I couldn't," I shook my head and shoved my hands deeper into my pockets.

"Why not?"

"Uh, I'm afraid of motorcycles." Oh, I have sealed my immortal place on the Wall of Lame.

"Why are you afraid of motorcycles?" she asked without condescension.

"I don't know," I said. Yeah, it sounds moronic, but truth is, I

27

really don't. There wasn't any logical reason I could fall back on.

"They're nothing to be afraid of. Not only can they save you a ton in gas money, they're fun to ride."

"Maybe so, but what if you need to pick up groceries?" Why was I trying to argue with a female who was not only beautiful, but actually spoke more than two words to me? The words "get lost" came to mind.

"If I need to pick up groceries, I rent a car."

I looked at her, puzzled. "Really?" Doesn't it defeat the whole purpose of saving gas money? I thought, but didn't add.

She laughed again, and I had the feeling she was having a grand time at the expense of yours truly. Even so, I found I enjoyed hearing her laugh. I can be such a masochist.

"Aren't you a gullible one."

"No, I..." I put my head down again, sure my hair was going to burst into flame.

"I'm not laughing at you, really I'm not," she said.

"Yes, you are," I retorted.

"Yeah, maybe a little. Come on, at least let me give you a ride." She patted another helmet strapped to the bike. "Got an extra, so you can feel a little safer. I promise I won't do any crazy stunts."

"Okay, I guess so." I gave in and took the offered helmet, though it was against my better judgment. I put the helmet on my head and fumbled with the strap.

"Here, let me help you with that," she said.

She reached over and adjusted the strap. I couldn't move, mortified and confused as to how this scenario could still be playing. She didn't even seem to notice. With a final tug, she got on the bike and said, "hop on."

Somehow, I managed to climb onto the seat.

I wasn't sure what to do, so I put my hands lightly on her waist. After all, I didn't want her to think I was some sort of creep.

I'm sure she already thought I was weird.

"You better hang on, or you might fall off.

"Okay," I said, though my hands barely moved.

I'm not going to bite you or anything."

"Really?"

"Why, do you want me to?"

"You're joking," I said.

"You might be gullible, but you catch on quick," she laughed. "Where are you going?"

"Home," I said.

"Where's home?"

"Not too far. Just a few blocks that way." I pointed in the general direction.

She nodded and started her engine, backed up and began smoothly down the street. I lost my inhibitions and gripped her tightly and proceeded to scream and whimper like an infant. (Yes, I am most definitely the king of all that is lame.)

I figured after she dropped me off, I would probably never see her again. If I did, she would turn and go the other way. I'd just be something she'd laugh about with her friends.

"This is it?" she asked, as she pulled into what I called, with humor, my parking lot.

I caught my breath, said "yeah," and got shakily off the bike.

I started to take the helmet off, though I didn't want to. My face was still flushed and I was sure there were the remnants of tears in my eyes. I turned my head and slid the helmet off and ran my arm across my face to wipe away any evidence before I handed her the helmet. I was sure I fooled no one.

She looked around. "So, this is your place, huh?"

Maybe she wasn't impressed. To be fair, there wasn't anything impressive about it, but she seemed a little curious.

"Yeah. Well, I keep an apartment on the third floor." I shuffled my feet in the gravel.

"Are there a lot of apartments?"

"No, not really. Just two on each floor. Well, except for the first. It's just an empty space with kind of an office. Only six."

"You could have just said six."

"I'm sorry."

"Stop saying that."

"I'm sorry," I repeated before I could stop myself. "Oh, damn it."

She smiled, her full lips framing even, white teeth. I wasn't staring, mind you, I just happened to notice when I chanced a quick glance.

"No big deal," she said.

She snatched my pen from my pocket and grabbed my hand.

"What are you doing?" I asked, but didn't protest.

"Shush," she mumbled and jotted a number on the side of my hand, just above the thumb. "Writes first time, every time," she said and slipped the pen back into my pocket.

I stared at my hand. "What's that?" I asked, like the complete dweeb that I am.

"My phone number, silly."

"But, what for?" If I were in front of a wall, I would repeatedly slam my head against it, as hard as I could.

"Umm, so you can call me?"

I must have looked utterly dumbfounded.

"Maybe ask me out?"

Let's forget subtle hints here.

I liked her smile, even if it was at my expense. "What, like a date?"

Head. Wall. Bam! Bam!

"Naturally. I guess it's what boys and girls do. So I hear. That your car? We won't have to take my bike," she said, as she nodded toward my beat-up Pontiac.

"Or maybe you could rent a car," I said. A meager attempt to interject some humor.

"Yes, I could!" She started the bike and wheeled it around. "Call me," she shouted over her shoulder as she revved her engine and rode away.

I wanted to hate her for getting Blondie stuck in my head, but as I watched her disappear, I knew there wasn't any way I could. I liked her immediately, and not only because I found her attractive —which I did, very much so. There was a carefree air about her that made me think she'd be a lot of fun to hang out with. What's more important, she didn't balk at my complete idiocy and my social clumsiness. I'd have to like anyone for that.

It struck me again how much she seemed to favor the girl I had seen in the house. I brushed it aside as a mere coincidence. After all, there wasn't any indication that she had ever experienced the kind of suffering I saw in that girl's face. I supposed I could be wrong. People deal with suffering in individual ways and just looking like someone doesn't mean you've had the same kind of life.

I glanced at the number she had written on my hand. Maybe I would give her a call. I only hoped it was a real number and not just some cruel joke. No, she didn't seem the type.

I headed to my building and walked past my Pontiac. Already, I was embarrassed with the idea of taking her in it on a date. I laughed at the thought. Normally, things like that don't embarrass me. I don't drive often, opting to walk or ride my bike—a bicycle that is—instead. It saves gas and I get exercise at the same time. I'm not interested in saving the environment or anything. The only green stuff I like saving goes in my wallet. I don't make a lot of money, but I do save some, since I work only a few blocks away and buy my staples at the corner grocery store. In fact, there's not much occasion where I need to drive anywhere. I'm content to stick around the area with the occasional junket into the world outside my neighborhood.

I took the entry key out of my pocket and started to unlock the door when I had a sudden sense of déjà vu. I felt the front of my apartment building was similar to the front of the house. Except, of course, my building had an attached door, intact windows, and doesn't stand in an eerie forest.

I was just imagining things. The apartment building was not the house. Gwendolyn was not the girl in the kitchen. I was making connections with things that had nothing to do with each other.

******

I like my building. Always have. Though I don't technically own her, I still feel like she belongs to me. (I always think of buildings as female.) I'm content with her belonging to me in spirit. She's been around a long time, and she has stories. Some are funny, some scandalous, and a couple of scary ones, too. Though she's falling apart now, I've come to love her. Some might say she should be condemned, but for now, at least, she is mine.

I started up the old staircase and listened to the sounds of old wood and pipes. Not many people come by and it's only myself and Mrs. Weatherman living in the building now. Mrs. Weatherman doesn't get out much. She's eighty-six and has outlived everyone who was close to her. At least she has me around to run errands and check in now and then. I've asked her why she doesn't move somewhere she could get around better and be with people. I worry about her taking those stairs when she does get a mind to go out. She just says she likes it here and can mind the stairs. With me around, she doesn't see the point moving somewhere that would be closer to a nursing home than an actual home. I'm flattered she feels that way, and I figure maybe she's right. She's still got all her faculties, that's for sure.

I decided to drop in on her as I got to the second floor, and rapped on her door a couple of times before I let myself in.

"Mrs. Weatherman, you here?" I asked.

"Hmpf, where else would I be? At the movie house? Dancing? Am I here indeed!" Her voice was surprisingly strong, especially from a body so small and frail, but it did not eradicate the beautiful woman she once was. She sat in her rocking chair next to an ancient gas furnace. A piece of quilting lay in her lap while her fingers deftly worked the needle and thread.

"Just thought I'd check up on you before I went up," I said as I stood in the doorway.

"Get in here and shut the door. You're letting the draft in," she said. "You know I don't need any checking up on, Harry. I can manage myself just fine."

"I know you can," I said. She could be stubborn and feisty.

"Why don't you sit down a spell? Would you like a cookie?" she said cheerfully.

The offer of a cookie was tempting, but I declined. "No, thanks, Mrs. Weatherman. If I didn't know any better, I'd think you were sweet on me, offering me cookies and all," I said with a smile.

"Oh posh, I'm old enough to be your grandmother."

"Really? You look younger than my mother," I countered.

She giggled into her hand like a schoolgirl. "I wouldn't let your poor mother hear you say that, so you stop on that now, you flirt."

"She wouldn't mind. Anyway, you love it when I flirt."

"Ah well, it does make me feel young again," she said wistfully.

"You are young."

"Oh, now. I'm a little old lady and I know it."

I laughed. "No. So, is there anything I can do for you? Anything you need?"

"No, no. I have everything and that nice young man, Sean

Hannity, comes on the radio in half an hour."

We chatted for a little while, and then I got up to leave. I didn't want her to miss her show, after all. "You call me if you need any-thing, all right?" I said.

"Of course, I will." Her smile grew wide. It made her look ten years younger.

"Okay, I'll see you later." I headed for the door.

"Such a sweet boy," I heard her say, before I closed the door and started up to my own apartment.

It made me smile. I enjoyed our visits and helping her out. It's not quite the obligation it may seem to be. She gets along fairly well and is in good health. She was here before I moved in and she's made her part of the building her own. It's probably the reason she stays here instead of in some newer place that insists every unit look the same. Apartment owners who allow individual expression are getting to be a rare breed, and retirement homes who let you do it are rarer.

Mrs. Weatherman loves to sew and knit. She's made window curtains and hand-stitched quilts, and her apartment shows the fruits of her efforts. My own apartment is not immune to the Weatherman touch, as I have one of her quilts covering my bed. It's full of color in a design she came up with herself. It is one of my treasures.

The fourth floor of my building is empty and has been for quite some time. No tenants can live there because it's in such a state of disrepair. The floor between the two units actually gave way a while back due to a liquid mishap, and you can see my floor below. I'll go in there from time to time to check up on things, fix what I can when time and money allow, and spray for bugs. I'm always careful, of course. I do it not only because it knocks a bit off my rent now and then, but because it gives me a chance to spend more time with the place.

Today wasn't a day I wanted to tinker around. My timing was

off and I wasn't sure what day it was until I took a look at my watch. I was tired and wanted to lie down. I let myself into my apartment and checked for messages. As usual, I didn't have any. I considered eating a little something, but decided it could wait until after my rest. I undressed, got into bed, and was passed out within minutes.

Chapter 4

Just after sunrise, I awoke refreshed. I couldn't remember ever having slept so well. Perhaps everything had been a dream, and I found myself curiously disappointed at the thought. I wouldn't mind having it again. Maybe next time I would know it wasn't real and wouldn't be so apprehensive.

I shuffled to the kitchen where I spooned instant coffee into my mug, stirred it briskly, and put it in the microwave. There was no point in using the coffee maker unless I was having more than a couple of cups, or had company over. I usually had neither, so it remained unplugged.

I took my mug from the microwave and blew on the coffee before taking the first careful sip. I noticed ink on my hand, somewhat smudged, and I tried to remember what it was. It took me longer than it should have to realize it was Gwendolyn's phone number.

Not a dream, then.

It was mostly rubbed off, but I could still make it out. I spent a few moments feeling stupid before I transferred the number to the notepad stuck on the fridge, lest I forget about it again and wash it into oblivion.

I was a complete and utter idiot, and no man in his right mind should expect to hear from such a girl again. However, I still had hope the number was real and I would have the balls to call it. For now, I just needed to jump into the shower so I could get to work on time.

******

After I arrived at The Bookworm, the used bookstore where I worked, I had a hard time keeping my mind on my duties. Instead of focusing on my job, my thoughts wandered all over the place. They made short stops at places I didn't realize I remembered, and some places I wished I could forget.

It was bad enough Carol, my boss, noticed my abstraction. It wasn't that big a deal, since it was a slow day and there wasn't an influx of merchandise to deal with. It was a good thing too, because I was sure my brain would not be able to handle any challenges today.

Finding the miraculous remnant of the number smudged on my hand made me realize how real all of it was, no matter how improbable. Whether it was Gwendolyn's number or the number for Big Dick's Gay Bar and All Night Picture Show didn't matter. I couldn't remember what I was doing prior to my appearance at the mysterious house, much less how I got there. Surely I wasn't doing anything that could have prompted a blackout. Maybe someone was running around, flashing people with those little wands Mr. Jones and Mr. Smith used in *Men in Black*. Bloody unlikely, that.

My mind had been so preoccupied, Carol had to tell me it was time to clock out. It didn't seem I had been at work for hours.

If only all my days went by as fast and without incident, I thought, as I hopped on my bike and leisurely pedaled home.

My bicycle is much like my car, old and beat up. I guess I could get myself something newer with more gears and such. It isn't anything fancy. It has one gear and I pedal back to brake, but I honestly prefer it this way. It's easy to maintain, which I'm all about. There's less to go amiss. And, of course, I have a fetish for older things.

I hadn't eaten anything all day, so when I got back to my apartment, I was famished. I threw together a simple bologna and cheese sandwich and ate it like a true bachelor, over the sink. I looked at the notepad stuck to the fridge. I thought about calling Gwendolyn while I argued the pros and cons.

I wanted to not only sate my curiosity as to whether yesterday was real, but because I was feeling uncharacteristically lonely. I have friends, don't get me wrong. But it would be nice to experience something different, and this certainly described Gwendolyn. I just didn't want to come across as desperate or too eager, and I had the feeling it might seem that way.

I popped the last bite of the sandwich into my mouth and chewed over my choices. To call, or not to call. Hell, what did I have to lose?

I picked up the phone and hesitated after I punched in the first six numbers.

"Come on," I said. "It's just a stupid phone call. Stop being such a wuss."

With the last number entered, I listened to it ring...ring...ring...

"Gay bar!" The voice on the other end sounded excessively cheery.

Well, shit. That's just the way.

"Uh," I managed.

I wanted to excuse myself with dignity, say I had gotten the wrong number, hang up, curse—do anything rather than hang on like an idiot.

"I knew it," I muttered.

"Hello?"

"Uh, yeah..." I said, unable to think of anything else, or hang up. Words were not my friends right now.

"Harry Harrison?" she asked.

"Yeah, it's Harry. Who's this?" I'm such a doofus. Like she called me. Where the hell is that damn wall?

"Ah, it's Gwen. What's up?"

"I don't know. I just wanted to call."

For the record, I'm really not this idiotic, but I'm going to have a hell of a time trying to prove it.

"Great. I thought you were going to call yesterday," she said.

"I'm sorry, I didn't think...think you wanted me to."

"You're apologizing again."

"Yeah," I said.

"Why would you think I wouldn't want you to call me?

"I don't know," I mumbled.

"I didn't have to, but I did give you my number. Usually people take that to mean a call would be welcome. Just thought you'd call earlier, is all."

"Oh," I said, and there was the kind of silent pause that makes you think what you just said sounded ridiculous.

"So..."

"Yeah, well, do you want to get some food?" I thudded my head against the cabinet. I hoped she wouldn't hear my self-inflicted punishment on the other end.

"I have to eat," she answered.

"Yeah, I know. I meant, you know, with me. Later. Sometime. Maybe."

She laughed. "Harry, are you trying to ask me out?"

"Uh, I guess so?"

"You aren't making plans to take advantage of me if I happen to accept your request, are you?"

"What! No!" My voice rose an octave. I heard her laugh.

"I'm joking. Don't need to take everything so seriously. I'm sure you're not that kind of guy. Anyway, I would like to eat some food with you."

"Okay," I said, with relief.

"Best of all, I do have this evening free. Should I rent a car?"

"No, I can drive. It's not very nice, so if you—"

"Hey, Harry?"

"Yeah?"

"It doesn't matter. I'm not that shallow. As long as you don't have anything growing in there and there aren't any springs that try to get fresh, what you drive doesn't matter. It'll be fine."

I was assured as she gave me her address and said she'd be ready by six.

Perfect. It gave me time to sweat, shower, change, and double up on the antiperspirant because I was starting to sweat again.

******

We had dinner at a casual restaurant by the lake and afterward drove to a little secluded spot where it was quieter. Don't get any ideas. There wasn't any funny business going on. It was all PG rated. The sun had already gone down and the breeze coming off the water was comfortable.

"I like to come out here now and then to watch the sunset," I said.

I had allowed myself to grow more comfortable and admitted to things most people would laugh at. Not laugh at in a good way either. Things like driving to a lake to watch sunsets.

"Too bad we missed it," said Gwen.

"The sunset?"

"Yeah," she sighed. "It's nice anyway, even if it does smell a little fishy."

"It's going to smell a little fishy. It's a lake. The lack of fish smells in a lake only exist in books and movies," I said.

"No need to go sounding all cynical about it."

"How am I sounding cynical? It's the truth. Actually, it's rained recently. The fishy smell gets stronger after a rain."

We were silent for a while, taking in the songs of the bullfrogs and crickets, and the occasional splash of fish. A small boat floated silently on the lake, the moonlight outlining two fishermen casting out their lines.

"So," Gwendolyn broke the silence. "Did you ever find Bugs Bunny attractive when he dressed up like a girl bunny?"

"Huh?" Where did that come from?

She laughed. "It's just sitting out here on the car like this reminds me of the scene in Wayne's World."

"But we're not at an airport. Wasn't that where the big jet flew inches from their heads?"

"I'm sure it wasn't inches. Anyway, things don't have to be exactly the same to remind you of something. Most of the time, it's the smallest things that bring something to mind."

"I guess that's true."

"It's nice to know you're able to hold a conversation without stuttering and apologizing."

"I don't stutter," I said. "I was just nervous, is all."

The truth was I still felt nervous.

"Nervous? Why would you be nervous?"

"Because you're beautiful." There we go, just blurting out what's on my mind without thinking first.

"You think I'm beautiful?" she asked with surprise.

"Sure, but you already knew that. Don't need me to tell you," I mumbled.

I could feel my cheeks burn.

"I think maybe you should get your eyes checked."

"My eyes are fine," I said.

She laughed. "You ought to send your resume to Santa in case Rudolph decides to retire," she said, as I grew even brighter. "You're cute."

"Oh no, I'm not," I grunted.

"Yeah you are, lobster boy. You know, your name reminds me of Humbert Humbert."

"Oh, first I'm cute and then she calls me creepy," I huffed and folded my arms.

"I'm not calling you creepy."

"He's the guy from *Lolita* and he's creepy."

She rolled her eyes and shook her head. "Same guy, but it doesn't mean I called you creepy. It's just your first and last names are so similar and they start with an H. That's all. Don't read too much into it. So, you've read Nabokov, I take it."

I relaxed and shook my head. "Afraid not."

"Oh." She sounded disappointed.

"But I do watch Kubrick and Nabokov wrote the script for the film."

"It's not the same. Books are always different from the films."

"True, but the concept's the same."

"There's a lot different with the concept too. Humbert was a very different personality in the book. Much more dark and, well, creepy."

"I think I'll cross it off my reading list just the same."

"Shooting star!" she exclaimed and pointed toward the sky. "Make a wish."

The shooting star was one of the largest I'd seen. Its tail streaked brightly across the horizon and blinked out before it hit the tree tops.

I made a wish on the star. I wished for happiness, peace, and a way back to the old house. In the back of my mind, I heard a little voice telling me to be careful what you wish for.

"What was your wish?" asked Gwendolyn.

"Don't you know if I tell you, it won't come true?"

"Yeah, yeah. People only say that so when their wish doesn't come true, they won't look like a horse's ass."

"Who's the one sounding cynical now?"

"What? Now, it's the truth and you know it," she laughed.

"Maybe. But also, if something really good happens to some-one else, you can claim it's what you wished for and get points for being unselfish."

"Don't tell me you've done that."

"Once or twice," I admitted.

"Good idea, actually," she said.

We sat a while longer in silence. I was comfortable with Gwendolyn, like I was with an old friend.

Finally, I glanced at my watch. "It's getting late. I can drive you home."

"Yeah, it would probably be best," she said. I thought she sounded a little disappointed.

"We can do it again sometime." I paused, and quickly added, "If you want to."

"I think I'd like that, Harry."

She smiled that little half smile of hers, the one that I could fall in love with. Funny, but I believed there was a good chance I already had.

Chapter 5

The sound of rolling thunder rumbled in the distance and the cool wind against my face woke me. I rolled over, and something sharp poked me as I sat up.

"What the hell?" I mumbled. I wondered what was in my bed until I looked around. I had been lying on the knotted root of an oak outside the old house, illuminated by moonlight.

I glanced at my watch. Just after eleven. That couldn't be. I would have just gotten home after dropping off Gwendolyn.

I tapped the watch and put it to my ear. It was dead. I tapped it again more forcefully, as if it would get it to work again.

"Just great," I said. I liked that watch.

I looked to the house. Once again, I'd returned and still didn't know how. Well, at least I got one wish. Peace and happiness must have been too difficult to fulfill.

A strange feeling came over me as I entered the house once again. I had done so without hesitation, as if it were something I did every day with full knowledge I would be welcome. The truth is, I wasn't sure I was welcome at all. I was feeling a bit mixed up on the subject.

Nothing had noticeably changed. The night sky could still be seen through the broken window at the top of the stairs and the musty, moldy smell still hung in the air like stale smoke. I strained my hearing, with the thought maybe I might hear the piano again. Only the silence spoke, save for the wind whistling through the gaps around doorways and windows.

I had a desire to look at the portraits again, though they had made me uncomfortable last time. I made my way to the paintings and shuffled through the dust layered over the creaking wooden floor. When I got there, I studied them.

Something seemed different.

Perhaps the doors of perception in my mind had opened. It happens sometimes when I look at art. At first, I couldn't see anything different. I felt some trepidation, but then I saw it.

The woman's portrait now seemed to emanate evil from beneath the pigments and yellowed varnish. I tried to shake the sensation out of my head, unable to do so. It was time to move on.

I went to the door between the two portraits and tried the knob. It was unlocked and opened easily, as if primed for my arrival. Inside, the sourceless blue light glowed. It offered just enough illumination to make my way around. Though I did not feel cold, I shivered.

The large room was paneled in light-colored wood, with a fireplace against the far wall and floor-to-ceiling drapes covering the windows. A long couch and two chairs, worn and faded, faced the fireplace. A low, curving table topped with shards of broken glass sat between the couch and fireplace. A grand piano filled the corner of the room near the door, with a large silver candelabra holding dust-streaked white candles atop the lid.

Over the fireplace mantel hung another portrait, and I went to get a closer look. It depicted a severely dressed man. He was portly and balding, with heavily creased skin and large jowls. It made him resemble a bulldog. If the gray beard he wore was an attempt to cover it up, it did a poor job. I thought maybe it was a portrait of Dr. Pierce, but I wasn't sure enough to put money on it.

Without the portrait looming over the space, the room could have been a warm, comfortable place where people would feel welcomed. A large rug, once fine but now tattered, covered the wooden floor, and all the furniture was thickly coated with dust.

I walked around and took it all in. The room was feminine. Paintings of flowers graced the walls. Vases holding long-dead stalks and desiccated petals were scattered throughout the room. A tall bookcase stood against a wall, next to a writing desk. The bookcase harbored old books, mostly novels, but there were a couple of reference books and an old Bible. I was afraid to touch anything or clear off the dust, so I left it alone.

Small porcelain figures were displayed on several shelves, mixed with a pair of binoculars, a compass, and other bric-a-brac. Some of the items seemed odd, but there are plenty of shelves in the world that hold stranger things. On the lowest shelf sat a long wooden box. I knelt down to get a closer look.

Reluctantly, I reached out and touched it lightly a couple of times before I finally picked it up. I blew the dust off the lid. Nothing terrible happened, but I still hesitated before opening it.

"What do you expect to find?" I asked myself. "A dead rat? A live one?" I shuddered at the thought, but decided I should be brave.

Carefully, I lifted the lid. I expected something creepy to jump out of the box and bite me on the nose. A loud clap of thunder crashed through the air and I screamed like a frightened little girl. I fumbled the box, but grabbed it before it hit the floor. I took deep breaths and tried to lower my heart rate to less than a thousand beats a minute. Then I had to check and make sure I hadn't soiled myself. Eventually I calmed down and threw open the lid. Damn the consequences.

There were no rats or anything living or dead to jump out. Instead, there was an antique 3-D viewer. Another box sat on the shelf, which I assumed held the cards for it, but I refrained from checking as it was too dark to use, anyway. It made me think of the View-Master I still had from my childhood. I didn't think I'd find He-Man, ThunderCats or G.I. Joe in this box, though.

As I slid the box back on the shelf, my heart rate shot up again as the piano began to play a mournful melody, like a dirge for a long-lost love. I forced myself to turn slowly toward the piano.

A woman sat at the keys, her head lowered as she concentrated on the instrument. The ethereal glow surrounding her seemed more darkness than light. It flickered in and out like bad television reception. She seemed oblivious to my presence. Her attention remained focused on her sorrowful song. Its volume grew louder and softer with the cadence of her flickering image. After some time, she looked up at me and without missing a beat, gave me a forlorn smile. I could feel her confusion. Her eyes were as melancholy as the melody she played. I recognized her as the somber woman from the portrait in the foyer, though she seemed younger here. In her presence, I felt a mixture of fear and wonder, and a sense that something deep within her was nefarious. I swallowed the lump in my throat as her lips moved. They spoke silent, unknown words. As she began to dissolve from view, the music faded close behind her, her eyes flashed fiery darts, and made my stomach twist with fear.

I kept watching the piano long after she disappeared. I don't know what I expected. I was torn between wishing she would come back and explain everything, and an abject fear of seeing her again. But she wasn't coming back, and I knew it. My frustration grew as I realized, once again, an apparition had spoken silent words beyond my understanding. If these ghosts wanted to tell me something, then why couldn't they find a voice, or at least write me a note? It would be much better than a ventriloquist act sans the ventriloquist. How is it possible, I wondered, for me to hear the music from the piano, but not hear the voice of the pianist? To not be able to hear anything coming from moving lips?

"Maybe the piano is real, but you're going crazy from seeing things that aren't there," I told myself. I countered with, "How can you hear something coming from something that isn't here? Huh?" By the gods, I was going crazy. I blew a frustrated gust of air from my lips and pushed my hair from over my eyes as I continued to argue with myself.

What the hell? The only positive was I was alone, and no one was going to call the white coats down at the funny farm to come and take me away, ha ha!

Was I really alone, though? Do mute flickering things that may or may not be figments of my imagination count? No, they weren't figments. They were definitely real. I was loath to find out how real they might be.

I touched the piano as I started to leave, mostly to prove to myself it was real, and found it was cold. Freezing, more like it.

After I left the room, I stood in the foyer and tried to figure it out. Suddenly the floor began to shake. My first thought was an earthquake. It wasn't just a little rumble, but not enough to knock me on my ass either. I froze and feared the house was going to crumble on top of me. I would be helpless. I hoped fervently that it would stop. It didn't look like the house would hold up in an earthquake of any magnitude.

A low, deep moan swept through the room and I could almost feel the sound push past me.

It stopped and I was still standing. The house hadn't crumbled around me. I didn't need to be told. I ran. Ten feet from the door, the floor cracked beneath me. I fell forward and twisted my ankle.

"Son of a bitch!" I cursed as I pushed myself up. I tested my weight on my ankle. The pain was slight, so nothing to worry about, thankfully. I didn't have time to assess the damage completely. I limped quick as I could out the door.

I stood on the porch with ragged breath as the wind whipped around me. Thunder rumbled in the distance, but it was closer than it sounded.

"It was only the wind. It was only the wind," I chanted to myself in vain. It wasn't just the wind. I sat down and felt my ankle. No real pain, just some discomfort. I'd be okay. Nothing a little aspirin couldn't take care of.

I pictured the bottle on the shelf of my old, metal medicine cabinet, a homely comfort that would be quite welcome. I shut my eyes and whispered, "there's no place like home. There's no place like home…"

Chapter 6

I opened my eyes. I thought I was still at the house since I wasn't on a sidewalk somewhere downtown, but the house was no longer there. In its place was a tall brick building, its doorway boarded up. The building faced an alley and looked something like my apartment building. A smaller door, covered in chipped white paint, was a few feet away from the boarded door.

I sat in an area mixed with gravel and knee-high grass. A concrete block wall, standing about eight feet tall, save for a few sections missing blocks at the top, stretched from the building twenty-five yards to another structure of red brick covered thickly in ivy.

The ivy was so thick I couldn't see an entrance and I didn't try to find one. Anything could have been mixed up in the greenery. I didn't think it was worth a rash to go look for a door. Anyway, one mystery building at a time was enough for me.

The wind blew strong and steady. The smell of rain and foliage drifted around me. I stood and tested my foot, finding it to be only mildly uncomfortable. If I needed to, I knew I would be able to run on it, though I hoped to hell there wouldn't be any reason to.

I walked away from the building to the narrow alley. It was dark, set with old cobblestones that peeked out from a thick layer of asphalt. A car might have been able to squeeze through. On each end, you could see streets, with a lone car occasionally driving by. For no particular reason, I opted to go right. The smell of rain hung strongly in the air, but I didn't think it would come down anytime soon. When I got to the street, I took a left, since I had just taken a right and thought I'd be fair. I began to have an idea of where I was as I walked along a sidewalk illuminated at even intervals by electric street lamps styled to simulate antique gas lamps. They looked like they were made of plastic, and probably were.

I walked past the post office and crossed a street to a tall, steepled building on the corner. It had wide steps leading to an alcove that hid large wooden doors painted a deep red. An illuminated sign proclaimed it to be St. Mark's Episcopal Church. I had never been to an Episcopal church before; as a matter of fact, I hadn't stepped foot in any kind of church in a long time. I admit I liked the red outdoor carpeting that rolled up the steps to the red doors. I smiled and thought perhaps the red carpet was a psychological tool, used to make parishioners feel important. Important people get to walk on red carpet, so you must be important if you go to St. Mark's. People have a stunning variety of ways to delude themselves, I thought, as I walked along.

"Hey," someone greeted me from behind.

I stopped and turned. She sat in a dark corner at the top of the steps. She could have been easily missed by anyone walking past. I would have missed her if she hadn't spoken.

She was short and chubby, not quite fat. Her hair hung in thick blonde curls that made me think of Shirley Temple. Her hair framed a face with a short nose and her eyes looked bigger than they actually were behind thick glasses.

There was an odd sort of cuteness to her, but if someone had asked you to describe her, you would most likely say she had a nice personality.

I nodded my acknowledgment and said, "Hello."

"So, whatchadoin?" she asked, as she swung her legs against the brick.

"I'm just out taking a walk," I said.

"We're having a party, you know."

"That's nice." I hoped I sounded more polite than sarcastic.

It didn't seem to matter to her.

"Would you like to come in?" she asked.

"Oh no, that's all right."

"Why not? You're not afraid you might have some fun, are you?"

She giggled at herself.

"Ah, no," I laughed politely. "It's just that I'm not Episcopalian."

"It doesn't matter, if you're not." She shook her head and her curls bounced against her cheeks. She leaned in and said in a loud whisper,

"I'm not Episcopalian either, so it's okay."

"No?" I asked.

She shook her head again. "My friend is. I come with her. It's fun."

I smiled and nodded.

"Oh! I'm sorry. You probably think I'm just some stranger and all kinds of weird for asking another stranger, who's just walkin' by, if they want to drop in on some party in a church."

She was correct, though she was nicer about it than I would have been. I wouldn't let her know, so I said, "No, not at all."

"My name's Belinda." She smacked her lips loudly. "Now ya know!"

"Yes, I know now. My name's Harry."

"Now you know my name, and I know your name. We aren't strangers."

You're a genius, Forrest, I thought.

"Now do you want to come in?"

"I don't know..." I said. She certainly was persistent. If she wasn't Episcopalian, I wondered if she was a Jehovah's Witness or something.

"What if I gave you a crispy treat?" she implored.

"Does that imply a concoction of puffed rice and marshmallow, or a burnt cookie?" I asked.

She laughed a loud, high-pitched machine gun fire laugh. It made me cringe.

"You're a funny guy, Harry. I mean Rice Krispies treats. Although Mrs. Jones did bring in some burnt oatmeal cookies." She chewed on her lip as her face grew thoughtful and said, "I'm sure you wouldn't want any of those. Not only are they burnt, they're oatmeal. Ick." She scrunched her nose in disgust and shuddered.

"Does she know they're burnt?" I asked.

"I don't think so. They're not very good," she said.

"Burnt cookies don't enthrall my taste buds, so I would have to decline those," I said. I put my hands in my pockets and scuffed the toe of my shoe on the sidewalk. "I do like Rice Krispies treats though. So, I guess it wouldn't hurt anything for me to step in for a few minutes and have a snack."

"Oh, goody!" She clapped her hands together like an excited child and jumped from her perch. She opened the door and I followed. She was strange enough to be a Jehovah's Witness. Maybe even a Mormon.

I could hear the noises of a small crowd coming from the end of a long hallway lighted with the harsh glow of fluorescent bulbs. A set of double doors to the sanctuary were topped by a brass plaque. Dark corridors led to other areas of the church.

"This way," Belinda called over her shoulder.

I nodded, though she couldn't see me. There wasn't much choice of places to go, save for outside, but I did say I'd come in for a few. I am a man of my word. I watched her walk swiftly in front of me. Underneath the fabric of her jeans, her ass looked like two basketballs pumping the handle of a railroad handcart. A chuckle threatened to burble up from my throat and I was unsuccessful in suppressing it.

Belinda didn't notice. She pushed open the doors at the end of the hallway and we entered the gym.

"Here we are," she announced. "Go get something to drink and I'll find you a crispy treat." She pointed toward a paper covered table with a large punchbowl and stacks of clear plastic cups.

Only punch. I was disappointed.

I ladled some into a cup and took a sip. Then I noticed the red cooler on the floor filled with cans of soda and bottled water buried in ice. No beer, but it was to be expected. Too bad, but I didn't mind as the punch was quite palatable. It tasted of sherbet and lemon lime soda. Unfortunately, nobody had come by to make it more interesting and I didn't have anything on hand. It would have been wasted, though the party would have been more lively if the punch was spiked.

Belinda came back with a sticky square atop a festive, colored paper napkin. I thanked her and relieved her of the treat.

"I hope you're not going to decide to take off now you've got a crispy treat." Her eyes looked even bigger and sad behind her glasses as if she had been jilted before when inviting strangers to a church party.

"No, I was going to eat it first and then leave," I said.

Belinda gasped and her eyes grew even sadder.

"I'm kidding. I'll stay longer." I actually felt bad.

"You promise?" she asked, with a tremor in her voice.

"I promise," I said.

If she had a boyfriend, I felt sorry for the poor guy.

"Okay." She looked at me as if not sure she should take me at my word.

She must have decided to as she said, "Well then. Have fun!" She left and joined a group of girls who cast glances in my direction as they whispered to each other.

I was sure they whispered about me, so I smiled and gave a little wave. They turned away quickly and giggled. I turned to my crispy treat and took a huge bite.

"Hey, there!" A guy called as he jogged toward me. Beads of sweat freckled his brow. He stopped and swiped them off with his forearm.

"Hey," I answered without feeling. I didn't really want to talk to anyone.

"So, we're all over there, me and the guys, playing some B-ball," he said between labored breaths. After a few seconds, he let out a long heavy sigh. "Saw you standing here all by yourself and got to wondering if you might want to come join in on the game. We could always use more."

"No, I'm not really what you'd call a sports kind of guy, but thanks just the same," I said, as I lifted the sticky square. "I'm just here for the treats."

He laughed as if it were the funniest joke he'd ever heard. "Funny. My name's Mark, by the way," he said, as he shoved out his hand.

Politely, I took it, gave it a couple pumps and discreetly wiped my hand on my jeans. "Like the church, huh?"

"What?" He looked puzzled for a moment, then laughed again. "Oh yeah. Mark. St. Mark's. I get it, ha, ha. Just like the church, yeah. Only I'm no saint."

It was a stupid joke, but I granted him a smile anyway. "I'm Harry."

I pointed toward Belinda's group and said, "Belinda invited

me."

"Oh, Belinda!" He smiled and gave me a wink before he glanced over his shoulder at her. "Belinda's a nice girl. Real nice."

"Yeah. She seems to be," I replied. I ignored the double entendre his wink and body language implied. It was clear what was going on in his mind. I didn't want to dig any further to find out if I was correct.

Mark clicked his tongue a couple of times. "Mm-mmm, nice." He snapped out of his little fantasy and said, "So, Harry, if you decide to change your mind about getting in on the game, you're more than welcome to just jump on in. No need to be shy or anything."

"Yeah, I'll do that. Thanks, Saint Mark."

I don't know why I made the joke. I certainly felt stupid for making it immediately after.

Mark laughed and pointed his finger at me like a gun. I almost expected him to make little bang-bang noises, but he didn't.

"You are one funny guy, Harry," he said, and jogged back to his game.

I looked around the gym as I ate my snack. I noticed how the people mingled only with their own sex. Most parties, the sexes mingle and sometimes even (gasp) dance! Here they kept themselves segregated, as if afraid of what mingling might lead to.

I watched Belinda as she sat in a circle with her group, playing some silly party game. I wondered if she went outside often and waited in the dark corner for some passerby to come along so she could pounce and invite them inside so their little group could get bigger. An attempt to increase the chances for good, clean fun. A creepy thought, but possible.

I tossed my empty napkin into the garbage, gulped down the last swallow of liquor-free punch and threw away the plastic cup. As I started to leave, I noticed Belinda waving frantically at me, so I waved back.

She smiled a big, stupid grin, jumped, threw her fists into her face and bumped her nose rather hard. She burst into laughter while the others followed suit.

I took the opportunity to sneak away, fast.

Chapter 7

I made my way to the front. On a whim, I tried the doors to the sanctuary.

They were locked.

It's a shame churches no longer left doors open so people could come in, meditate, pray, or light candles. In an ideal world, maybe, but it's not ideal. Vandals and thieves don't discriminate, so even churches are afraid to leave their doors open.

I noticed a narrow stairwell beside the sanctuary doors. They weren't blocked off, so I climbed the stairs. The door at the top opened and I stepped through. It was the balcony overlooking the main sanctuary.

The sanctuary below was dimly lighted. Stained glass windows along the sides depicted religious scenes. The pulpit, carved with a gilded cross, stood a few feet above the raised chancel. A much larger cross hung from the ceiling behind it, doing its best to look imposing.

"You know, this is where they made black people sit, not so very long ago."

I recognized Gwendolyn's voice before I saw her. She sat in the front corner. I responded, "And now they ordain women and homosexuals. What is the world coming to?"

She gave a short, nasal chuckle. "You took the words right out of my mouth. You just waltzed up in here and stole them. I hope you realize."

"What can I say? The truth doesn't belong to just one person."

"You could say you're sorry."

"I could, but you got me out of the habit," I said, as I took a seat beside her. "How did you know it was me?"

She shrugged. "I just did. Maybe I recognized your walk."

"Recognized my walk? It's carpeted. Anyway, my walk isn't noisy. That can't be true."

"You'd be surprised the things you can hear in silence," she said.

"It is quiet. What are you doing here?"

"Me? I sneak in here sometimes when the young adult group has their little get-togethers."

I smirked. "Adult?"

"I know, right? They hang out in the gym and the door's usually open. So I come up here to think."

"How'd you discover this?"

"I have a friend close by. She had something come up one night, so when I came by here, I saw something was going on and stopped by to see what."

"Ah. You Episcopalian?"

She laughed. "No. Are you?"

I shook my head. "I guess you could say I am a worshiper of the god, I."

"Me, too," she said.

"You worship me? Awesome."

"No." She shook her head. "I meant me, myself."

"It's okay if you do. No one will blame you."

"Oh, hush. I come here because there are no interruptions. At least there weren't until tonight."

"Maybe I should apologize."

"No, you're fine. Anyway, you've done enough apologizing for a lifetime."

"Wait until I really screw something up. I'll hold you to it," I said. "I'm surprised they haven't interrupted you at some point."

"Who?"

"The group down there."

"They don't bother me."

"That's good. Keeps it quiet up here."

"Really great for thinking, being alone. Come to think of it, I'm amazed they haven't figured out this would be a fantastic make-out spot."

"Are you hinting?"

"Pervert," she muttered and punched my arm.

"Hey!" I rubbed the spot. "Am not."

"That remains to be seen. Anyway, I'm saying when they do figure it out, I won't have a nice quiet place to think and I'll have to hunt up another."

"I doubt it's something you'll have to worry about. They segregate themselves like they're afraid of each other or something," I said. "Anyway, it doesn't seem too safe, sitting up here all alone."

"What? It's a church. What could be safer than a church?"

"You'd think, but churches get shot up just like anywhere else. They're not immune to psychos with guns. It's not quite the sanctuary it once was."

"Yeah," she said, sadly. "A shame."

"I still can't believe it's an adult group down there," I said.

"Hard to believe, isn't it?"

"I thought they were teenagers. Older teenagers, but still. They haven't figured out places to fool around? Their own place maybe?"

"Maybe their parents are home."

"Ah yeah. They seem a bit immature."

"Adults can be immature too," she said.

"I guess that's true. I just never noticed."

Her eyes sparkled as she glanced at me. "Haven't noticed in other adults, or yourself?"

I thought a moment and admitted, "Both."

"What are you doing here, by the way?" she asked. "Are you stalking me, or something?"

"Or something. I got bribed," I said.

"Bribed? You don't say."

"Yeah. Belinda drew me in by offering Rice Krispies treats."

"You're cheap. I'll have to remember that," she said. "She's the one with the head full of Slinkys?"

I laughed. "Yeah, she's the one. I think she stalks strangers and lures them into churches to partake in snacks."

"Maybe. She seems strange to me. Not easy to forget, but nice."

"That's what I heard." I pictured Mark winking and wanted to gag. "What religion do you think she is?"

"Episcopalian, I'd assume."

"She said she wasn't. I thought maybe Jehovah's Witness."

"Couldn't be," Gwendolyn said with assurance.

"Why not?"

"Jehovah's Witnesses don't have, or go to parties. Goes against their religion."

"I wonder why? Some people like to get rid of any kind of fun. Maybe she's a Mormon then."

"Why a Mormon?"

I shrugged and said, "They're weird and usually a friendly

sort."

"Maybe that's it."

We sat there, listening to the quiet together and watched the streetlights shine through the stained-glass windows. Subtle, tinted shadows drifted over the sanctuary below.

It was peaceful and conducive to thinking. I could see the allure.

I looked sideways at Gwendolyn. She had her long, dark hair tucked around her ear. It brought attention to the soft lines of her cheekbones and her full lips. Dark lashes batted occasionally over moist, green eyes. She was dressed comfortably in jeans and a T-shirt. Whatever she wore, she'd look incredible.

Her hands, with slender fingers, and short, well-manicured nails, lay folded on her lap as her long legs hung carelessly over the rails.

"Why are you staring at me?" she asked.

"Oh well, I..." I lost my tongue and wondered how she knew. She didn't even move her head. "I didn't, wasn't staring."

"Bullshit."

"I wasn't!" I exclaimed. "I was...I was studying."

"Another way of saying you were staring."

"Really, I was just watching you think." I said.

"Still bullshit, but okay."

"Can't get anything past you, is that what you think?" I said.

She didn't pursue it any further, but I continued to watch her anyway. I realized she had been crying before I showed up and her sarcasm was only a mask.

I enjoyed a spot of sarcasm from time to time with her, but if it was a cover, then it was different. I felt insensitive for not thinking she could hurt, too. For not noticing. I could have let her know I was here for her, but who was I to interfere? Sure, we're friends, but how presumptuous to think she felt close enough to share deep, dark secrets with me.

Maybe in time.

Silly as it may sound, I wanted to reach out to her. To hold her and be a strong, sturdy ship in the storm. Maybe it isn't silly at all. I wanted this, but didn't think I could do any good. I wear masks myself and my own anchor was still far above the seabed.

How many of us are really that strong? At our core, we all pretend. We all wear our masks only to take them off when we are alone and secure in the thought no one else is looking. Some wear theirs better than others. Gwendolyn might be one who wears hers well.

I wanted to get to a point sometime where we could take them off and say to each other, "This is what I am. This is the me no one else sees." A point where there are no secrets and nothing is so sacred it must be hidden from each other. I wanted to let loose now, but I feared it wasn't the proper moment. I'd probably fail. Tonight, I was lucky to succeed in small talk.

That's better than nothing at all.

"You know," I said, "black people had the best seats."

"What?" She shifted and looked at me.

"Black people. Best seats were here. Don't know why neither the blacks or whites realized it. They wanted down there, when the whole time, it was better up here."

"Yeah, the best seats. You could see it all from right up here," she murmured.

"Not to mention you could cough up some serious phlegm bombs and drop 'em down on the snooty white folk."

"That's disgusting!" she said with a laugh.

"Sure, but it made you laugh."

"As disgusting as it is, you could do that. I'd have never thought of it, but of course, leave it up to a guy."

"Yeah, you're too refined and delicate to come up with it. That's why you need me. I have no such reservations."

She smiled as she took my hand into hers and said, "Thanks."

I looked down and felt the warmth of her hand infuse into mine and travel up my arm. My face began to flush as I asked, "For what?"

"For coming here."

"Ah, I wouldn't have even come if it weren't for being bribed. Coming up here, it's just, I guess it's just a coincidence."

Gwendolyn shook her head. "There's no such thing as coincidence."

I looked at her, a little bemused. "I always assumed there was. Are you saying nothing can happen by chance?"

"Yes," she said. "Coincidence says things happen as they do for no good reason. For no reason at all, most times."

"Don't they?"

"No." She took a breath. "Things happen because of choices we make."

"I never knew you were a philosopher," I said.

"We all philosophize. If you're human, you're a philosopher."

"I might argue that."

"Philosophy isn't reserved just for guys with a Ph.D. and thousand-page tomes on the meaning of life, or whatever."

"Maybe so," I said, more to myself than her.

After a moment she asked, "What are you thinking about?"

"Nothing."

"Come on, I'm not stupid. Tell me."

"Just thinking about what you're saying. Coincidences and all. Maybe you're right. I just never thought of my Gwendolyn waxing philosophical on me."

Her expression was unreadable and I wasn't sure how to feel about it.

"So I'm yours now?" she asked, and I could tell she was trying to be sarcastic, but it didn't quite come out that way.

I looked away. "I didn't mean it in that way."

"Even if you did, it doesn't matter." She sighed, then said, "I think you're a nice guy, Harry. I'd even venture to say you're a great guy. That's the reason you wouldn't want someone like me to be yours. Not really."

"Why not?" Of course I thought she was wrong, but I was curious.

She squeezed my hand in hers. "Different things. I don't know. Things I don't want to talk about and even if I did, you might not want to know. Not if you want to keep everything friendly and innocent."

"What, you kill somebody or something?" I asked, only half joking.

"No, nothing like that," she said with a weak smile.

"I get lost," I said.

"Lost?"

"Uh-huh. Lost."

"What are you talking about?"

"I don't know. Just sometimes I end up...never mind."

I couldn't say it. I wanted to tell her about it. How I ended up in places, and didn't know how I got there. Strange experiences I still perceived to be coincidences. About how I was, in a way, lost right now.

I had the strange feeling she tied into it all somehow, but I didn't know the answer, nor how to find out if it were true.

"It doesn't matter," she said, and patted my hand. "I'm still glad you came." She stood and stretched, her T-shirt hiked up to reveal her navel. I couldn't help but admire it. "I'm going to go. You have a ride?"

I didn't remember seeing her bike parked in the front. Maybe she had it in the lot behind the church.

"I walked. I can walk home, no problem," I said. I didn't want her to feel burdened and I'm still not a fan of motorcycles. Besides, my place wasn't far and the weather was nice enough.

"Just as well. I'd insist, but I am on my bike," she said.

"Is this a challenge?" I asked.

"A challenge? Of course not. Just an innocent offering. Would you like a ride?" A smirk pulled at her lip. "Or would you be too chicken?"

"That is a direct challenge!"

"Maybe," she laughed. "So, yes? No?"

"I think maybe I can trust you enough not to kill me, so I'll say yes. Just to prove I'm not chicken."

"We'll see."

We went down the stairs. The muted sounds from the gym could still be heard.

"Still going at it," I said.

"Want to go back and have some fun?" she asked. "Maybe we can put on some music, dance, and really make them crazy."

"I don't think I'd want to go back there again. Not even for another crispy treat."

"Just as well. Let's jet."

I stopped. "I don't know about that."

"What are you talking about? Come on."

"No way. I'm a Shark and we don't have anything to do with Jets."

"Oh no! Not *West Side Story*! Next, you'll be singing *I Feel Pretty*."

"No, I don't have the voice for that."

"Thank hell," she said, as we left the church.

The wind had picked up a bit outside, but it wasn't much cooler. The treetops swayed heavily and the leaves clapped together, as if applauding our appearance back into the real world. The scenery seemed different, although I knew we were still in Carson. A lot of things had started to seem different lately. I ignored it, lest it confuse me further.

I slid on the helmet before I climbed on the bike and took hold of Gwendolyn's waist. Then, I closed my eyes tight and willed myself not to scream or cry. At least, not audibly.

Now, one may think it isn't manly for a guy to ride a motor-cycle behind a girl. I have no argument. I realize it isn't manly, I just don't care. It's a big step for a guy with a fear of motorcycles. I was proud I didn't start bawling right away this time.

I swallowed a lump the size of a tennis ball when the bike surged forward. I swore I would not be tight-eyed this time and cautiously opened my eyes one at a time. I timed my breathing and tried all the relaxation techniques I knew.

All was forgotten when we hit a turn. I suppressed a squeal and slammed my eyes shut. They remained firmly sealed until the bike came to a complete stop in front of my building.

"Hey, you didn't cry this time," Gwendolyn said, as I shakily let myself off the motorcycle.

"Inside, I was bawling like a giant baby," I admitted. "Because you didn't know, it only shows my great ability to hold it all in."

"It's a start," she said. "You should be proud."

The sky lit up in a series of flashes.

"Wow. You think it'll rain?" she asked.

"Nah, just an electrical storm, I think."

"Maybe I should get out of here, just in case."

"Yeah," I said, though I didn't want to see her go.

"I'll see ya," she said and motored off.

"See ya," I said and watched her disappear.

I started to my door. I hoped she would get home safely. I was tired. The hours of the day now seemed to have been very long.

I checked my watch and found it was working again. I thought it odd and stumbled through the door. I tripped over a piece of loose flooring and made a mental note to fix it before someone got hurt. I trudged up the stairs with my bed foremost in my mind. I got inside, locked the door and decided to ignore the pangs of hunger rumbling in my stomach. Breakfast would come soon enough. I got to my bed and fell like a giant tree, as if a lumberjack had hacked off my feet.

The last thing I remember was I looked at the clock radio beside my bed and wondered why I felt I'd lost a whole day—and whether tomorrow would be just as strange.

Chapter 8

I tried to look busy as I manned the info desk at The Bookworm. As busy as one could look while playing spider solitaire on the computer anyway. There are those who surf the net for news, horoscopes, or stupid things like, I don't know, recipes. Some ride the waves for pornography, which I'm sure shocks people who never knew such vile, sinful things were available in a sleepy little town like Carson. Me? I don't go for any of that. I'm perfectly content to waste my time with spider solitaire. I don't even need the internet for it.

"*Hola*, Harry!"

I looked up as Gary DeVille swished his way through the door as only Gary could do.

"How do, Gary," I said, and cursed silently as I lost another round.

"Harry! Harry, darling! You shouldn't answer with something so banal," Gary said. "It's vulgar. You should greet people with something charming. Or foreign. Foreign is always charming. You should do the same when you take your leave."

At the risk of being offensive, Gary was a self-proclaimed, flaming queer. He's also my best friend.

"I would Gary, but saying 'ciao' always makes me think of food," I said.

"Ah, my simple, simple friend. There are many ways to say hello," he said. "You could try something like, for instance, *bonjour*, *aloha*, *buenos días*, or any other flavor that happens to tickle your fancy."

"I could, but what would you say when you're in Spain? What do you do then?" I asked. I knew I had him and I was ready to bask in the victory.

Gary shrugged. "In that case, I just say hello and goodbye."

"But it's not foreign."

"It is when you're in Spain."

Denied. "I guess you've got a point. So, what brings you into this fine establishment today?"

Gary leaned on the counter and said dramatically, "I must know if you have gotten my book in."

"No, not yet. I'm still looking out for you, but I guess nobody has *The Joy of Gay Sex*. You'll have to buy a new copy, I'm afraid."

"Someone has it. They just don't want to give it up. New is just too expensive. It's a conspiracy."

"Maybe, but I don't think there's much of a gay community in Carson."

"Oh, honey, there are gay communities everywhere. Some are itching to get out. They just can't find the closet's doorknob."

"Or maybe they don't want to come out. Not every place is accepting of others. And what about homeless gay people? They don't even have a closet to come out of." I grinned.

Gary cringed. "That old joke needs to be put to death. It's painful and not even funny."

"I think it's funny."

"Anyway, the time will come. Native Americans, women, and African Americans went through the same things. They're all still dealing with prejudices and cold shoulders."

"They used to have to sit in the balcony," I said, thinking of last night with Gwendolyn.

"Those were the best seats."

"That's what I said."

My stomach rumbled loudly.

Gary arched an eyebrow disapprovingly. "I take it you haven't had lunch yet?"

"I haven't even had breakfast," I admitted.

"Let me buy you lunch next door."

"Mexican?"

"Unless there's another place next door," Gary said.

"I think you're just trying to use me for your own nefarious purposes. Plying me with food."

"I'm taking the fifth," he laughed.

"Okay, I'll let you buy me lunch, but you'd better not just sit there ogling the beefcake."

"*Moi?* I would never!"

"Yeah, you would, but whatever. Hang on a couple minutes so I can let Carol know and clock out." I got the okay from Carol and met Gary at the door. "I got an hour."

"I'll have to ogle fast," Gary sighed.

******

The restaurant was half full so we were able to grab our usual booth and order the lunch special. I attacked the complimentary chips and salsa as soon as they were set on the table.

"Hungry?" Gary asked.

"I thought we already established that," I said.

"So, *mon ami*, you must come by the gallery soon. I've taken on some new work from an artist I think you'd appreciate." Gary's eyes lit up with excitement.

I'd assumed this might have been the reason he'd come into the bookstore today. "I can try, but I'm not going to make any promises."

"Do more than try. What else are you doing anyway?"

I shrugged. "I don't know."

"Then no excuses, Harry. I can say these pieces are rather Kevorkianesque."

"Did you just make that up? Kevorkianesque?" I asked.

"No, I made it up last week."

"I see. Wasn't Kevorkian the freaky little doctor who wanted to legally kill people?"

"He wanted to help people."

"By killing them."

"If you say, but he was also a freaky *artiste*. I have some photos of his work at my place somewhere. I'll dig them out if you'd like to see them."

"How about I just take your word for it. I'm trying to eat here."

"You can do that, too."

"Good. Then I will."

Ashley, our regular waitress, brought our food to the table and set the plates in front of us. "Careful, it's hot."

"Thanks. Busy today?" I asked.

"Not yet, but we're expecting to be in a bit. Anything else for you guys?"

I smiled. "Maybe later."

"Let me know if you need anything," she said and went to check on her other tables.

"You were flirting," Gary whispered.

"I don't know how to flirt," I said. "So, if I do come by the gallery, I might bring a friend along."

"Oh? Would this be a boy friend, or a girl friend?" Gary asked with interest.

"The latter."

"Do tell!"

"There isn't much to tell. She's a girl and she's a friend."

"When you go as long as you have without a special someone on your radar, it constitutes a major event."

"Geez, Gary! She's a friend. You make everything into a major event. Anyway, it hasn't been that long."

Gary ignored the comment. "Are you going to tell me about her or what?"

I rolled my eyes, but told him about Gwendolyn and how we met, which led me to mention the house. I hadn't seen Gary since it started, so I told him everything freely. I felt a little weird, but he was a good listener and wasn't judgmental. Not a bad quality in a small town like Carson.

Gary's story is he swooped on the scene about four, maybe five years ago. He came to town and opened his little gallery, DeVille's. Carson isn't a very artsy place and probably would be the last place in anyone's mind to open up an art gallery, but as you've probably already guessed, Gary's not just anyone. He wasn't doing the gallery for money. Art was a hobby for him. He managed to live comfortably on what he already had. He used the gallery not only to show and sell his own work, which he put out slowly, but also to showcase the work of new artists he felt were talented and had an independent and unique voice. Somehow, he managed to get a good amount of traffic into the gallery on a regular basis, despite Carson's status as a town where just about all the businesses were closed, save for a few hardy survivors and several fast food joints. Like Gary, his customers were charmed by the quiet and quaintness of small town America.

Carson isn't a very open-minded place. Gary had a rough go of it when he first moved here. Gay just isn't something to be in Carson, just like being an atheist isn't. Gary is both. However, he did have something going for him. He had class and a contagiously sunny personality. He wasn't one to shove his religious views or sexual orientation in anyone's face and accepted people for who they were. With that and his artistic talents, he eventually won most people over.

Gary won me over from the beginning. I think it was mostly due to the fact I'm not close-minded and my view on the eternal soul isn't the same as most folks around here. We had a lot of things in common and became fast friends. Gary's place became a favorite spot for me to pass time every now and then.

We finished our meal and Gary handed his credit card to Ashley. I placed a few bills underneath a glass.

"Oh, honey, you don't have to do that. I already added a tip," said Gary.

"You don't think she deserves more than whatever measly pittance you might have added? Yours is counted. This, my friend, is tax-free income."

"*Touché*," Gary said.

I knew Gary always tipped well, but I liked doing my part. Anything tax free is good and Ashley always did a great job and college isn't cheap. Every dollar counts and I could afford to let a few go on occasion.

Outside the restaurant, Gary said, "Don't forget to swing by the gallery."

"I won't forget. Don't worry yourself too much about it," I said.

As he started to get into his silver Infiniti, I shouted, "*Adios, Gary!*"

Gary laughed. "Bravo, *mon ami*. When you swing by the

gallery, don't forget to bring your friend." He punctuated the word "friend" with a kissy face.

I shook my head. "I won't forget," I said, but he had already shut his door and started to back out. I looked at my watch and realized my hour was up. I had to get back to The Bookworm and spider solitaire.

Chapter 9

Since the weather was nice and breezy, I decided to take the long way home after I got off work. I strolled and sorted through my mental filing cabinets and tried to figure out what to do. It wasn't easy, but nobody ever said life was easy.

I thought about coincidences. Maybe Gwendolyn was on to something when she said there wasn't such a thing. I wasn't sure, because my mind still wanted to side with the idea there was. Maybe I was looking at it from the wrong perspective.

I thought about the old house and wondered if there might be something tied to it I needed to do. Maybe it was the reason I was being mysteriously transported there. Or, I thought, it could just be I'm going insane. I didn't want it to be true, but it made sense. The whole thing was like a Dali painting. Dreamlike. But, all I felt the past few weeks was confusion.

It only got like this after I stumbled onto the house.

The house: I knew not its location, how I found it, nor how I could go back. It always seemed to be accidental. I never saw a street or a distinguishing landmark. Nothing I could use as a point of reference. I thought of every explanation I could. Was there a connection to where I was living now? To myself? It would make an interesting episode of *The Twilight Zone*, but I hated the feeling of being lost while knowing where I was at the same time. I could try to investigate whether the house actually existed, and where. Surely if it were a real place, in this town or nearby, there should be some record of it. I just didn't have much of a starting point.

I'd mentioned some of it to Gary, but he wasn't sure what to think. He said he'd try to find out something, given some time, but I didn't want to burden him with it. At the time, he was really busy with the gallery and some other projects he'd been working on. The busyness was good for him. He had been going through a slow period, but I had no one else to share with.

Gary was my only real friend. I could talk to him about it. I might be able to tell Gwendolyn, but with her, it was a brand new relationship and I wouldn't feel comfortable sharing something so strange with a person who was still new to my life. I was sure she had her own issues and didn't need to be dragged into mine. Plus, it was too weird.

I was thirsty so I ventured into the Quick Stop and purchased a fountain drink. Even though I wasn't hungry, I bought a sand-wich and sat at the table next to the big plate glass window to rest and eat. There was a decent enough view of the street and parking lot, even though the window was covered with advertisements for beer and tobacco.

I looked outside and watched people pump gas and come in

to purchase the advertised beer and tobacco along with snacks and soft drinks. As I watched the activity, I allowed myself to get lost in thought. Turned out I was hungry after all and was glad I got the sandwich.

With all that had happened lately, I thought it would be a good idea to take a fishing pole to the lake and watch the sunset. I had a couple days off, which only made the idea more attractive. Not only would it get my mind off things for a while, I might get lucky and have catfish for dinner. If I caught enough, I could have a little get-together and feed everyone. I'm not a bad cook, if I do say so myself.

I wiped the crumbs off the table into a napkin, threw my accumulated debris into the garbage can and started to walk home. I looked forward to getting out my pole and fishing paraphernalia and going the lake.

******

The lakeside was peaceful. The water lapped against the rocks scattered along the bank and the smells of the lake floated along the breeze. I unfolded my canvas chair and set it up a few feet from the waterline next to my equipment and a cooler. I didn't have any idea how long I was going to want to stay, so I prepared for all night.

I took my net out to one of the boat docks to try and catch some bait. I had bought chicken livers as back up, but I found pleasure in catching my own bait, casting out a net like my grandfather taught me when I was a boy. I felt a childish joy in catching the little fish, even though there wasn't any great skill involved.

I recalled memories of coming here and fishing with my father and grandfather as I cut bait before I went back to my chair and settled in. I listened to the music of nature as I rigged my line and cast it into the water. I watched the lake ripple as the bait hit and the bright orange and yellow bobber moved up and down with the incoming swells. I popped the top off a soda and relished the first cold sip while the cool breeze washed against my face, and I inhaled the smells of earth and water. The moment carried with it a feeling of peace I wanted to linger for a while, if not forever.

I fished through the night. At one point I had a scare when a beaver swam under my line. I had seen beaver before, but never in the area and never that close in the dark. It sneaked up on me. I was startled enough to be glad there were no witnesses.

When I'd caught enough fish, I cleaned them on a rock we had used for years. It was sort of a family tradition to clean your catch on that rock. I entertained the thought I might one day have a son to take fishing here and have him do the same thing. Meanwhile, I'd let first things come first.

After I finished, I packed everything into the car and took a last look at the moon and the star-peppered sky, their soft light illuminating the water, before I drove home.

Chapter 10

I awoke the next morning from a dreamless sleep. I felt good. I took my time getting out of bed. In the mood for some morning big band jazz, I padded to my record player and put on some Gene Krupa. I turned up the volume, glad I didn't have any neighbors to complain. There was only Mrs. Weatherman one floor below, and I was sure it wasn't loud enough for her to hear it.

I adjusted the player, went to the kitchen and attempted to make myself an omelet. I say attempt, because I've yet to actually make one. Today was no exception. I threw peppers and onion into my now-scrambled egg breakfast, poured a glass of milk and sat at the table to enjoy food and music.

I had planned a busy morning for myself, though after I had gotten around to finishing my breakfast, the morning was halfway gone. I mixed up some bug spray and went to the fourth floor to spray the units and check for any issues.

I liked the fourth floor. Granted, it was a wreck, much more so than the rest of the building, and it wasn't going to get serious attention any time soon. Renovation costs, especially in older buildings. The floors and moldings were original, put in when the place was built, at least a hundred years ago. The windows here, unlike the other floors, were old glass, inefficient but large, and let in a lot of sun. The other two floors with living space had re-placement windows in hopes of making the apartments more energy efficient. It was a lost cause, but at least it looked nice. Since this floor was unsafe, I wouldn't want to live on it, but the old embellishments, paint and wallpaper gave it a sort of charm, or at least a distinctive character.

After I finished up, I went to visit Mrs. Weatherman. I let her feed me a lunch of sandwiches and cookies while I admired her latest work in progress, another hand-stitched quilt. She talked about her late husband's love of the outdoors and fishing when I mentioned my own outdoor excursion. I felt sad as she talked about him because you could tell she missed him terribly. She lost him to a stroke ten years ago. I had never gotten to know him my-self, except through her stories, but I could tell he was someone I would have liked.

I invited her to come up for dinner, but she declined. I offered to bring her a plate, but she vetoed that idea as well, saying she was afraid she would swallow a bone, but I suspected she just wasn't a fan of catfish.

She did take me up on my offer to pick up some groceries, as I was going to the store for myself anyway. When I got back I refused the ten spot she tried to pass along. I told her the cookies were more than enough payment. But she insisted, so I took it. She can be quite stubborn.

I put away my groceries and thought it was a good day to swing by Gary's gallery. I called Gwendolyn and invited her, as per Gary's demand, but I would use any excuse to spend time with her. She claimed she had nothing better to do and would like to come along. I was sure she had plenty she would rather do, so I finished up quickly and went to pick her up before she had a chance to change her mind.

****

Gary's face lit up as if he hadn't seen me in years. He always got so excited I couldn't help but feel a little special. He spread his arms out wide and shouted, "Howdy thar, pardner!"

I smiled at him. "*Hola*, Gary. What happened to your charming foreign phrases?"

Gary shrugged and said, "I thought I'd go for more of a southwest patois today. It's still foreign."

"I don't think people really talk that way except in the movies."

"Have you been to the Southwest?"

"No," I admitted.

"Then don't go raining on my parade," he said, and turned his attention to Gwendolyn. "Harry did mention a friend, but he didn't mention you're gorgeous. I absolutely love your hair!" Gary squealed and impulsively ran his fingers through it.

I made a hasty introduction. "Gary, meet Gwendolyn. Gwendolyn, Gary."

Gwendolyn giggled as Gary took her hand and kissed it. "And perfect skin," he gushed. "If only I were born with different genes, but alas!" he cried, as he went into a mock swoon.

"You're okay." I rolled my eyes at his dramatics.

"But I do like the ones I have now. Aren't they cute?" He gave a twirl, showing off his new jeans.

"Ravishing," I agreed.

"I found them on sale. Can you believe it?"

Gwendolyn could only giggle again.

"If I had pulled that, you'd probably slap the shit out of me," I muttered to Gwendolyn.

She said nothing, only shrugged.

"How about a little tour, Gwen?" Gary asked.

"Sure," she agreed, and followed him.

Gary showed her around and I tagged along. I had seen most of it already, but there were a few new pieces, some of which were already marked as sold.

Gary talked about the artists and spiced it up with some gossip and history. He always created an experience. I thought Gary's gallery could be on par with some of the ones you might find in New York, or some big city.

"Okay, what you've been waiting for," Gary rubbed his hands together.

"What am I waiting for?" asked Gwendolyn.

"A first look at some new art," Gary answered, as he took his keys and opened a back door. He flipped on a light and went to a sheet covering some canvases and yanked it away dramatically.

"Bloody hell," I intoned.

It was a dark painting of a skull. The skin over it was being pulled to the sides in the beaks of dingy white doves subtly speckled with dark red dots. It was done with a heavy hand, using broad strokes that only enhanced the effect.

Gwendolyn's breath stopped. After a moment, she said, "It's rather ghastly. People buy this sort of thing?"

"Of course. They do it all the time. It's more popular than you might imagine. People have a thing for the macabre and have been known to buy stranger things. Monkey paws, shrunken heads.

82

Things of the sort."

Gwendolyn cringed. "That's disgusting."

"I like it," I said with enthusiasm.

"I love his work myself," Gary said. Then more to himself, he added, "I can't think of a good time for a show."

"How about Halloween?" Gwendolyn said in jest.

"Not a bad idea," I said. "It seems fitting."

Gary seemed to mull over it for a moment as his long fingers played with his sparse goatee. "I like the idea, but I was thinking maybe I should have the paintings on the website exclusively. Show them only to serious buyers. I've done it with a few in the past."

"You should show them," I said. "Are you thinking about not doing it here because of the content? If that's the case, I wonder when you started shying away from something controversial."

"I can't remember, but this is Carson. These make Goya's paintings look like things you'd hang in a nursery."

"Isn't he the guy who did paintings of witches eating people?" asked Gwendolyn.

"Indeed, it's the same guy," said Gary.

I chuckled, "You've already decided to show them, huh?"

"Of course," Gary gave a flip of his hand. "They're not all blatant."

I agreed with him. In some works of the horror genre, the gore was implied rather than shown, but you knew it was there, and that alone disturbed the psyche. Think Tobe Hooper's *The Texas Chainsaw Massacre*, or David Lynch's *Eraserhead*.

Disturbing without being blatant.

"The artist is actually from the city," Gary started. "I think he's got something. He came to me asking if I'd put them up. I feel lucky and honored he thought of me, especially since I love showing local work. He's good enough I'd like to give him a one-man show, but not right away. I'd like him to bring in a few more pieces, but there's already a lot of interest."

"Really? Who would you get to come?" Gwendolyn asked.

Gary looked at her with narrowed eyes. "Just who do you think I am, little missy?"

"You're Gary?" she answered.

"Damn right I am," he said, with a narcissistic smile as he covered up the paintings and led us back to the main gallery. "That's it. That's DeVille's!"

"It's very nice," Gwendolyn said.

"Thank you, sweetie."

"So, I caught some catfish last night—" I began.

"Oh, you're a brutal, brutal man!" Gary interrupted.

I rolled my eyes. "Anyway, I thought maybe you guys would like to come and eat them, or something else if you don't like catfish."

"What about me?" Gwendolyn asked.

"I just invited you."

"You said, 'you guys,' and last time I checked, I'm not a guy."

"Oh, why must you be so literal? Let me rephrase. How would you 'girls' like to come to my place to partake in a catfish dinner?" I asked with a grin.

"Smart ass," Gwendolyn muttered.

"I do rather like profiting from the brutality of man, so I'm game," Gary answered.

Gwendolyn shook her head. "I'd be happy to come, but why can't you invite all genders?"

"Gary accepted."

"But Gary isn't a girl."

"He's gay, so he doesn't mind the category at all."

"Why don't you let him speak for himself," Gwendolyn said, her hands on her hips.

Gary laughed and clapped his hands together. "Bravo! I could be convinced you two were a married couple!" He looked at

Gwendolyn. "Sweetie, I am all things, so if the situation requires femininity, then I shall make myself more feminine. If masculinity is called for, I can be just as manly as the rest of them."

I let out a snort.

"You, young man," Gary pointed at me. "Don't you say a word."

"What?" I shouted. "I didn't say anything."

"You wanted to, don't you deny it. Don't think I didn't hear that stupid snort of yours."

"Don't be offended," I pleaded.

"Feed me dinner and I won't be."

"You got yourself a deal."

"What time should I be there?"

"I don't know. Whenever. Six? Seven?"

"Six-thirty then," Gary decided. "I'll be there. Make sure you bring your beautiful self, Miss Gwen."

"I'll be there," Gwendolyn giggled. "I like your gallery, Mr. DeVille."

"Gary, please. All that mister stuff makes me feel old and, well, manly."

Gwendolyn flashed a smile. "Okay, Gary."

"See there? Not so hard, is it?"

"Not at all."

Gary walked us to the door and let us out. "I'll see you later," he said, as he wiggled his fingers.

"Don't forget," I said.

"I'm like an elephant. I never forget. *Ciao!*"

We waved and walked to the car.

"I like him," Gwendolyn said after she shut her door.

"Me, too," I agreed. "He's quite the character. He's also the best friend I've ever had."

"A very flamboyant character at that."

"Indeed. Should I drive you home, miss?"

"If you feel you must. If you'd rather, we could go to your place and I'll help with dinner."

I didn't think it was such a bad idea. In fact, I thought it was a damn good idea. More time with her, and less work for me. "Sure, if you want. I won't complain," I said, nonchalantly.

"I want," she said.

"It's settled."

We made a quick stop at the grocery store to pick up a few things to go with dinner and found a couple of bottles of wine to go with the fish. I'm not much of a wine guy, to be honest. If it were up to me, I'd just get one of those boxes with a built-in spout and call it good. I was more than happy to let Gwendolyn take charge of that part. From there we went to my place, put on some music, and went to work on dinner.

******

Punctuality was typical of Gary, and he showed up right at six-thirty with a container of store-bought potato salad. We had finished dinner preparations, so we were able to eat straightaway.

Gwendolyn handled the fish. I had planned to just fry it like normal and call it good. I have to admit she made it much tastier than what I had in mind.

After we finished the meal, we played cards and talked. Gary and Gwendolyn got along splendidly. So much so that I kind of felt left out. I just can't get into fashion and girly things. To be frank, I felt awkward, but happy at the same time. You always want your friends to get along with each other. Gary seemed to attract everyone and they all called him a friend. I wasn't completely left out, but I was the odd man for certain.

The evening drew to a close and Gary made a big production of leaving. We made promises to do it again soon, only Gary wanted to host the next one. After he finally left, I took Gwendolyn home and we chatted a while in the car.

She leaned over and kissed me on the cheek. "Thank you for today."

I blushed heavily. "Aw, shucks. It was nothin'."

She laughed. "It's way too easy to make you blush!"

"Glad I could be entertaining."

"Oh, don't get like that. It's a good thing."

"Yeah?"

"Yeah. Thanks again. It was a lot of fun," she said softly. She got out of the car and I watched her walk away, and kept watching even after she shut the door behind her.

I sighed with content as I started my car and headed home. In this moment, I was happy and all was right in the world.

The moment didn't last.

Chapter 11

For reasons I can't explain, the mellow mood created by fishing and eating with friends dissolved overnight. The house once again haunted me, my dreams and my reality. I wasn't sure I wanted to know more about it, even while a secret desire drew me to it. I craved it like a kid craves a cookie he's not supposed to eat.

Following the theory there is no such thing as coincidence, that there is a reason for everything, I tried to think of how it connected to me. I tried to think of all the things in my life I could pin down as an absolute result of choices I had made.

Maybe it was true. Gary was my best friend because I decided to befriend him. I started working for Carol at The Bookworm because I made the decision to fill out an application, go to an interview and accept the job. My home and friendship with Mrs. Weatherman I could trace back to choosing my apartment over two others I'd looked at.

Meeting Gwendolyn? I don't know about that. Maybe I was in the right place at the right time—catapulted there by the house.

A reason why the house kept calling to me? I couldn't think of anything I had done to bring it on. It frustrated me to the point it made me sick. I still went to work and did all the stuff I had to do, but my heart wasn't in it. I allowed the house to take over my thoughts and emotions, even though I knew relinquishing control was a bad choice.

At the base of it, I was just feeling sorry for myself.

People tried calling. Gary, Carol. My brother, Jim, asked me if I wanted to go out on his boat and do some fishing, thinking it might help me get out of my mood. It usually would have, but I didn't feel like driving that far to do it. I knew if I did, a good time would be had, because it was always that way when I went fishing with my brother. He provided the beer and he was a genius with the grill.

Jim is the only guy I know who puts a grill on his pontoon boat. He loves going out on the water to fish and camps with regularity on his boat. I've joined him on more than one occasion. If I ever win the lottery, I think I'll buy him a house boat. He'd really like that. Then he could just live on the lake and fish all night and day, and not have to worry about getting wet when it rains. Not that he does now, but sleeping on his boat is a pain.

It's just a silly pipe dream. Bloody unlikely that I'll ever win the lottery, even if I actually bought tickets. I was feeling pretty down to decline an invitation to spend time with my brother. I'll make it up to him sometime soon, I decided.

Gwendolyn called a few times, but I couldn't get into it with her. I couldn't explain anything, especially since I wasn't sure about it myself. To be honest, she frightened me a little. She shouldn't, I knew, but she did just the same. It wasn't through any fault of her own, but I wasn't sure we had gotten to the point where I could share those things on my mind. Not that I thought I couldn't trust her, I just worried it would make her disappear. I didn't want that to happen, but she stirred feelings inside me which had caused me some degree of pain in the past. I don't want to sound like a wuss, but I don't like pain.

Normally, I tend to get nervous around women. Especially beautiful ones, just like I did with Gwendolyn. It's probably the reason why I rarely dated. She was one of those exceptions. Not only was she beautiful, but funny and intelligent. I loved being around her and the way her smile made me smile. Everything was better when she was near. Even the sound of her name...holy hell, I'm already in love. How did I let it sneak up on me like that? As much as I tried to avoid it, it seemed I'd set myself up to be hurt. No way around it.

It seems strange, but the fixation on the house while I also thought about Gwendolyn made me feel guilty. Foolish? Yes, I knew it was. Maybe I was trying to make an excuse for wanting to go back. If I did, perhaps I could get it out of my system and forget the whole thing. Put it out of my mind forever. Focus on things that mattered. Stop feeling like I was in thrall to something beyond explanation.

I really think I am going insane.

Before I could even try go back and get it out of my system, I needed to figure out how I managed to get myself there in the first place. What was I thinking or doing, the first time? Was I awake or asleep? I couldn't remember.

I had a crazy thought. I sat up in my chair and closed my eyes. I used some of the self-hypnosis techniques I'd heard about. I'd never used them to any great degree before, but how hard could it be?

I let myself relax, from my toes to the top of my head. I took deep breaths and released them, as I put Her facade into my imagination. As I breathed, I visualized the house into existence in my mind. The emptiness around Her. The smell of Her.

I couldn't say how long I sat like that. I had lost all sense of time, but I eventually felt the wind whip around me. It brought with it the smell of wildflowers. I held fast for a few moments before I opened my eyes. I blinked several times. I had to make sure I was really there, that I had done it.

There She was, right in front of me, in living color.

I had solved one of the mysteries. As far-fetched as it may sound, it seemed all I needed to do was will myself there, like a crazy kind of whole-body astral projection. Now that I'd figured it out, I wondered how difficult it would be to learn the rest. It did not escape me She made the choice somehow of what would and wouldn't be easy. Still, I felt relieved to know this particular secret. This was how I had been doing it all along. It meant that anytime I wanted, I could go back.

So much for my resolution to end things with one last visit.

Without hesitation, I entered Her recesses again, consequences be damned. She had changed from the last time I was here. She was darker. Colder. Less welcoming than She had been before. It entered my mind that I had perhaps gone too far, moved too fast. I shook the feeling off and allowed an invisible force to pull me to the kitchen. I didn't know why I was going that way, or what I was supposed to be looking for.

I gasped as I opened the dining room door. The room had changed. The meticulously placed china was smashed, not a piece spared. Bugs, big ugly things, crawled over and under the debris, searching for any leftover crumbs. The chandelier that hung above the table now lay cockeyed and broken in the middle. Candles were scattered, some fallen to the floor. My immediate thought was it was the work of vandals, but I knew it wasn't true as soon as the thought hit. Something else was the cause.

Maybe I was seeing different stages of decay, snapshots over the advance of time. Whatever it was, it felt sinister. I swallowed my rising fear and pushed through the swinging door into the kitchen. Straight into a scene that could have been from one of Hollywood's earliest films. I saw the room as though I were watching faded, scratched film in sepia tones. A fire blazed in the hearth, and something bubbled in the cauldron, but I felt no warmth.

A plump, black woman with a kerchief knotted in her thick hair was cutting vegetables on an old chopping block. She seemed to be singing as she swung her ample hips from side to side. I also recognized the same girl I had seen on my first visit, washing vegetables in the sink. She had a smile on her face and was singing along with the woman. It was nice to see her happy. To see there was at least one time when she had reason to smile. Neither of them noticed my presence.

Carefully, I stepped further into the room and let the door close behind me. Suddenly, I was pushed with violent force by someone shoving the door open behind me. I flew forward with the wind knocked out of me and caught hold of a countertop. A large rolling pin fell to the floor.

Two men stumbled in, tangled together in a human knot and fell hard onto the floor. One was a portly, bearded man. He gripped the neck of the other, younger man as his face distorted with violent anger, his lips shouting out silent curses.

The younger man, his eyes bulging, fought for breath under the grip of the older man's hands. He struggled as he tried to pry the older man's thick fingers from his neck with one hand as the other snaked across the floor, searching for something that would help him free himself from the vise-like grip. Blindly, his fingers grasped the heavy wooden rolling pin. His fingers wrapped around the handle tightly as he swung his arm in a blurred arc.

The rolling pin connected with the bearded man's temple and his eyes widened in shock and pain. His fingers grew slack and loosened their grip on the young man's neck. The young man rolled out from underneath and tried to catch his breath.

The bearded man, dazed but not out, grabbed the rolling pin and smashed it against the young man's nose. I imagined the sickening sound of cartilage breaking as blood gushed out. He instinctively raised his hands to his damaged nose as the rolling pin made a return trip, breaking fingers as they pushed into the broken nose he was trying to protect. Though I couldn't hear it, I knew he was screaming in pain.

As he tried to recover, the bearded man swung again and connected to his temple. The young man's eyes rolled back as he fell over. His head bounced as it hit the floor. The bearded man drove the weapon down onto the top of his victim's skull to make sure his foe wouldn't be getting up again, then caught his breath and righted himself.

The door slammed open again. I quickly moved out of the way to keep from being flattened as it flew at me and bounced off the wall. A woman burst through, her clothing disheveled and her eyes wild with fury, fear and insanity. She grasped the handle of a large butcher knife wedged in the chopping block and yanked it out forcefully.

The black woman and the girl were silently screaming in terror, pleading with the woman and warning the man. Neither seemed to hear, caught up in their own drama. The woman ran toward the man and brought the knife down, cutting him deeply in the neck, just above his shoulder blade. He turned, his eyes widened in shock. She lifted the knife again as he raised his arms, his whole countenance pleading with her as she brought the knife down, madly hacking and stabbing his body in wild abandon. Blood gushed and spattered. Her face and hands stained with his blood and gore as it sprayed the room.

The knife blurred as it came down repeatedly. The fallen man was dead by now, but the woman cleaved into his neck and severed his head from his body. She kept at it, her body convulsing as if she were laughing uncontrollably.

I knew I could never forget that face, coated with another human's blood and laughing like a mad woman. It was probably best I couldn't hear it. I imagined if I could, it would probably be a crazy cackling like the wicked witch, only ten times more frightening.

A bright flash came out of nowhere. When I regained my vision some seconds later, the kitchen was void of people, void of death, and the color restored. I remained in shock from what I had witnessed.

Murder.

Even with the old movie feel to it, I knew it was real, an event that had actually occurred in this house at some time, somewhere in the world, if not in Carson itself.

Chapter 12

It wasn't only the sheer brutality of the event that left me in a state of shock. I had also recognized the woman. Even with her muddled appearance and the eyes filled with insanity, I knew it was the same woman who graced the portrait in the foyer. The same woman who had played her sad song on the piano in the parlor. I couldn't deny it. The similarities were too great.

Who was she? What had caused her to commit such an atrocious act? Who were the men? What riled them up?

More questions to be answered.

I backed out of the kitchen. I couldn't trust anything enough to look away from the room until the door was closed. Even then, I cast furtive backward glances as I left the dining room with the smashed dishes and the bugs hunting for a meal.

As I reentered the foyer, I looked for a place to sit and found a chair mostly held together, hidden in the shadows. I sat down carefully and relaxed only when I was sure it would hold my weight. I couldn't get the woman and the bloody scene out of my mind. What had happened? What were these people going through? I pushed myself from the chair and walked to the portrait to examine it, as if it would hold answers. The woman stared at me through the painted eyes, still hard, but different somehow. They weren't any kinder, but neither were they bereft of reason, as the specter's eyes were. This made it hard to reconcile that they were the same person.

Why was this being shown to me? Why did I have to see it and what was I supposed to do about it? These things had happened a long time ago, before I was even a thought, much less born. I was sure of it. I had no knowledge of any personal connection to the place, nor was there a logical explanation as to why the hell I had the ability to come here. I was bewildered and lost, not to mention more than a little afraid. I wasn't sure I wanted to continue, but if there was some reason I was brought here that I was not privy to yet, brought into Her confidence and allowed a glimpse of Her terrible secrets, then I guessed I should face my fears and try to be brave. I should at least continue until I learned my purpose in all of this. I must, though whatever interest I held was quickly turning to terror.

"You know the secret."

I heard it, but did not know where it was coming from; whether it was inside or outside my head. My heart was working overtime. It beat as if it had a speed metal drummer banging away inside. I swallowed my fear and tried to think. What was the secret I was supposed to know? Surely it wasn't stumbling onto a murder in a time warp.

"Why me?" I moaned. I looked at the door beside me, apprehensive at what might be behind it. I grasped the doorknob. I turned it and threw open the door and entered before I could chicken out. I hadn't realized my eyes were closed until I opened them.

The eerie blue light illuminating the rooms had now turned a violet color, though I could still see clearly enough. The walls were lined with floor-to-ceiling shelves filled with books. A painting hung above a stone fireplace.

I moved closer to get a better look at the painting. It was of a garden, with a house in the background. I realized with a start that it depicted the house I was in, though it looked much better in the painting. The garden was splashed with bright colors, and nymphs danced in a circle around a satyr playing a Pan pipe. It was a happy scene where all eyes were bright and dancing, as were their feet. The painting seemed to be alive, like I could step in and join the festivities. I wondered if it could mean something, but I didn't have an answer. I had a feeling there was more in the painting hidden from the casual viewer. It reminded me of a painting hung in my grandfather's house, where you looked for Indians and they kept appearing in places like rocks and trees. Places I hadn't noticed them before, though I had looked at the painting a hundred times.

I eventually tore myself away and looked around the room. A writing table sat flush against a wall with several books stacked on it, as if someone were working and had stepped away for a moment. Only the dust said otherwise. I walked across the threadbare carpet to the heavy drapes that covered the windows flanking the fireplace and pulled them aside to look out. After a couple of dust-induced sneezes, I tried to see outside, but it was too dark, as if the windows had been blacked out. Stuffed chairs were at an angle facing the fireplace, the upholstery torn and moth-eaten. A table was set in front of the chairs with an unfamiliar game set upon it. It looked as if the players had abandoned their game midway.

I did not feel the desire to touch it. Instead, I scanned the books housed on the shelves. I pulled a few out. Though some were worn, the pages yellowed with age, they were in better condition than I'd expected, although I observed that most of the tomes had been visited by silverfish. I had an odd compulsion to protect the place and its contents from pests, especially to preserve the old books, though I had the feeling I was only seeing what She wanted me to see; that I was perceiving only limited visions, with others hidden away. Underneath the makeup, there was something else, and quite likely, it was something not benign.

I looked at the old, rotted rugs covering the wood floor and thought of how they had once been beautiful and expensive. Now, every step threw up puffs of dust that had long lain dormant. I felt like I should clean it up, but I didn't see anything resembling a broom. Not that I made a habit of cleaning up after ghosts.

I noticed the shelves across from the door held books with brightly colored bindings, which could have been sets, though they were mixed up. I didn't want to stay, so I filed it away to perhaps look into later and left the library.

I paced around the foyer a while and considered my next step. I was developing a morbid sense of reverence for Her, even as I feared Her more. Maybe reverence is the wrong word, but I don't know what else would be appropriate.

I began to wonder if I could go home at will, just as I was able to arrive. Just will myself to go back to my apartment, back to my bed and back to my life. I stood at the entry door, closed my eyes and did the same thing as when I came. I felt nothing and after a few minutes, I opened my eyes. I was still inside the house.

"Of course, it wouldn't be that easy. At least I gave it a shot," I said.

When I stepped off the porch, I was in downtown Carson. I felt disoriented and ran my hands over my body to check if I was still intact. There was no one around to see my materialization, if that's what had happened. The building behind me was up for rent, so it was empty and no one would have been inside to see my miraculous appearance.

None of it mattered. I still had the lost feeling. The travel agency still stood across the street, unchanged except for a few travel posters advertising new cruises. The Carson Historical Center stood next to it. I was too physically and mentally exhausted to do anything now, but I made a mental note to pay it a visit sometime to see if I might be able to dredge up some information. I didn't expect it to have too much and I wondered if it would be worthwhile to visit. The town was rather small and uninteresting and I assumed it had always been this way. Maybe the Historical Center was someone's idea of a joke. Or maybe I was wrong and it would be worth looking into, at least once. All I had was Dr. Pierce's name, but perhaps it would be enough to get started. I didn't even know where the house had been located. I pushed it all aside, took the familiar air of the town into my lungs, and started to walk toward home. I was beginning to feel a little better.

Chapter 13

I thought it would be nice to drop in on Mrs. Weatherman and see how she was doing, after making a brief stop at the grocery on the way. When I got back to my building, I went to her apartment.

"Well, well. Don't you look a bit more chipper," Mrs. Weatherman said as I came in the door.

"Thanks. I do feel better," I said. I pulled a bottle of strawberry/kiwi sparkling water from my bag. "I brought you a present."

"Oh my, Harry. You shouldn't have done such a thing!" she exclaimed, as if I had brought her a handful of diamonds. "I do appreciate it. How nice."

Though her reaction made me feel a bit embarrassed, I was glad something so small could bring her so much pleasure.

"Could you please fetch me a glass?" she asked. "Just put a little ice in it."

"Yes, ma'am, I can do that," I said, and headed toward the kitchen.

"Thank you. You're a gentleman and a scholar, two bits shy of a dollar," she said brightly.

"My grandpa used to say that," I commented.

"It's just an old saying. Make a glass for yourself, why don't you?"

"No, it's okay," I said. I found a juice glass in the cabinet and dropped in several ice cubes, poured some of the fizzy water in, then put the rest in the fridge. The bottle would most likely last her a week, whereas with me, it would be lucky to be alive for the six o'clock news.

I took the glass to her and she took a sip before setting it down on a coaster decorated with butterflies.

"Mrs. Weatherman, you've been here a long time, haven't you? Here in Carson, I mean."

"Well, sure. I guess you could say I've been here a while," she said. "Bill, that would be Mr. Weatherman, and I moved here, I'd say about fifty years ago, thereabouts. We were newly married and had the future and all the world to look forward to. I can still remember the day. It was the happiest day in my life, don't you know." She smiled at a silent thought before she continued.

"We moved here when Bill got on at the steel mill over on the other side of town. 'Course, the mill isn't here anymore. It seems a lot of these places just pick up and move anytime the fancy takes them and don't pay any mind to the people put out of work, with families to feed. Of course, it's their business what they do. I'm sure there are advantages to picking up and moving, but they should at least give their workers a bit more notice. Especially if they put in years of their lives making money for the company. We got lucky, Bill and me. He retired ten years before they packed up and moved overseas somewhere. He'd been with them for thirty years. Hard to believe, but it went by so fast. I guess you can say I've been here a spell."

"Yeah, that's a long time," I said. "You ever hear of a big house being around here? An old one? Maybe owned by a doctor?" I asked.

Mrs. Weatherman laughed. "Well, that sounds like a good number of big and fancy houses."

"It does. So, did you ever hear of a guy named Dr. Pierce? A Henry Pierce who might have lived here before?"

She rocked a little in her chair and took a thoughtful sip of her water. "The name sounds familiar, but I can't rightly recall. Probably a story of one kind or another. I didn't grow up here, mind you. It may have been before my time. Carson is an old town."

"Yeah," I said with disappointment.

"Well dear, if it's something of any significance, you might try the library, or the Historical Center downtown."

"I was thinking of that earlier. I'll probably go and check it out. I just thought maybe you might have known something about it."

"What is this about, this interest of yours?" she asked.

"It's nothing, really. Probably just heard someone mention it, or overheard it in the store, and it just stuck in my mind."

"There's more in this town than meets the eye. Lots to keep one curious."

"Surprising, isn't it?"

"No, no. Not at all. Most small towns that have been around a time have interesting things happen and interesting people who live in them. You know this."

"You're right, Mrs. Weatherman. You're interesting," I said.

"Oh, posh, I'm not at all interesting. Just an old lady. You are an odd one, because most folks don't much look for those interesting things. They think nothing ever happens in little towns."

"True," I said, as I glanced at my watch. "I think I should go on up."

"Would you like to take some cookies with you?"

"I probably shouldn't. You're going to make me fat," I said.

"One or two isn't going to hurt you none. Let me get you a few wrapped up and you can nibble on them later," she insisted, and started to push herself up.

"No, you don't have to get up," I said. "I can get them."

"All right then. Just take as many as you'd like," she said, and settled back.

I went to the kitchen, took a few cookies, and made sure to thank her before going up to my own apartment.

******

"This is nice," Gwendolyn said, as she lay back on one of the cheap vinyl lawn chairs I keep on the roof of my building.

"Don't lie. They're not at all nice. These chairs prod your back and are uncomfortable as hell. I should get rid of them."

"Then why don't you get something less uncomfortable?"

"Because I'm cheap and lazy."

"At least you're honest, but I wasn't talking about the chairs. I was talking about being out here. The open air and the view of the sky."

"Yeah, it's not too bad," I said. "I keep chairs up here for the times I want to be out in the fresh air and don't feel like driving to a better spot. A little bright at night for my tastes, but it's good enough. And I guess you get used to the chairs."

"By saying you don't feel like driving, you're really saying you're too lazy."

"Why does it have to mean lazy?"

"Because that's what it means. 'I don't feel like' is just a euphemism people use. A longer way of saying lazy. Why sugarcoat it? Just be out with it. Laziness isn't as bad as people want to make it."

"Sloth is one of the more pleasurable sins," I said with a grin.

"It is, but it doesn't matter. I still like it up here; you just have to rethink your seating arrangements."

"I've thought about getting one of those hammocks. If I ever got around to doing it, I would probably embrace laziness all the more. A hammock would definitely be more comfortable than these crappy old chairs."

"You should get two of them," she said.

"I assume one would be for you?"

"Sure. Why should you be the only one to have all the hammock fun?"

"I guess it wouldn't be fair, me lounging away while you're stuck in a cheap lawn chair, getting your back prodded."

"Wouldn't be fair at all." She stole the last sausage roll and took a huge bite. "You weren't kidding about these things," she said, through a mouthful.

"I never kid," I said.

"Yeah, yeah. These are fantastic! I bet I gained a couple pounds tonight."

"I have noticed you're getting a little fat," I teased.

"You shut your mouth!" She swatted me on the arm.

"Hey! I was only kidding," I laughed, as I blocked another attack. "Calm down!"

"You're not funny," she muttered.

"You're right. I'm not funny and you're not fat. You're perfect."

"Let's not lie," she said. "When you said sausage rolls, I was expecting a link inside of baked bread."

"That would be a pig in a blanket."

"Same thing. Like shit on a shingle is just gravy over toast."

"Yeah, but gravy over toast sounds more appetizing than shit on a shingle," I said.

"Not much more. Come on, it's freaking gravy on toast."

"True." I didn't offer any arguments.

"I'm glad you're feeling better." She glanced over at me. "I was a little worried about you."

"There's nothing to worry about, but it's nice to know some-one was thinking of me. I've thought about you, too."

"I hope you haven't overtaxed that brain of yours," she said. "So, how much have you been thinking of me?"

I thought a moment. "I guess if every time I thought of you, a star fell from the sky, there wouldn't be any stars left."

Gwendolyn burst into laughter. "That's the cheesiest thing I ever heard!"

"Then I'm the king of cheese." It was a stupid thing to say, but I didn't let it bother me. I was content to hear her laugh again.

Since I had been feeling like going out and doing things again, I had gone to pick her up for dinner. She did seem to be concerned and I figured it to be a good thing. It's always nice to know people worry over you, but I didn't want her to ever worry about anything. Not even me, no matter how good it made me feel.

We'd gone to a mom and pop pizzeria where I introduced her to their one-of-a-kind sausage rolls, which I placed in the top five tastiest foods. After eating, we shot some pool, which I am terrible at. She wasn't much better, so the game lasted awhile. It was fine with me, because I hate spending a dollar on a game that lasts for only a few minutes. I like to get my money's worth. If I wanted to work on my skills, I would go to a place where they rent tables by the hour.

After we finished there, we drove around for a bit, though not too much, what with the price of gas and all. We ended up on the roof of my building, on cheap lawn chairs and munching leftover sausage rolls.

I admitted to myself I was developing stronger feelings for Gwendolyn, but I didn't know what to do with them. I wasn't sure how she felt about me, and I wasn't sure I wanted to. I wanted to keep this relationship friendly. I feared the dreadful phrases "You're my good friend" or "You're like a brother." Those might be the responses if I raised the prospect of romance. I'd heard those words more than once before. The relationship becomes uncomfortable afterward, and eventually fizzles out.

With Gwendolyn, I would rather be just a friend or like a brother than nothing at all, so I determined I'd keep my feelings to myself. She was Jenny to my Forrest Gump, and we all know how that turned out. It sounds stupid, but I can't imagine my life without at least her friendship. With me being only twenty-five, it could be a very long time.

"What are you thinking about?" she asked.

"Uh, I'm not thinking about anything."

"Bullshit," she said.

"Why'd you say that?"

"Because you stumbled. You only do it now when you're nervous, or up to something. Also, you're blushing."

"Move on over Sherlock Holmes, we've got a new detective in town!"

"Three, you're being sarcastic." She crossed her arms and lifted her chin. "Out with it. What were you thinking? I bet it was something bad about me, wasn't it?"

"You think you know me so well, don't you?" I said. I felt I'd only embarrass myself if I told the truth.

"Oh, come on and tell me. I promise I won't laugh," she pleaded.

"That's not what I'm afraid of," I said, but I was. It's the kind of laughter which crushes hearts; the kind of laughter friendships do not often survive.

I was indeed afraid of it.

Gwendolyn turned toward me. Her eyes shone. Her perfect green eyes. "If not, then tell me what you're thinking."

"Okay, so I was thinking about you," I admitted.

"I knew it!" She shouted and clapped her hands together.

"Yeah. Just how I really like having you around and don't know what I would do if you weren't. That I'm blah, blah, blah. It's stupid." I tried to pass it off as a joke, but I didn't pull it off. I'd probably messed it up now.

The quiet became uneasy and I could feel the heat rising in my cheeks. I almost wished she would laugh.

"Oh, Harry. I like you. I really do like you a lot. You're an American original."

"Thanks, I guess," I mumbled. I should have made something up. Should have said I was thinking about politics, religion, war. I knew where it would be going now, so I prepared to give myself a huge, Rush Limbaugh-style, "See, I told you so!"

"I think I understand, but really..." She closed her eyes and sighed. "I'm not going to say something stupid like you're my best friend, or whatever people say to blow off someone. I like you too much for that. But the fact is, I do think of you as one of my best friends. Honestly though, I don't think you'd really want anything more."

"Why not?" I asked, secretly relieved it wasn't as bad as I'd feared.

"I have my reasons."

"What kind of reasons?" I prodded.

She didn't say anything for a moment. I began to feel bad for being persistent. If she didn't want to say, she didn't have to. I really had no business prying into her private thoughts.

"Maybe sometime I'll tell you, but not now."

"Okay," I said quietly, and felt like a jerk when I noticed a tiny tear, a crystal drop mothered by an emerald sliding down her cheek.

"I think the Ramones said it best," I said.

"And what did they say?"

"Hey little girl, I wanna be your boyfriend," I said, and smiled.

She laughed and took my hand. "And you are, Harry. You are."

"I'm sorry about all that."

"It's okay. Honestly, I wonder what it would have been like if you weren't standing there, looking all lost and ogling me."

"I wasn't ogling you," I said, as I rolled my eyes.

"It looked that way to me."

"Whatever. Did you talk to me because you thought I looked lost?"

She thought a moment. "Yeah, I think so."

"Yeah? Well, I was a dork that day."

"You're still a dork." She punched me lightly on the arm. "Are we okay?"

I nodded. "Yeah. There wasn't anything wrong."

I was glad it turned out the way it did. It beat what I was imagining.

I just needed to remind myself things don't always go the way you expect them to, and sometimes it is best to get things out in the open and out of the way. This way, you know where everyone stands. Because of this, I was able to say we were okay without any hidden doubts.

Chapter 14

I thought a lot about friendship that night. It was still on my mind late the next afternoon as I sat in a sleek-but-comfortable chair in Gary's living room. The space where my host spent most of his at-home time was nothing less than I expected, his embrace of the stereotype extending to impeccable home décor.

Gary came from the kitchen, carrying a silver tea service. He set it on the coffee table and poured two steaming cups of tea.

"Nice little tea set you have there," I said.

"It is, isn't it? Sugar? Cream?"

"No, thanks. Matter of fact, it seems too nice for everyday use. Most people would only bring something like that out for special occasions."

Gary looked at me askance.

"You know, like a party, or when people are over they want to impress. Something like that."

"Any time a friend visits is a special occasion," Gary said.

"You know what I mean."

"Honey, nice things are meant to be used."

"I guess that's true," I said, as I tested a sip of the tea. Too hot.

"Of course, it is. If you have it, you should use it and enjoy it. There's no sense in fretting if something gets scuffed, chipped, or tarnished."

"Yeah, I don't know," I said. I glanced at a large, bright painting hanging over Gary's sofa.

"I never understood people who have books they don't read, toys they've never taken out of the box, much less played with, records they never listen to, et cetera, et cetera." Gary sipped his tea and lay back on the couch. "It's enough to make a boy weary."

"It's because they collect those things," I said.

"What's the point?" he asked.

"They're valuable. That's the point."

"Look at you, playing devil's advocate. You use things yourself some would say are valuable. Your records for instance."

"Maybe they would, but I'm not collecting them. I got them on the cheap so I could listen to them. They're not in collectible condition. Some of these people spend a lot of money on their collections. Hundreds of dollars sometimes, for something that originally cost a few bucks."

"I just think if you're going to spend money on something, you should use it. If it's so valuable, then they should sell it off and buy something they're not going to be afraid to use."

"Maybe they enjoy just looking at it now and then."

"I can't imagine how they just enjoy looking at things. Not unless it's a painting, or a sculpture. I can understand that. Use it or lose it, as the Crüe sang."

"I don't think they were singing about collectibles."

"That's up to interpretation. Drink your tea before it gets cold."

I obliged him by taking a sip of the Earl Grey. It went down my throat, warm, bitter and strong. I set my cup on the table and looked at Gary. He didn't look too well. A little thin and pale. He was probably working too hard.

"Are you okay, Gary?" I asked.

"Of course. What makes you ask such a silly question?"

"Looks like you might be coming down with something. You're on what is probably the world's most comfortable sofa and you don't look comfortable."

"It's nothing. Just a little headache. Could be coming down with a cold, or it's just my sinuses acting up again."

I didn't think he was being completely honest with me, but I left it alone. "Maybe you should see a doctor. "

"No," Gary waved it off. "Nothing a little rest and a couple aspirin can't take care of. A doctor would just charge me to say the same thing. I'll wait it out."

"It's enough for me to notice, and anyway, you've not been looking your best for a while."

"Thanks." Gary grinned.

"I didn't mean it like that. You should see one anyway, just to make sure."

"Okay, Mother. Enough. How have you been?"

"I'm all right. Not complaining any."

"How is the gorgeous Miss Gwen?" His eyes sparkled as he fished for gossip. "Tell me, are you two an item?"

I lowered my head to hide the color rising to my cheeks. "No, nothing like that. We're friends, is all."

"If I'm any kind of judge, I would think you two were more than just friends. I've seen you together and the vibes I get tell me there's more."

I wrestled my thumbs and avoided his gaze. "Really, we're

only friends. I'd like to be more, but you know how it goes."

"Nope. I have no idea how it goes. If I want a date, I ask. If I want more, I pursue it. I understand that, but not this. You two have chemistry. Anyone looking at you can tell, but both of you are fighting it. Is it a straight thing, or what? You're going to have to explain it to me."

"I don't know," I said.

"Come on now. I love both of you and I want to see you happy."

"Ah, I brought it up. It was an accident, just came out. She seemed put off by it. Said I wouldn't want that kind of relationship with her, but wouldn't tell me why. I'm okay with it."

"Are you really?"

"Yeah, I guess. We're still friends and I've seen too many friendships end because one blurts out his love for the other. I guess I got lucky. I'm perfectly satisfied being friends. Really, I am."

"Ah, the song of young love," Gary smiled and hummed a couple of bars from a tune I didn't recognize. "I've seen this kind of thing before. She's afraid to let you in."

"Why?"

"Honey, I don't know. What I do know is her feelings for you are just as passionate as yours are for her."

"I doubt it." I wondered how he could see this stuff and I couldn't.

"Believe what I say and give it some time, *mon ami*. Eventually, she'll come around. Just be patient. You never know what kind of baggage someone has. It's not all bad, but sometimes people need a little time and understanding. You are quite the catch, Harry. If only you were gay. I'd snatch you up and hug you, squeeze you, and never let you go."

"Come on, you're just trying to embarrass me."

"How can I embarrass you when it's just us chickens?" he said. "Anyway, I think you came with something else on your mind, so tell Gary about it."

I finished off my cup of tea and set it back on the service. "You remember me telling you about that place?"

"Yes, of course I remember."

"I found out how I got there and how to go back anytime I want. Actually, I'm not sure how the first time, but it's probably the same thing. Fact is, I know how to do it now."

"How?" Curiosity danced in Gary's eyes.

"I can...oh hell, this sounds so stupid," I started, but didn't want to finish.

"It doesn't matter if it sounds stupid or not. It's just you and me here. Anything said here doesn't leave my body, so go on."

I smiled, because Gary was always able to get things out of you by his rationalizing. "All right. I will myself there."

"You what?"

"I told you it sounds stupid," I moaned.

"No, I just didn't understand. What do you mean, will yourself?"

"I mean, I can go there at will. All I have to do is wish for it and poof, I'm there. Sort of."

"Okay, go on," Gary pushed.

"That's it. I don't leave my house and drive there. I just think of it and want, wish, to go and I'm there. But I can't leave the same way. I have to physically exit the house, and then I end up somewhere in town. It never takes me back home, even though I start there."

"Interesting. It seems too fantastic to believe."

I explained it the best I could, everything I'd seen and felt, my thoughts as to why it haunted me.

Gary let me talk and he listened. I didn't leave anything out, as he was the only person I trusted to listen. He wouldn't think me insane, even when I thought so myself, which was becoming more common than I liked to admit.

Maybe it's a key reason I hadn't gotten around to saying anything to Gwendolyn about it. I wanted to, many times. Not that I didn't trust her, because I did. I just didn't want her to think I was as crazy as I sometimes felt.

"Wow, that's quite a story," Gary said, after I finished. He wasn't condescending. He was calm, as if it were something he heard every day.

"I know," I said.

"You saw a murder, in cold blood, like it was in an old movie? I'm trying to understand."

I nodded. "Yeah."

"You have to admit, it does sound crazy," said Gary.

"I know."

"Maybe you're meant to do something. Things like you witnessed are usually for a reason."

"Maybe they are, but what am I supposed to do?"

"I don't know, *mon ami*," Gary said. "Have you looked at the library? Gone through old newspapers? Any research on it yet?"

"I asked Mrs. Weatherman if she might know something."

Gary looked at me dubiously. "That's not what I meant when I said research."

"Hey, she's old and she's been around a while," I said.

"She's not that old. From the way you talk about it, it was near the turn of the last century. Early 1900s at the latest. Mrs. Weatherman's what, seventy? Eighty?"

"Yeah, well it doesn't hurt asking. She didn't know anything, but she mentioned the Historical Center. I'd already thought of it, though."

"You might be able to find something out there. History's what they do in a historical center."

"I'm not even sure the house was in Carson," I said.

"Don't give up before you start." Gary clucked his tongue.

"I'm not. It's not something I've thought about until recently.

I just always assumed the house was in town since I always end up in town when I leave it. Hell, I just assumed the place existed sometime in the past, but isn't around anymore."

"I think it wouldn't hurt to check the center and see if they have something. Are you going to go back to the house and try to find something you might be able to use to solve the mystery?

"I'm thinking about it."

Gary's voice dropped, as if someone were listening. "Can other people go, too?"

"To the house?" I asked.

Gary nodded.

"I don't know." I eyed him. "You want to go or something?"

Gary sat up, waved his hand and laughed nervously.

"No, no, no. I wouldn't want to go. Frankly, the idea scares the bejeesies out of me. Spooks, bugs, and rats? Creaky old houses filled with dust and cobwebs?" He shuddered. "Not to mention the hell it would be on my sinuses. Thanks, but no thanks."

"Yeah, I don't blame you." I started to reach for my cup, but remembered it was empty.

"Would you like another cup?" Gary asked.

"No, I'm fine. I should get going anyway."

"You sure?"

"Yeah," I said. "Say, maybe you could do me a little favor?"

"Does it involve spooks?" he asked.

I laughed. "No, no spooks. Well, not directly."

"What?" he asked, leery.

"Maybe if you get some time, you could do some checking?"

"Oh, Harry, I'm pretty busy, but if I find time I'll try, just for you. It might be fun, but you don't give a boy much to go on."

"Thanks," I said. "I appreciate you, Gary. I don't know if I ever tell you that. You're a great friend."

"Oh, sweetie. You're a great friend, too."

"Thanks. I better get out of here."

Gary got up to walk me out and I thought I saw his eyes beginning to mist.

"Are you all right?" I asked.

"I'm fine."

"Did I say something wrong?"

"No, of course not. Just my sinuses. Go on, get out of here."

"*Ciao*," I said.

"Bye," Gary said, and shrugged.

I got on my bicycle and waved at him again as he stood on his front porch. I pedaled for home, lost in thought.

Chapter 15

My thoughts flowed with the rhythm of my bicycle's wheels as I pedaled down Carson's back streets. Sometimes, I thought, information is nil. It is a commodity that often has to be traded or bartered. It's the way it works most of the time. It comes from various sources. Stories caught by an inconspicuous ear. Sometimes, information comes from a gut feeling rather than facts. Of course, neither of those methods are what we'd call scientific. They're not grounded in concrete fact, but sometimes you have to play with whatever pieces are handed to you.

For the record, I believe in ghosts, spirits, or whatever you might want to call them. I believe this while knowing I probably will never be able to offer conclusive proof they exist. It isn't a recent development; I've believed this since long before I discovered the house. I've had some experiences, though not as dramatic as this, but for me it was all the proof I needed.

I remember hearing stories back in my early years about a small school. It was said it was attacked and burned down by the Klan sometime in the thirties or forties. It was a little school for "colored" children, in the vernacular of the time. Segregation was the rule then. One day, classes were in session when a large group of Klansmen charged in and tortured and killed everyone in that little school—twenty-eight children and five adults. The only fact I can verify is the ruins of the place claimed to be the school still stand. I've been there and walked through the charred remnants. I swear the place felt haunted as hell. In the corners of my eyes, I saw what I thought were apparitions, and I heard the barely discernible cries of terrified children seeping from the walls. Maybe it was my imagination in overdrive, powered by the story of the murders. I could believe that argument. Hours of research failed to find any mention of the building, as a school or otherwise. I had to wonder whether the horrific incident ever occurred.

The house was different; Her impression was like a body blow to the senses. I knew there was something there for certain, and it was unlike anything I had experienced before. Now if I could only find out something about Her.

"Conflicted" is inadequate to describe how I felt. Part of me wished the whole experience wasn't real, while at the same time I dreaded the thought the house never existed in this, or any other, reality.

I admit I can be a man of some complexity.

Gary had asked something which I had not considered until he brought it up: Could others be transported with me to the house? I knew I could carry small items, such as keys, back and forth, but had never thought about it extending to something like people. I had already ascertained I could will myself there, but could others do the same? Could someone be transported with me if I held on to them? The idea was intriguing, though I was loath to test the theory. Not that I would have anyone to test it with anyway, save for Gary, and he had already made it clear it was an invitation he would decline. I didn't blame him, because I probably would have declined it myself, if I hadn't already been taken in by Her. I didn't want my morbid fascination with the house to rub off on anyone else. Best to keep things the way they were.

I made my decision. It might also be a good idea to take a break from my admitted obsession. Get away and clear my mind. Maybe then I could go back to Her and be more able to figure something out.

I thought I'd take the time to go visit my brother, Jim. Perhaps do a spot of fishing. I'd already put off a visit with him many times, even though it didn't seem to deter him from offering invitations. I thought we'd both like that. He would, for sure, especially if fishing were involved.

******

My brother and I sat on the boat and watched the sunset color the clouds in a brilliant display. George Strait sang softly in the background about a woman hijacking his chair as we lazily cast our lines into the water and reeled them in, without a care if we actually caught anything.

We had just finished a dinner of burgers and onions cooked on the grill Jim kept on his boat and we sipped on bottles of beer, just enjoying the kind of moment that didn't happen as often as we'd like.

"Glad you came out, bro," Jim said.

"Yeah? I only came out so you would stop whining and crying about us never going fishing anymore."

"Well, all that whinin' got you out here, didn't it?" His laugh was deep and sincere.

"Maybe, but don't expect it to work every time," I said.

"It never does." Jim took a deep swallow of his beer and sighed.

"Yeah, yeah. So, how are things?" I asked. I knew he wouldn't tell me if things weren't going well. It didn't matter, because I was able to read him better than he thought. That's what brothers do.

"They're all right. Just workin' here and there. Gettin' out on the boat when I get the chance," he drawled in his slow, easy way.

He pulled up on his rod suddenly. I watched him as he stood to reel the catch in.

"Man, oh man! This 'un's a fighter!" he exclaimed. He played with the fish, letting it tire itself out, and reeled it close to the boat. "Get the net."

I grabbed the net and scooped up the fish. It was a decent sized bass, about six or seven pounds.

"Ain't he a beaut?" He held it up and admired it.

"Not too bad for a first catch. You ought to marry it, since you think it's so pretty."

"Marry it? Shit, I'm gonna eat it," he said, as he started to work the hook out.

"Now?"

"Hell yeah, I'm gonna eat it now."

"But we ate not more than an hour ago. How can you be hungry?" I said.

"Why shouldn't I eat it now? If you let it set too long, it's not gonna taste as good. Eat it while it's fresh."

"Right, I just thought it would keep until at least breakfast."

Of course he'd eat it now. He was a human garbage disposal. His talk like he's some kind of connoisseur is only a cover. If he could put it in his mouth, chew and swallow it, it was eaten. It almost didn't matter what it was, or if he had just finished eating. There were some things I was sure he wouldn't eat, but the only thing that came to mind was shit. Maybe sushi.

At least he'd cook it. I don't think I could handle seeing him eat it raw.

Jim picked up the fish, holding it up to his face and looked it in the eye thoughtfully. "I guess he'll keep. That's what my livewell is for."

"Maybe you do have some sense after all," I replied with a smile.

"Sometimes. Hey, we should go to the ocean and fish," Jim suggested.

"We should, but I got to work tomorrow," I said.

"Not now, dumb ass. You think maybe sometime this year?"

"Yeah, maybe. We'll see what happens. Deep sea fishing could be a lot of fun."

"Yeah. I've never been, so I'd like to do that soon."

"There's no hurry," I said. "We might be able to catch us a shark."

"Shit, if we do, I'm a gonna eat that sumbitch."

I laughed. "I know you would. Show that shark a thing or two."

"You betcha."

We sat in silence for a while.

"Business good?" I asked.

"Good as it can get," he said, his eyes on the horizon. "You know how it is with this economy and all. People aren't able to spend their money like they want. Hell, like I want them to spend it. I'm gettin' by. It'll pick up more once things settle."

"Seems to always work that way," I said.

"Yep." He knocked back the last of his beer and reached for another and sighed with satisfaction as he popped the can open.

Jim ran something of a handyman service. Self-employed, because he had always shunned the idea of working for other people. He did small repairs, roofing and things people either didn't have time for or didn't want to do themselves. It didn't make him a rich man, but he never wanted for anything, and even in harder times he managed to eke by. I envied him a little for his ability to find work anywhere and his easy manner with people.

He was like a modern Will Rogers, who never met a man he didn't like. Everyone, in turn, liked my brother. We had our moments, of course, but Jim and I had always been able to quickly work things out. We'd bloodied each other plenty when we were kids, like we were a couple of extreme fighters, but as soon as a skirmish started, it was over and forgotten. It was always something stupid, I'm sure, because we never remembered the cause of it.

Jim and I fished long after the sun went down for the night. Eventually we dragged out the sleeping bags he kept on the boat. We looked up at the night sky. The stars were truly countless out on the lake where there was no traffic or bright lights to dull the view. It was always easy to forget your troubles as you stared in awe at the vastness of space.

"Makes you feel like you're just an itty bitty speck that don't mean nothin', huh?" Jim asked.

"Sometimes it does," I agreed. "This is perfect. No clouds or anything. We need to do this on the next meteor shower."

"I don't know nothin' about that kind of stuff," Jim said sadly.

"It's all right. I'll let you know when there's going to be one."

"You going to be okay to go to work if I pull in early in the morning?"

"Yeah, just make sure it's early enough. You don't mind?"

"Nah, I don't mind. I kinda like having you out here."

"I like being here. You do this a lot, don't you? Come out here like this?" I asked.

"Every chance I get. Good clear nights like this are the best."

"It's nothing like this at my place. The street lights and the cars ruin it."

"Hell, I'd just as soon live right here on this lake, if I could."

"I bet you would," I said, and smiled.

I didn't blame him. I would do the same thing, if only for nights like this.

Chapter 16

Early the next morning I drove back to Carson, maybe not exactly obeying the posted speed limit. Though I had taken all the precautions I could think of, I still managed to oversleep. I made it home with barely enough time for a quick shower, which I couldn't do without unless I wanted to offend everyone who crossed my path.

"I ought to plan these things out better," I said.

The truth was, I was glad I had done it. It might have been nicer and more relaxing if I had spent time with Jim when I had the next day or two off, but sometimes, stolen opportunities are much more fun. I could plan a lot of things better, but if I spent all my time planning, I probably wouldn't get to a lot of the actual doing.

The short trip did what it was supposed to do. It cleared my mind and allowed me to temporarily forget everything that had been happening at home. I didn't talk to Jim about this kind of thing, and he certainly wouldn't get it. It made it easy to forget for a while.

I would have liked to spend more time with Jim, but I worked for someone else and didn't have the luxury of being able to choose my days off. Jim set his own hours and though he worked long and hard, he could afford to take a few days here and there. He didn't take advantage of it very often, but I also envied that about him. It really didn't matter because I still liked my job and there are plenty of people who would envy a job they liked.

After I quickly scrubbed down and threw on some reasonably clean clothes, I rushed out, hopped on my bike and pedaled like a madman to get to The Bookworm with a couple minutes to spare.

I entered the building short of breath.

"Did you run all the way here?" Carol asked when I came in the door.

"No run. Rode bike," I answered between gulps of air.

Carol rolled her eyes. "You look worn out, Harry. Did you oversleep? Party too hard last night?"

"No, went fishing with my brother and slept on his boat."

"So there was drinking involved," she said.

I shrugged. "What fun is fishing without a little drinking?"

"True," she conceded. "You went and slept on a pontoon boat all night?"

"Not all night. We fished and drank some," I said.

She laughed. "Oh, the folly of youth. You better enjoy it while you can. Once you get to be my age, you won't have that luxury anymore. Well, so long as you're here, get clocked in. There's a bunch of boxes that need to be sorted in back. The task should let you catch your breath and maybe sober up some," she said with a wink.

"Yes, ma'am." I started to the employee lounge to clock in, then, when out of earshot, muttered, "I'm not drunk."

I went into the small room we laughingly called a lounge and clocked in after finding my time card. I stole one of Carol's root beers out of the fridge and took a long swallow before going to the sorting room to start my task. It ate up my whole day. There were a ton of books from a recent buyout.

I was halfway through the boxes when I found a book that made me chuckle. I set it aside to buy as a gift for Gary, whose birthday was coming up in a couple of weeks. Of course, once he had it he would never be able to come into the store and ask for it again. Of course, he'd still come by, but at least with this book in his possession, he wouldn't be able to embarrass me anymore by loudly trumpeting his request for the title.

Oh yes, he was getting the damn book—a bona fide copy of *The Joy of Gay Sex*.

Chapter 17

"You have been away...too long." She said in my mind as I stood in the foyer.

The air was stuffier and noticeably cooler, though still not cold. I gave no reply, unsure if I could. I might have been talking to myself anyway, so no reply was necessary.

I looked up at the empty window. It was as if someone had hung a thick black fabric over it from the outside to keep the light at bay.

"You brought yourself here," I said, as I walked to the foot of the stairs. Waves of doubt washed over me. Her pull was strong and compelled me to move further into Her. Though I had spent some time with Her already, it didn't quell my troubled feelings.

I placed a foot on the first step and tested it. From the looks of it, I had every reason to be nervous because it didn't look particularly safe. I thought it would be able to handle my weight as long as I was careful.

My hesitation was becoming second nature.

For a short second, I thought I saw the stained-glass window atop, complete, without so much as a crack. It disappeared as quickly as it came, so I didn't have enough time to discern any specific design. It lasted only long enough for me to see the predominant color was red.

"What are you trying to tell me?" I asked with frustration.

I heard a thud behind me, as if a giant tree had fallen. I jerked around, fast enough to feel a pull at the muscles in my back, but I saw nothing. It was on the tip of my tongue to ask again, but I knew there wouldn't be an answer. I grasped the wooden rails and with carefully placed steps, made my ascent to the second floor.

A few of Her steps creaked loudly and protested my intrusion. It was enough for me to pause and test them more. I changed my footing so they wouldn't crumble beneath me. To my relief, none did.

A carpeted runner, worn all the way through in many spots, eaten away by time in others, softened my footfalls, and between the creaks and moans, I listened for noises that would tell me if I was truly alone. But then, I had never felt alone in this house. There had always been a feeling of someone—or something— around me, invisible, but ever-present. I discerned no audible sounds, but couldn't trust a spectral level of sound was not calling to me.

When I finally found myself at the apex of the staircase, the stained-glass window seemed much larger, the jagged teeth of broken glass framed only the silhouettes of treetops. At the center of the lower edge, a half-moon of red shards rose like a sinister, hungry mouth, its teeth stained with the blood of some unfortunate prey. Remnants of fallen glass crackled beneath my feet as I crept closer to the window. What I expected to see as I peered out, I couldn't say; the darkness revealed only the blackest of shadows.

I pulled back from the window and looked down the long hallways flanking each side. Three small steps led to the passages from the landing and the same eerie light, morphed from blue to violet, illuminated both hallways. I felt pulled toward the hallway on the right. I didn't try any of the doors, just walked the length of the hall. The dark wooden panels encasing the walls brought on a claustrophobic feeling, like the walls might slam together with me in the middle. There were three doors and a narrow staircase leading up, presumably to an attic. At the end of the hall there was a pedestal that stood waist high and held a black urn, with white trim encircling the top and bottom. I touched it, thinking it was made of glass, then realized it was carved from stone, possibly onyx. I didn't take the lid off; whatever the contents, I preferred to leave them safely confined. No way was I going to be a modern-day Pandora.

I turned and looked down the entire length of both hallways. They seemed to go into infinity, narrowing into the darkness. I thought I saw someone walking across on the other side. I rubbed my eyes with the heels of my hands and looked again, but it was already gone. I was sure it was a person, although I couldn't make out any features.

Maybe it was just a trick of my mind.

I tried the handles on the doors opposite the side with the staircase and found them both locked. Although frustrated, I didn't allow myself to dwell on it. There were other doors.

I tried the door opposite and it swung open without a problem. Inside was a decrepit bedroom, windows decorated with heavy drapes at the center of the outer walls. I tried to push one aside to see if I could look out, but dust rained and I sneezed, so I gave up the idea. A simple four-poster bed sat against the far wall.

The mattress sat askew and sagged heavily in the middle. Next to the headboard, a small table held a lamp and a small book. I picked up the book and thumbed through its brittle pages. It contained pages of handwriting, but the ink was faded to illegibility, and some fragile pages crumbled at my touch, so I put it back down. An armoire leaned awkwardly in the corner, its back legs broken and the doors spread open, half off the hinges. A folded quilt sat on the bottom, a couple of faded, simple dresses hanging above it. The room belonged to a woman, but there were no clues to her identity. I poked around a little more and then I heard a sound like water splashing, coming from behind another door that stood slightly ajar.

I pulled the door open and stepped carefully into a dingy room. A claw-footed tub, spotted with dirt and rust, abutted the wall. I went in for a closer look and felt as if I walked into mud, my feet sinking into the mire. I gasped and looked down. The floor was dry, though it was rotted and sagged in places, as if it had been flooded at some point.

I feared I would fall through and break bones in this isolated and unknown place—a danger which, for some reason, I hadn't considered before. My only excuse? I'm a guy, and guys sometimes act first and think later.

Without warning, the violet light shut off. I was in complete darkness. My heart seemed to stop as panic swept through me.

Then just as suddenly, the light flashed back on.

The figure of a woman knelt at the tub, her hair tangled and wild. Water geysered up as she shoved her arms downward. Her shoulders heaved with effort.

I stumbled back, aghast as I realized she was drowning a little girl in the bathtub. The girl struggled, her tiny legs kicked and her arms flailed at her attacker. I could not see her face.

Suddenly, the woman whirled and faced me. Her eyes glowed in an empty skull. I could feel them burn into my flesh.

I fell backward into the bedroom as the light flickered. I hit the floor hard and screamed, almost crapping my pants. A large rat —my least favorite of all creatures—scurried out from under the bed and ran for the door, no braver than I was.

I forced myself to take a few deep breaths. I wasn't going to let the murderous apparition spook me away. I got up and dusted off my jeans. I told myself firmly She wouldn't throw anything at me I couldn't handle.

On the other hand, it was probably time to get out of there.

Chapter 18

I had not expected the rain. The skies hadn't given the slightest hint of it. The setting was familiar, but I was getting soaked and ran into the alley, toward the street. I passed the post office, and wondered if St. Mark's had something going on tonight. Maybe I could get out of the rain for a moment.

The door opened and I stumbled in. The church was warm and dry. I felt glad to be out of the rain. On a whim, I went up to the balcony. I wondered if I might find Gwendolyn there. I stood there, water dripping on the floor as I scanned the seats, but saw no one. I shouldn't have, but I felt a little disappointed. Just because you go somewhere sometimes doesn't mean you're going to be there all the time. You don't see me at The Bookworm on my days off, for instance. Well, not all of them, at least. Most likely, Gwendolyn was at home and staying out of the rain. Smart.

I went back down the stairs and thought I should leave. The rain wasn't going to stop and walking in it isn't the worst thing in the world. I hit the bottom of the stairs and ran into someone. If I hadn't caught the wall, I would've hit the floor.

Where the hell did she come from?

"Hi," she said.

I only recognized her by the thick glasses and the nasal squeak of her voice. She was as soaked as I was, her large bouncy curls plastered to her head and shoulders with the wet. The white button-down she was wearing clung to her like a second skin. As she was not wearing any undergarments, there was nothing left to the imagination.

There are many things better left to the imagination. This was one of them.

"Hi, Belinda," I sighed.

"Oh!" she squealed. "You remember my name!"

"How could I forget?"

"You came back to see me?" She moved closer. "I hoped you'd come back. I forgot to give you my number and all, so I thought you would."

"No, I was just getting out of the rain, really. Looking for someone else, but she's not here."

"She?" She frowned, but stepped closer still. "Does this mean you don't like me? Who is it? Why don't you like me?" Her lips quivered as she fired the questions at me. It looked as if she were going to cry.

She moved closer until my back was against the wall. Her breasts were pressed firmly against my chest. "I like you," she whispered.

"Ah, yeah, well, I've got someone I'm seeing," I stammered. It wasn't exactly a lie, nor was it exactly the truth. I just hoped it was enough, and she'd back the hell off.

She moved her face toward mine. I smelled French onion dip on her breath. It made me want to gag.

"No one needs to know." Her breath hot in my ear I as she spoke. "I'll never tell," she whispered.

"Jesus would know," I said. I hoped it worked.

She giggled as she put her arms around my neck and moved in to kiss me. "I don't think Jesus would mind."

"I bet he does," I said and twisted my head. I couldn't back up any further. I really didn't want to push her, but it was exactly what I was going to do.

"Oh, Harry," she breathed, as her lips approached mine.

"What are you doing?" A voice boomed.

Normally, a guy would freak out if someone walked in on a situation like that, but I'm not most guys. I was relieved. I offered a silent thank you to the gods as Mark stepped out of the shadows.

"Hey, Mark," I laughed nervously.

"Don't you 'hey Mark' me! Just what do you think you're doing, huh? What are you doing?" His face reddened with anger as he enunciated each word.

"I just came in looking for someone..." I broke off as my voice betrayed me. Given the situation, it wasn't a good thing.

Mark jerked toward us, grabbed Belinda by the shoulder and yanked her off me. Her arms flailed as she lost her balance and crashed to the ground.

"You stupid whore!" he screamed at her. "You're nothing but a low down, dirty slut!"

Belinda blubbered.

"Hey now, there's no need for all that, Mark," I said. I felt sorry for her.

Mark scowled at me. "Belinda's my girl, you hear? You don't

have any business here."

"Actually, I was coming in to see about becoming a member of the Episcopal Church, but..."

"You think this is a joke?" Mark gaped at me stupidly.

"I'm sorry. My humor isn't very appropriate, I realize. You're absolutely right. I don't have any business here, but it's no reason for you to act out toward her. She didn't do anything wrong."

"I saw you kissing her!" he shrieked.

"No, no. You saw wrong, Mark. I wouldn't do that."

Mark's lips moved as if he were going to say something, but he apparently decided to launch his fist at my face instead.

Luckily, I saw it coming and was able to sidestep before he connected.

Instead of my nose, his fist went through the wall. He gasped in shock and I wasn't sure if it was because he missed, or because he just put a hole in the wall of a church. Or because it hurt like hell. He pulled his fist out from the wall and swung with the other.

"Stop! Please stop!" Belinda cried.

The thought crossed my mind she might be enjoying what she thought was a fight over her.

I blocked Mark's second swing easily and landed a solid blow to his gut. Steamy breath rushed from his lips as he doubled over.

"Come on now, Mark. Let's just call it even and be friends, all right?"

"Fuck you," he hissed.

"Now, that's no way to be talking inside a church. What would Jesus say, eh?" I didn't really care what he said in a church. I didn't think Jesus did either. Perhaps he'd be more worried about the destruction of church property. After all, it was supposed to be his house.

Mark scoffed as his fist rounded again toward my head. I grabbed it, gut punching him again. I know, unlike my opponent, gut punches are more effective in a fight. Luckily, I don't get into fights very often, but when I do, it's my stand-by. Less of a chance of breaking fingers on a skull that way.

"Seriously, Mark. Let's not do this. I have no interest in coming between you and your girl. Frankly, my friend, she's not my type and I wouldn't want her on my worst day. You can have her for all I care. I'd like to think I have my own girl, who is much more attractive. I have no desire to graze on inferior fields, know what I mean?"

Belinda looked like she didn't know whether or not to be insulted.

Mark just looked like he was going to curse me again. It seemed the Jesus argument had no effect. Instead, he charged toward me with his head lowered like a raging bull.

I laughed and wished I had a red cape to wave around. It would be much more fun. Anyone with a smidgen of intelligence could win a fight against Mark. His fighting style was predictable. I could read his moves and counter them without thought.

As he came at me, I stepped aside and let him slam his head through the wall. He stood up, a little wobbly, with white dust falling from his hair.

"I tried to be nice," I said, and smashed my fist into his nose.

I cringed as the cartilage broke and blood poured from his nose like a waterfall.

He crumbled to the floor in a heap. Maybe it was a bit much. He already looked like a fool.

"I really didn't want to do that," I said to Belinda, who huddled on the floor crying.

"It's my fault," she sobbed.

"Don't say that. It was more his fault than yours or mine. He's kind of a moron."

Why was I placating her?

"Well, I guess I should probably go."

"He needs a doctor!" she cried.

"Call one," I said, as I waved and left the church. I supposed it sounded cruel, but it wasn't my place. I would have liked to stay and warm up a bit, but it didn't seem advisable. I didn't want to involve myself anymore, so I went back outside.

Instead of going straight home, I walked for a while in the rain. I wandered into the part of town locals called The Swamp. Every time it rains hard, the area floods and water will still be standing after a couple of days. It's quite the haven for snakes and that sort of thing.

You would think people wouldn't build here, would live somewhere in town where you didn't have to wade in knee-deep water. A small boat wouldn't be out of place. Not surprisingly, poorer people lived here. The houses were all built close together, some on stilts, in proclamation of the inevitability of flooding. A veritable forest of trees surrounded the rundown houses.

I wandered between houses and trees, not really going anywhere in particular. I remembered Gwendolyn mentioned a friend lived around here, but I knew she wouldn't be out riding in this weather. She was at home, dry and warm, which was where I should be. Instead, I was being stupid.

I turned to head home and struggled through the fast-rising water. Debris pushed past my legs and I tested spots in front of me with my feet so I wouldn't fall into a dip and run the risk of drowning myself.

I felt eyes on me so I looked around. I spotted an obese woman staring at me through the screen of her front door, a bucket of chicken clenched in her arm. She just stood there, and watched me with suspicious eyes. She probably wondered why the hell someone was crazy enough to come traipsing through the neighborhood in this weather. A stranger, of all things. She finally lost interest and turned away.

I wished I had just gone straight home. I was tired, cold, and hungry. I hurried toward my building, just up the next block. I would get there, dry off, and maybe call Gwendolyn, like I should have in the first place.

Ten minutes later, I stood in my shower beneath jets of hot water. I let the heat sink into my skin and deprive the cold of its hold on me. It felt good after being in the rain and I lingered in the shower a little longer than usual. I got out and wrapped myself in my worn terrycloth robe, wriggling my feet into my slippers with big gorilla heads on the toes. I looked ridiculous, but I didn't care. I was alone and I was warm. And I like gorillas. Anyway, one shouldn't have to be concerned with what they look like while at home.

I heated up a can of soup and made myself a grilled cheese sandwich. In my hunger, I devoured most of it in one large bite. I scolded myself for staying out in the rain, in the flooded neighborhood. There was no point to it. Maybe I subconsciously wanted to get wet, but if I wanted to do that, I should have come home anyway. It was wet enough from there to here and taking the detour was not a necessity. What did I suppose I was looking for?

I hated to admit it, but the bathtub scene back at the house might have shaken me up more than I liked to think.

After I finished my simple dinner, I called Gwendolyn. She was smart and stayed in, of course. I told her I'd been out and she nagged a bit. I didn't mind so much. It was nice to know she cared. Not that I go out and do stupid things just to get someone to care. Don't get me wrong. I go out and do stupid things because sometimes, I'm a moron.

We talked about nothing important. She mentioned having something for me, but wouldn't tell me what it was. Something about ruining the surprise. I told her I hated surprises. It got me nowhere. All she would give up was she had found it while out shopping with Gary. I didn't know if I should be scared. I just had to wait and see.

I was glad to hear her voice, even if she did nag and refuse to pass along secrets. I was glad to be home. Glad to be safe, warm and with food in my belly. At least I could be assured I was safe for now, not knowing what tomorrow might bring.

Chapter 19

I finished my shift early at The Bookworm, so I decided to take the rest of the day to do some hard-core relaxing. I got home and threw open the window and set a fan in it to pull in the fresh air. I put Mozart and Wagner on the turntable and mixed myself a rum and Coke. I settled into my chair and stuffed my favorite clay pipe with a vanilla blend. I took a puff and sighed contentedly. It seemed ages since I'd allowed myself such an indulgence. Even when I had the chance, I didn't take it. Why do we deny ourselves the opportunity to enjoy even the simplest pleasures?

I sipped my drink and watched the blue-grey smoke spiral toward the ceiling while I thought about life, the universe and everything. I'm not convinced the answer is forty-two.

I thought about bad days. We all have them and I've had my share. I expect to have more in the future. Maybe it's pessimistic, but not really. I believe one should hope for the best and prepare for the worst. I've been accused of being negative. I've been called cynical. I won't deny it. I do feel that way about a number of things. When you look at the whole, which we should always do, I'm not that way at all. People tend to focus on the negative and remember it. Nobody seems to remember the good things. At least not until you're dead and that's not a guarantee.

Maybe I've got a split personality. Who knows? I never claimed to be normal, and current circumstances didn't help.

I thought about the house again, of undiscovered parts and the people who might have lived there. What did they do, and who were they? I wondered what part I was meant to play, and that was still the biggest mystery of all.

"Yeah, that's what I should think about when I'm trying to relax," I said. I turned my attention to the music, closed my eyes and let it soothe my mind into a meditation.

I must have fallen asleep because the buzzer awakened me and the arm of the turntable was trying to pull music from the record's label. I went to answer the buzzer. I hoped it wasn't a salesman, a Mormon, or one of those Jehovah's Witnesses. I didn't want any of them, but a salesman was the most appealing of the bunch.

I punched the intercom. "Yeah, who is it?"

"It's Gwen. Let me in."

"Why should I?" I asked.

"Because you've been dying to see me. Let me in, or else!"

"Okay, it's open," I laughed and pushed the button to let her in. I started another record and settled back into my chair.

I was happy. Gwendolyn was much better than a salesman, religious or otherwise.

"Are you going to just sit there on your ass, or are you going to help me with this?" Gwendolyn asked as she came through the door. She was out of breath and sported droplets of sweat on her brow.

"Help with what?" I asked, and pushed myself reluctantly out of my chair.

She wiped her forehead with the back of her arm. "With your present, that's what."

"Present? It's not my birthday or a holiday. Unless there's something I'm not aware of," I said.

"Who made the rule you could only get presents on special occasions? Why can't somebody give a gift without having their motives called into question?"

"I haven't questioned your motives." I laughed when I saw the hammock and stand she had brought.

"What's so funny?" she demanded.

"Nothing's funny. I just...why didn't you tell me? I would have come down and helped."

"If I'd told you, it wouldn't have been a surprise."

"So you were just bitching on principle," I said.

"I wasn't bitching."

"Then what do you call it?"

"I call it...oh, I don't know."

"You were bitching, but it's all right."

"Fine. Are you at least surprised?"

"I must say your plan has worked perfectly."

"Good. Don't think you're going to get to hog it all the time."

She pointed at me. "I shall use it whenever the mood hits me, you understand?"

"So you did have ulterior motives."

"What?"

"Nothing, I understand. Of course, I wouldn't think of not letting you use it."

"Good. Now take it up and put it together."

"Now? But I'm hungry," I pouted.

"You can eat while I'm testing the hammock."

"Let's order pizza."

She perked up. "Only if you get those sausage rolls."

"Okay, deal."

"I'll order. You assemble."

"Do I get a break when food gets here, at least?"

"It shouldn't take long, but I'll think about it. Now go."

"Fine." I pretended to mope as I dug for the necessary tools and took everything up to the roof.

Chapter 20

"It looks sturdy enough," I said and eyed the assembled hammock.

"You don't sound so sure," Gwendolyn said as she polished off a sausage roll.

"I'm sure."

"So, try it. That is, if you're not too chicken."

"What are you saying?"

"I am saying nothing."

"It sounds like you're saying my manly put-it-together skills are lacking. We'll just have to see." I sauntered over to the hammock, my thumbs in my belt as if I were some sort of bootless, hatless cowboy. "Watch and see how this is done," I said, as I started to lie back on the hammock.

Instead of lying back in comfort, I flipped and landed on my back, much to Gwendolyn's delight.

"That's what you get for being cocky."

"There's something wrong with the hammock," I said.

"Not from where I was watching. It didn't do anything but throw you off and I saw nothing wrong with that."

"You're a sadist."

"Try again, cowboy."

I tried again. And again. After several attempts, I got the hang of it and was able to lie back without mishap. I folded my hands behind my head. "Now all we got to do is get you one of your own."

"Are you kidding? Do you really think I brought this big ol' thing for you to use by yourself? While I'm relegated to one of your hideous plastic lawn chairs?"

"They're vinyl," I said, brainlessly.

"Is there a difference? You're not that big, mister."

"I guess I could take the hideous lawn chair." I wondered if getting out of this thing was going to be as hard as getting into it.

"Scoot over. This thing is big enough for both of us." Gwendolyn stood at the edge of the hammock and nudged it with her knee.

I grasped the netting as it started to rock. "Hey! You trying to throw me off, or what?"

"Go on, scoot over," she demanded and ignored my plight.

"Fine, hold your horses," I said, and tried to move without upending myself.

Gwendolyn slid herself into the hammock like a pro and nestled into the crook of my arm.

"I can tell you've done this sort of thing before," I said, impressed.

"I used to have one when I was a kid. I love 'em. Comfy, don't you think?"

"Indeed. Much better than those lawn chairs. I could get used to this."

As I took in the air, I caught the aroma of strawberry-scented shampoo in her hair.

"Are you sniffing at my hair?" she asked.

"Maybe," I answered guiltily.

"You're a weirdo."

"Am not. I just like the smell of strawberries. If you'd use a different shampoo, I wouldn't be sniffing at your hair."

"What if I used peach?"

"I like peaches."

"I guess if I used motor oil, you wouldn't be sniffing."

"I am a guy."

"You're a freak." She giggled.

"A super freak." I began to sing the song's chorus, badly.

"Oh, stop! Rick James you are so not!" she cried, and covered her ears.

"I take it you don't think I'll be landing any recording contracts any time soon?"

"No way."

"There's been worse."

"Yeah, but you're still a weirdo freak."

"Hey, you're still here, so it's got to count for something," I said.

I enjoyed the feel of her against me, small and warm. I could have died happy right then as we lay there. The hammock swung gently and we watched the setting sun light the sky with bright reds, oranges and yellows as it turned slowly into black night.

"My uncle once told me if the skies are like this in the evening, it meant good weather, and if they were red in the morning, there'd be storms," I said.

"I heard that too, somewhere. Never paid it much thought, but maybe it's true."

"It seems to be," I said.

The first stars of the night began to twinkle while crickets broke the silence.

"I think I maybe should tell you now." She said it so quietly I almost didn't hear it.

"Tell me what?" I asked.

"What I said I'd tell you before."

"What did you say you'd tell me?"

"You know, about me."

"You don't have to tell me anything. I know enough now and I already like you and everything."

"Sure, you say that now," she said, with underlying anxiety. "It's why I should probably tell you."

"Nothing you tell me could make me like you any less. It's no big deal."

"Maybe it isn't, but I like you and think you should know before you decide."

"What, are you really a man or something?"

"No, it's nothing like that." She didn't smile, so I knew this was really bothering her and now wasn't the time to make jokes.

I made myself be serious. "Okay."

"Just let me talk without interruptions."

"Why?"

"Please?"

"All right."

"No interruptions," she said.

I kept quiet and let her go about it the way she wanted.

"Okay," she sighed, probably waiting to make sure I wasn't going to open up my trap.

"I come from a larger family, but nothing you'd call traditional. I know a lot of people don't come from traditional families anymore, but mine was less than most.

"I lived with my mother, sister and brothers until I was seventeen. I moved in with some girlfriends then, because I couldn't stand to be at home anymore. I have one sister and three brothers. None of us has the same father, so we're all actually half siblings. My own father died a week before my eighth birthday. I can't prove it or anything, but I know my mother killed him. None of us had seen our fathers since we were very young. Until he died, I saw mine regularly, like every week, at least once. Thinking about it, I guess I was the only one who actually had a daddy. My sister had never seen hers. I don't even think my mother knows who her father is. She was only half sure with my brothers until she got some paternity tests done. It's the only way she knew for sure. All of our fathers are either missing, in prison, or dead. Two of my brothers' fathers are in prison. One over drugs and the other is on death row for murder. My oldest brother's father was killed. Drugs. Every one of them had something to do with drugs. Using, selling. All except for mine. My daddy was a good man, and I'm not just saying that. It was true. He was kind and loving. I don't know how he got mixed up with a woman like my mother, because he wasn't the type she normally went for. It was probably for money, though he wasn't rich or anything. Maybe she got the crazy idea to go straight.

"He had a decent job and was steady, but she couldn't change. He used to tell me he was glad he met her because he got to have me. I'll never forget him, not for as long as I live.

"We used to make up games and stories. He'd make me laugh. Anytime I was sad, he could make me smile. Stupid things, like he'd make faces at me, and I'd mimic it. It got really silly and I laughed so I wasn't sad anymore. My daddy's the reason I love stories.

"Anyway, I was with him and my mother had come to pick me up. I didn't want to go. I cried and begged him to let me stay. He said I should go on, because it would make her feel better and I'd come back before I knew it, anyway. That, and he needed time to finish the plans for my birthday.

"It was going to be huge, he said, so I could look forward to the next weekend.

"My mother went inside. She said she needed to talk to him about something, so I stayed in the yard and played with my dog. He was a mixed terrier my daddy got for me. Daddy kept him at his house because my mother refused to let me keep my dog at home. I called him Doggie." She laughed a little, and wiped her eye. "What a stupid name it was, so unoriginal. My mother wasn't in the house very long. Ten, fifteen minutes. When you're a kid, ten minutes seems forever. We left and the next day, I was told he was dead. They said it was heart failure. I'm positive she did something. I was as sure of it then as I am now. He was young and healthy. There wasn't a reason for it, but it's what they listed it as. Heart failure.

"That's something about my mother. She was able to get away with anything. I think she prided herself on it. She even bragged about it several times, how she would get away with things and beat the system. I think it had a lot to do with her willingness to spread her legs for anything that moved. Some might say it's terrible to talk about your mother like that, but it's the truth. Sometimes truth isn't pretty. I think people who ignore it and try to hide it are worse off.

"My mother, she was always high on something and there were always men in the house. A lot of them were creepy and one of them tried to do things. I bit him on the arm as hard as I could. Made him bleed. He screamed and cussed me, but he never tried anything again. There were more who probably would have, but they didn't bother me. I don't know about my sister, or my brothers. I hope not. I said something to my mother about it, but she accused me of lying. Said I was keeping her from having any fun. She'd turn the dime on anyone else, even falsely, but if you tried to get her to take a little responsibility, she'd just say that. Stop her from 'having fun.' She'd even have the teenage neighbors come in and use her. Some were no older than thirteen. Really disgusting. My mother had five kids and four abortions. Those are only the ones I knew about. I wouldn't be surprised if there were more.

"She'd get into some trouble here and there with CPS, but she was always able to con them somehow, and even turn the blame on others, if there was something that caused enough concern to bring questions. Like there was this time my sister, she was five, about a year after my daddy died, she had gotten into the cookie jar and it fell off the counter and broke. It was one of those jars that looked like a cow and mooed when you opened the lid. It startled her. She hadn't seen it before and when it mooed...it was only an accident. She never meant for it to fall and break. It made my mother angry. She heard the crash and ran into the kitchen where Bella was still standing on the chair and already crying. Mother screamed at her, calling her a 'thieving little cunt' and slapped her. She slapped her so hard she..." Gwendolyn stopped. Her voice choked and she wiped her eyes on her sleeve.

I didn't say anything, because I had promised to let her talk without interrupting. Instead, I gave her a little squeeze and let her continue.

She took a halting breath. "The slap, it knocked her off the chair, but thankfully, she didn't break an arm or a leg. She got a black eye and bit her tongue. She cut herself on the glass where she fell and was bleeding.

"Mother backhanded her. 'Stop bleeding on the goddamn floor!' she screamed at her, as if Bella could've helped it.

"Mother's ring, it cut Bella's cheek open. Deep. Blood was coming out of different places. It must have shaken her up a bit, because she took Bella to the hospital.

"At the hospital, they asked her what had happened and she

said Bella fell. When they doubted the story, she started crying and told them her friend, Michelle, had done it. Told the right story and all, but only named the wrong people.

"Michelle was a woman who stayed with us sometimes. I guess she and my mother were friends, but I think they just used each other. Mother sobbed and wove a story and the police arrested Michelle and took her to jail. Mother told us kids if we didn't tell them Michelle hit Bella, and made her bleed, or told them she had done it, she was going to get her gun and shoot us until we were dead. There wasn't any reason for us not to believe she'd do it. She waved her gun around, threatened us with it all the time. Especially when she was high. With all the drugs, the men and all, I was freaked out most of the time. Eventually, I got the chance to get the hell out of there.

"She has three sisters and they're all the same way. My grandmother, too. Even my baby sister Bella's along the same path. The thing I'm most afraid of, and it might sound stupid to people who haven't had my life, I'm afraid I'll end up being just like her. That's my greatest fear. It's bad enough I have to watch Bella on that path, if she's not full-blown already. She's still young, so there's always a chance.

"I don't do drugs. I don't drink except on rare occasions. When I do, it's never enough to get me even a little tipsy. I don't smoke. I've never had a steady boyfriend, or even dated much. I've been on a couple dates, but all they wanted was to get into my pants. It's not that I...not that I can't, I just don't want...I'm afraid I'll turn into her. I'm afraid to become my mother." She broke.

I stayed silent. I didn't attempt to say anything, though I wanted to. Badly. I only held her close, not minding her tears soaked my shirt. I wanted to tell her she was too good to ever be like that. I cared about her. Not where she came from, nor who she happened to be related to. I loved her and no matter what her past was, no matter what happened, or what she might be afraid of, I'd be willing to stand by her and help her face anything that comes. I think these things have made her a stronger person, and her strength was part of what I loved about her.

Maybe I didn't know how it felt. I was lucky to have a mother and a father who both loved me and cared for me and my brother. They loved each other and did their best to keep us from harm and were happy in their life together. I may not know what it was like, but certainly, I could sympathize.

Eventually, she calmed down and kept talking.

It was at least an hour before she finished. When she did, she seemed to deflate, as if all the pressure had been built up and was only released by talking about it. I remained silent. I wanted to make sure she was finished.

"Are you going to say anything?" she finally asked.

"All I can say is I don't think you can be anything like the woman you described. Not even if you tried really hard." I should have thought of something better to say, but when the time came, I couldn't think of anything profound.

"But they say it's in our genes and it seems just about every female in my family has turned out that way. Even my sister. She's been pregnant once already and she's only..." She stopped. Fresh tears ran down her cheek.

"There's still hope for her," I said.

"Yeah, but it's slim."

"You're not like that," I said and wiped her tears with my finger. "Who says it's in our genes, anyway?"

"All those doctors. Psychologists."

"Oh, who gives a crap what they say. It's all just guesswork at a hundred and fifty an hour. Have you ever wondered why they call it a practice? They're just like the rest of us, trying to figure it all out. The meaning of life, or what we have to do with it. They just happen to have a little more academic experience and a piece of sheepskin saying they paid the money and took the time to put the word doctor before their name. They make mistakes and are wrong sometimes, just like the rest of us. So, you shouldn't have to worry what people think, or say. No matter what their title may be."

"You're right. I'm just so afraid."

"I understand."

"Do you?" She sounded skeptical.

"Sure. Sometimes you have to face your fear and take a chance. Otherwise, you'll end up wondering 'what if' the rest of your life. Anyway, you have me." Perfect. I was spouting out the same old platitudes I try to avoid.

"You sound like you've had some experience."

I shrugged it off. "Anyone who spends time in this world has some. Everyone's got at least one 'what if' in their life. Fear can be a motivator, or a destroyer. You make the choice." I should listen to myself.

"My Harry, the philosopher," she said, with a smile in her voice.

I felt relieved. "So, I'm yours now?" I asked.

"Was there ever a doubt?"

I thought briefly and said, "No." Then I asked, "What made you talk to me?"

"Talk to you?"

"Yeah, when we first met."

"I really don't know. It's weird, because I don't normally chat up strangers." She smiled at me. "I'm glad I did, though."

"Yeah, me too. We wouldn't be here together right now, if I had given in to fear."

"Yeah?"

"I wanted to run away."

"You did?"

"Uh-huh. I was even afraid to call you."

"Get outta here! No way!"

"I thought you'd given me a fake number. When you answered with 'gay bar,' I was going to hang up and never call again."

She grinned. "I'm glad you didn't run away or hang up. You were so nervous. It was cute."

"What if I hadn't been nervous?"

"I don't know. Probably wouldn't have given you a second thought."

"Makes me glad I was nervous. Got a question."

"Okay?"

"How did you get here?"

"What do you mean? Is this a god question?" She eyed me suspiciously. "You getting all religious now?"

"No, I meant get here. Like walk, or drive."

"I came on my bike," she said like she didn't think it was a stupid question.

"I mean, how did you get the hammock here without renting a car." Bloody hell, I felt stupid.

"I put some pixie dust on it and it flew behind me," she cracked.

"Seriously," I said.

"I had a friend bring it. She followed me. Is it important?"

"No, just curious."

"How did you think I got it here?"

"I thought you rented a car."

"You're a nut."

"You think I'm a nut?"

"Yeah, but a lovable nut."

"Better than a hateful one."

"Much better."

She leaned back into my arms and we lay there together. We gently rocked in the hammock, too comfortable to get up.

Naturally, we fell asleep.

Chapter 21

I awoke just as the sun was beginning to paint the sky with light. The air was clean and brisk, with a slight breeze. The birds sang their morning songs and Mother Nature was awakening to begin a new day of wonder.

Gwendolyn still slept, so I didn't move. I didn't want to wake her just yet. I watched her and marveled at how beautiful she was. She looked peaceful, like she had never seen any trouble in the world. She had childlike innocence, as if she lived in a world with no violence or guilt. I would have been content to let her sleep as long as she wanted while I watched, but the truth was my arm had fallen asleep and I really, really needed to get up.

******

"I can't believe I fell asleep," Gwendolyn said. She stifled a yawn as she shuffled into the kitchen behind me.

"You were tired," I said.

"Why did you let me fall asleep?"

"Let you? I fell asleep too. I can't help you also succumbed to the Sandman's charms. How do you want your eggs?"

"Mmm, scrambled with sausage."

"I only have bacon." I wished I had some sausage.

"I guess I'll have to suffer with bacon," she sighed.

"They're both pork products, so there's not much difference."

"Are you kidding me?" she said. "I can't believe I'm letting you cook for me. There's a whole lot of difference. They're nothing alike save for they come from the same animal. And then, different parts! You men can't tell because you just shovel everything in without tasting it."

"That's not fair. I'll have you know I'm quite the connoisseur when it comes to food."

"Of gas station food," she said. "If you were such a connoisseur, then you would know the difference between bacon and sausage without me having to tell you."

"Fine, so maybe I'm not so great in the breakfast category, but I am when it comes to pizza."

"Just because you were right about the sausage rolls doesn't make it so, but I'll let you have it."

"At least I have something," I said. I felt I'd won a small victory.

"Although I must point out that sausage rolls are not pizza."

Denied! "Same thing. Bread, meat and cheese."

"Not the same, but I'm not going to argue."

"Better not. I haven't drunk my coffee yet." I scraped the eggs from the sides of the pan with an old spoon and turned down the heat.

"You're not going to go off and tell all your friends we slept together, are you?"

"What kind of guy do you take me for?" I tried to sound offended as I popped some bread in the toaster.

"Maybe the kind of guy who might make something innocent look like something more, just so he can make himself look like a stud when he's just a sweet, fuzzy teddy bear."

"Get serious," I said. "I'll have you know I'm not at all fuzzy."

"I am being serious. You need a shave." She ran a hand over my cheek. "Maybe not fuzzy. Just prickly."

"I'm going for the rugged look," I said, as I put the eggs and bacon with a slice of toast on a plate and set it on the table in front of her. "Eat your breakfast."

I made myself a plate and we ate breakfast in comfortable silence. I thought about what she'd revealed the night before. I felt sad about it, but glad she trusted me enough to share it. Whatever had happened in the past had no effect on how I saw her as a person. If anything, it improved my view. I couldn't see any trace of the qualities she feared would surface.

Often, we wear different costumes when we're with others, along with the masks. I didn't think she was hiding behind any false exteriors with me. I believed when I looked at her, I saw most of the real Gwendolyn, with no intentional hiding.

Admittedly, we all have a secret life that remains private. A life never to be discovered unless it is with our knowledge and consent. Everyone has the right to that life. The right to share it with only the people they wish to share it with. It's what contributes a sense of wonder and curiosity about others. It allows us to seek companionship and have the ability to continue in relationships for the long term without getting bored.

Private lives are important, even to those who share a life together—probably essential. I'd be willing to bet every marriage that manages to last does so only because both partners have a separate life. A life together doesn't have to include both people in every activity or thought. If a couple spends all their time together, have the same friends, enjoy the same things, go to all the same places without having anything setting them apart as individuals, then the relationship is doomed from the beginning. It will never have the longevity of a relationship that maintains separate lives. Not to mention, things get awkward if the couple splits. Not only for the couple, but their mutual friends.

I wanted Gwendolyn in my life. I considered possible consequences of giving her some information on what was going on with my secret life. It was feasible to think she might somehow be able to help. I thought I should give it more time. I didn't want to endanger anything. Not her, not this relationship. I wanted to let her see I wasn't going to run. Her past wasn't going to determine my thoughts and feelings. I wanted to be with her.

I guess it's why she told me what she did. It was some sort of test, whether she realized it or not. I guess she's had others in her life who thought there were enough reasons to run. It's their great loss. I'd give it more time so we could each show the other we weren't going to run off screaming. I might, if she turned into a rat, but that seemed unlikely to happen. I'd stick around.

"I better get out of here," Gwendolyn said. She took her plate and rinsed it in the sink. "You're not so bad at making eggs."

"Just don't ask me to make an omelet," I said, as I looked at my watch. "I need to get to work, but I'm glad you came by and slept with me." I grinned at her.

"You better watch yourself," Gwendolyn pointed at me and

actually blushed. My grin grew even wider.

"Kidding, but really, thanks for the hammock and the company."

"Yeah, sure, but I'll have you know the hammock was gotten for selfish reasons."

"It's okay. Selfishness is a virtue, no matter what people may think."

She smiled. "Rand."

"What?"

"Ayn Rand," she said, but I must have looked confused because she added, "The philosopher?"

"Right, of course. *Atlas Shrugged*."

"There was a book with some of her essays called *The Virtue of Selfishness*, and you reminded me of it."

"I haven't read it," I admitted.

"I have it at my place. If you'd like, you can borrow it."

"Maybe we have a copy of it in the store. If not, I'll borrow it. I really need to get going."

"Yeah. Hey, you want a ride? It's on the way, so no trouble."

I thought she looked cute, being all hopeful. I couldn't really resist, so I said, "I'll let you give me a ride if you have an extra helmet."

"I always have an extra, so you can't back out."

"No, I'm not backing out."

"Are you going to cry?" She was making fun of me now.

"I'll try not to, but no promises."

"Good enough," she said.

I locked up and we went downstairs.

"Why don't you get a car?" I asked, as I managed to put the helmet on my head.

"I like my bike. And I hate paying for gas."

"Fair enough," I said, and climbed on.

"If there's ever a reason I need a car, I'll just borrow yours."

She started the engine and I began to tremble a bit, but not too badly. I was beginning to get used to this. I must take a moment to brag. Not once during the short ride did I scream, and I had my eyes open for over half of it. I was rather proud of myself.

******

"Am I crazy?" Carol asked, as I walked into The Bookworm.

"That's a very dangerous question. I'm not sure how I should answer it. If I tell the truth, you won't fire me, will you?"

She rolled her eyes. "Just tell me if I saw you getting off the back of a motorcycle, or if I'm seeing things."

"In that sense, you are not crazy."

"What in the world are you doing hitching a ride on a motorcycle?"

"I was coming to work," I answered.

"Maybe I was hearing things, but I seem to recall you saying you wouldn't be caught dead on one. Something about being 'uncomfortable' with them."

"Did I say that?"

"You did, though I knew you were really saying you're scared of them."

"That is exactly what I meant. I'm getting over it. Conquering the fear. Maybe one day I'll get really brave and actually drive one!"

"We'll see," she said doubtfully. "What brought on this bout of bravado?"

"She asked me if I wanted a ride. I said sure, and here I am."

"Oh, so it's a girl, is it?"

"Yes," I nodded. "Not one of those plastic ones either. A real live one!"

"Oh, for heaven's sake, Harry, it's about time!" she said with genuine relief. "People were starting to ask questions."

"Questions? What kind of questions?" I asked, though I suspected it.

"You know…" she stalled. She looked uncomfortable.

"People think I'm gay?" I voiced my suspicion.

"Well, naturally." Carol broke off to check out a customer.

I took the opportunity to clock in. I couldn't understand why people would think I was gay and whispering behind my back about hell knows what. Not that I thought it mattered much, but gay? Me? I never thought I put off gay vibes. I went back up to the front where, for now, there weren't any customers.

"Why would people 'naturally' think I'm gay?" I restarted the conversation. I was confused. Did this explain why I'd always struck out with women until Gwendolyn?

Carol's face flushed and I was sure she wished she never mentioned it. "Well, Harry, you're always running around with that DeVille character."

"You mean Gary?" I asked. "Yeah, I hang out with Gary, and yes, he's gay. We're friends. That's it. A straight guy can have gay friends and not be gay, or even bi, you know."

"Of course, you can. Of course." she studied me. "Also, you…" she lowered her voice to a whisper. "Not that it matters, but you did pick up that gay sex book."

I laughed loud enough to attract the attention of some browsers. "I got the book for Gary. His birthday is this week. It's kind of a joke. Every time he comes in, he asks if we have the book. I'm sure he's just kidding around, but I thought it would be funny to get it. That way he couldn't ask for it anymore." I rambled on as if I had to defend myself.

"I am relieved, I must say," she said. "Though it wouldn't make a difference to me."

"Uh huh." If it didn't make any difference to her, why was she relieved? Honestly, people can be so clueless.

She wiped her hands on the front of her jeans, and looked around the store. "I'm going back to the office. I've got a pile of paper on my desk I must get through by the end of the week. Don't know how I'm going to do it, but I must try. Do you think you can handle it up here?"

"What do you think?"

"You're right. I shouldn't have to ask."

"I'll be fine. If a super-hot hunk comes in and I can't resist taking him right there, I'll be sure to give you a call."

"Yes, you do that," she said and headed to her office.

I chuckled to myself. Yep, clueless.

Chapter 22

"She told me people thought I was gay!" I exclaimed to Gary as we sat in his living room. "Me, of all people. I don't look gay, do I?"

"Oh, honey, gay doesn't have a look. It's not always as obvious as someone being of a different race. You obviously are not, and it should be apparent to anyone."

I had the idea he was placating me.

"I always thought so, but it seems it's not obvious to every-one. Carol said people assumed, because we hung out together."

"When you assume, you make an ass out of U and me." He chuckled. "I still get a kick out of that one. I guess I'd better start getting all the laughs I can now."

"There's no sense in not taking the opportunity when it comes your way," I wondered what he meant, but didn't pursue it. "I brought you a present."

His eyes brightened. "A present? I do so love presents."

"Happy birthday." I pulled a bottle of his favorite wine out of a bag and handed it to him.

"I should have known. This must have unnecessarily dented your wallet. You shouldn't have, Harry."

"Why shouldn't I get you something you really like for your birthday?"

"I'm shocked you even remembered. I'm happy with just that." He took the bottle to the kitchen.

After he left, I took the book out of the bag and set it on the coffee table. He came back shortly with two glasses of wine.

"I almost didn't remember myself," he said. "I took the liberty of pouring you a glass. If you don't want it, I'll just drink both."

"You'd be allowed today, but I think I'll have some." I took the glass. "Thanks."

Gary sat down and sipped. He rolled it in his mouth before swallowing.

"Mmm, that's good."

I agreed, but it really wasn't my taste.

"I just don't like being reminded I'm getting old."

"You're a long way from being old," I assured him.

"Still, every year, it's just a step closer. A yearly reminder we're all going to age. Most of us, anyway," he said, ominously. "It's not like when I was a child. When we're children, we get ex-cited about it. Life is big and majestic. A whole world is out there to discover. Then you become an adult and reality smacks you in the face. Slams you back to earth and shatters all your fantasies."

"I thought you liked your life?" I asked. "Anyway, I think life can still be pretty wonderful," I thought of Gwendolyn.

"I'm not saying it never is. I'm no negative Nancy. For the most part, it's been wonderful for me. Not everyone can say they've been as lucky as I have. There's plenty who's had more luck, but I don't begrudge them."

"I think everyone's in the same boat."

"Maybe." Gary set his glass on the table. He noticed the book and picked it up. "How did this get here?"

"The gay fairy brought it while you were pouring wine."

"Come now." Gary smiled as he leafed through it.

"It's your other present. It finally, by some miracle, came into the store and I picked it up because you're always asking for it. Someone, somewhere, gave up their book just for you. Probably knew you needed to learn how to do it right. Happy birthday."

"Oh, Harry," Gary put the book back on the table and shook his head. "I was only kidding, *mon ami.*"

"Okay, so it's a gag gift. Either way, you can't keep asking for it. If you give this one up, you don't get to ask for another."

Gary teared up a little. "It's friends like you who make it so hard."

His voice was so quiet; I almost didn't hear him.

"What are you talking about?" Panic rose up in my chest.

"Harry, you do know you are my very best friend, don't you?"

"I've always thought I was in your top ten." I tried to suppress the panic from showing in my voice. I was unsure what was going on, but I knew it wasn't good. "What's wrong, Gary?"

"I don't know how to tell you this." Gary's eyes moistened and he looked toward the ceiling.

"Say what? Seriously, Gary, you're starting to scare me."

He didn't say anything straightaway. He lowered his eyes and held his hands together. He seemed to be trying to get the cooperation of his vocal chords.

"I'm dying," he finally said.

"Oh, stop playing around. We're all dying. You're not funny." My voice cracked.

Gary shook his head slowly, deliberately. "I wish it were a joke, but it's not. It's true."

I could see in his eyes he was scared. I moved to sit by him and took his hands into mine. "What is it?"

"Those headaches. Normal, right? I didn't worry about it, figured it was just stress, but it happened all the time. Like migraines. Finally went to the doctor and he ran some tests." He paused and wiped his eyes. "They found a tumor. Pretty big," he finished in a whisper.

"What the hell are you talking about?" I immediately regretted my tone and wished I could take it back.

"Cancer, Harry. That's what I'm talking about. I have brain cancer."

"You don't know it for sure." I didn't want to believe it.

"Yes, Harry. I know for sure. The tests don't lie."

"They can fix it, can't they?"

"The chances aren't good."

"You're not even going to fight it?"

Gary gave a choking sigh. "I'm not just going to roll over, but the odds aren't good. Not at this point. Most of what they can try is experimental."

"You say you're not going to give up, but you don't sound like you're serious."

"I do have to be realistic."

I put my arms around him and hugged him close to me. I felt his hot breath on my chest as he began to sob.

"They said I may have only a few months, but they were being optimistic."

He broke and clutched to me as if for his very life. In a way, he was.

He shook as he sobbed like a little boy. "I don't want to die, Harry."

"I know." I really didn't know what to say. I just held him, stroked his hair and tried to comfort him while we cried together.

I cried with my best friend.

My dying friend.

Chapter 23

Days seemed to drag along and I stumbled through in a daze, unable to separate them. I tried to spend as much time as I could with Gary, with the knowledge that the time we had was limited. He, from all outside appearances, seemed to accept his fate. He was still sad and frightened, not by death itself, but by what he might miss. He didn't dwell on it. He took opportunities to do things he always wanted to do, but never got around to. Trips and things, before he couldn't do it anymore. Gwendolyn spent a lot of time with him too. We'd go out together as a group. Gary brought along a date most of the time. I don't think he ever had any of them stick around long, and I'm sure he never told them his situation. I could understand. Why get close to someone new only to end up hurting them?

Gary and Gwendolyn had grown quite fond of each other. A lot of guys might have become jealous, but not me. It wasn't just because Gary is gay and no real threat in that department. It pleased me my two best friends got along so well. All they ever really talked about was fashion and chick flicks. They'd shop together and Gary would get her to indulge in more classic fashions. Gwendolyn liked to wear little skirts and strappy tops when she wasn't riding, and Gary wanted to "expand her horizons." Timeless, he called it. Bright red lipsticks, stockings, high heels. Things of the sort. I don't know a thing about that stuff, only I liked it. Judging from the looks she got when we ventured out, I wasn't the only one. Sure, I felt like the odd man out a lot of the time, but I can't say I was jealous.

Since learning of Gary's illness, I'd put the house on the back burner. I figured a break was needed. I was still uneasy, but I still felt Her pull. I never brought the house up with anyone else besides Gary, but I didn't want to concern him with my own worries. Especially not now. I knew I'd eventually have to face it. It was something I needed to do, even if only to ease my troubled mind. Everything these days seemed to be a nightmare I wished I could wake from.

Eventually, I decided I would pay a visit to the historical center. I hadn't found out much of anything. Gary offered to try, though I protested. He didn't come up with anything either.

The historical center was the next logical step. Someone there might have knowledge, or at the very least, dredge up information.

I didn't know what to expect. I had lived in Carson most of my life. Far too long, I sometimes thought. In all this time, I had never set foot in the Carson Historical Center. I'd never felt the urge to, until now. I went in as anyone might their first time. It looked like a typical small town museum. I looked around for a living person, but didn't see anyone.

I wandered around and looked at some of the things on display in the glass cases. There were photographs, old and faded, of the town and her people. All the items related to something of Carson's history, though I thought some of it was stupid and not worth keeping. Such as old, yellowed bills of sale or something. The ink had faded away and most of it was illegible, so why keep it? I didn't think Farmer Brown's purchase of watermelon seeds a hundred years ago warranted a space. Unless they happened to be giant magical watermelons. Maybe then they'd deserve a place of great honor, but of course, there are no such things as magical watermelons.

At least not that we know of.

The best thing I saw, and I realize it was best merely for the novelty, was an old box of something called Sa-Tan-Ic Laxatives. It had a little picture of a red devil, complete with horns and a pointed tail. I wished I could have it. Not that I needed, or wanted, a laxative. I just wanted to say I had Sa-Tan-Ic Laxatives. Maybe I could find one at an auction or something.

"Why, hello there." A short, stout woman greeted me with a broad grin. I guessed she may have been somewhere in her seventies.

"Hello," I said.

"I'm so sorry I didn't greet you sooner. Seems our little doorbell isn't working again. Really should just get a new one put in, but haven't got around to doing it. I'm sure you're not interested in any of that though, are you?"

"It's all right. I was just looking around."

"I don't remember seeing you in here before," she said.

"No, haven't been in. It's very interesting," I lied. I didn't have much interest in anything here. Well, except for the Sa-Tan-Ic Laxatives.

"It is that. For a small town, anyway. Have you been here long?"

"In town, or here?" I asked.

"Here."

"Only about ten minutes or so. I haven't had time to get bored." I grinned.

"That's good. No shortage of things to look at in here."

I suspected she was talking more to herself than me.

"So, what brings you in today? Anything I might be able to help you with?" she asked, with seeming genuine sincerity.

"Maybe you can," I answered. "I was wondering if you might have some information on a person, or a house."

"Do you have a name? A location?"

"I don't know where it's at, or even if it was in this town."

"I see," she said.

"I do have a name, though. Henry Pierce. I think he was a doctor." I felt like a dullard and wondered why I even pursued it.

"The name does sound familiar."

I grew hopeful.

"Why don't you look around a little more and I'll go see what I can find."

"Okay," I said, as she trotted off to the back.

It looked like there might be a possibility I'd find something here, after all. I figured she was going to check a computer. Perhaps she was of the old school and kept a filing system using folders and cabinets. Kind of like the card catalogs they used to have in libraries. Those are a lost art, taken over by computer databases. I guess the computer makes it faster and easier to find out things, and it saves a lot of space, but I still like the idea of doing things the old way. Manually go through cards and files to find what you're looking for. For me, there's more of a sense of accomplishment. Makes you appreciate it more.

I browsed through more local memorabilia, though I found nothing more to pique my interest. Carson seems to have always been a dull town. No interesting artifacts. Maybe the townsfolk kept all the stories to themselves, or they just moved away to more exciting locales. I suspect it's a bit of both. It's part of what I like about this town. It's so dull you have to use your imagination to override it. Like playing pirates in a featureless suburban back yard.

"You know, I do have something for you," the woman returned with papers in hand. "I couldn't be certain about the name at first, but now I'm sure it's the same family."

"You are?"

"Yes, yes. Of course, it's only stories and legends and I don't put too much stock in that sort of thing. I'm sure nothing's been verified, but you know how rumors go."

"Yeah, I know how it can be." I waited for her to continue. She seemed to be sorting out the things that should or shouldn't be told.

"I remember hearing this story about a doctor. He had a big house on the far edge of town. A nice, fancy house, though not as big as you might see of those who are well off today. He'd bought up a lot of the land surrounding the property so he wouldn't have close neighbors." She paused, and tilted her head to one side. "It seems odd, though, a doctor not wanting to be around people."

"I don't think it's all that strange," I said. "Maybe he got tired of people always asking for advice, or to diagnose things while he was off the clock."

"Yes, I can see where he would enjoy the solitude," she said "He had a practice in town. I think he also kept an office at home. Mostly though, he took care of the people in town. He was very good, from accounts. He was also doing a little work and research in..." She paused and tapped her finger on her temple. "Oh, what do you call it, where they study the brain and such?"

"Psychology?" I offered.

"Yes, yes. That's it," she said. "He seemed to go along with the theory that body and mind were related, which they are. The good book tells us that, but these things he was studying, most folks around here didn't think much in that direction. Just simple folk, really. What got him interested was his wife. She would get ill and he couldn't find explanations for it."

"What was getting her sick?" I asked.

"Drugs," she answered.

"Drugs?" I was a little surprised. "How did he know?"

"We can only speculate, but if he did know, he denied it. From what they say, she had become addicted to opium and absinthe. She was able to hide it from him at first, but it did a number on her mind. Hallucinations and what have you. She got violent toward her husband. Even with her children. She Lashed out at them. Threw things. Screamed. She must not have realized she was doing it, because she never seemed to remember, or so it was said."

"So, there were children? How many?"

"Three, I believe. Though they may not have all been hers."

"No? Whose were they?"

"I think the oldest was a married daughter. The younger ones could have been hers, but I'm not sure."

"Sounds strange to me," I said.

"Oh, it is. It surely is." She leaned over and lowered her voice as if someone might be listening, said, "She was also quite promiscuous and had all sorts of affairs. Probably a result of the drugs. I don't see how her husband could have missed it, but he often gave the impression he had no idea anything of the sort was going on."

"Why didn't he notice?" I asked. She seemed to have a lot of gossipy tales about these people. I wondered where she got it all.

"He did spend a lot of time in his work, but I guess he was in denial. His wife, Lydia her name was, got steadily worse. To the point that she had these delusions demons were torturing her, trying to steal her soul and drag her into hell. Until then, she had been somewhat discreet about her affairs, whether she thought he knew of them or not. There was a time she began to take men into her home while her husband was working in town. Don't know how long that went on. One day, he came home early and, needless to say, he found her with another man. Not just any man, but a young friend and colleague of his. I reckon he did just what any other man would do if he found his wife with another man. He got up in a rage and attacked that young man. There was struggle and the doctor killed him. His wife then killed the doctor with a butcher knife. Story is, she cut his head clean off his body."

"Wow, that's just crazy," I said. But I already knew it was true. I'd seen the murder with my own eyes. "What happened after that?"

"Ghastly business if you ask me, but nothing came of it. Only the good Lord above knows why not. I'm guessing she had her way of doing things and kept most of it out of the records. Maybe it's just all talk. It must be, because there's not much at all, except for talk.

"After that, it was like anyone who would have her ended up with a death sentence. She even murdered her children. They say one survived, but no one seems to know how, and of course, there aren't any records. Now that I think about it, I'm sure she had a daughter, who was grown, with two little ones. If any survived, I'm sure they have passed on by now.

"There's a curse, they say, on all women folk who're descended from her, but chances are good there aren't any descendants. If that were true, then there wouldn't be a curse anymore. But, if any of the girls around town get into a spot of trouble, the old timers wonder and talk as though they might be under the curse."

"A curse?" I thought this woman seemed to know an awful lot for someone who claimed to not know much.

She laughed. "Oh, that's just what they say, but as I've said, I don't put much stock in that hogwash. That's what I think of the idea of curses and the like. Hogwash. That ol' devil, he gets too much credit for things and most of those are nothing. Not real. Just something he likes to put into people's minds to get them to forget about the one their mind should be on. The good Lord above. He's the one who should get all the credit, not that wicked ol' devil. Do you know the Lord?" she asked.

"I was raised in church," I said, using my standard answer for people who ask the question. Most assume you've said what they wanted to hear. I think that's super fantastic.

"That's wonderful," she said. "Church always does a soul good. Let the Lord get his due, is what I say."

I nodded politely.

"Now, I don't want you to run with all I told you. As I said, it's just hearsay. Don't want you going off taking it as gospel truth."

"No, of course not, ma'am. Is there anything else you can tell me? Maybe other places I can look?"

"Not that I can think of." She handed me a couple of pages. "I made you a copy of the article I found. Don't suppose it'll help much, but it's all that's there. You can keep it."

"Thank you," I said, as I took the papers. The print was diffi-cult to read, but one can't be choosy. "I appreciate your time and the information, Ms.—" If she had given me her name, I'd already forgotten it.

"Call me Pearl, and I'm more than happy to do whatever I can." She smiled broadly. "The pleasure is all mine. Now, when you decide to leave, don't forget to sign the book. I like to keep track of how many people come through and visit."

"I actually need to get going, so I'll go ahead and sign it now.

Thanks again," I said.

"You bring yourself back real soon." Pearl smiled again and went back into the other room.

I found the book and a pen chained to the pedestal. I read the scant few names written on the page. I didn't recognize anyone. I signed my name and slipped a couple of dollars into the donation box. I figured the information was worth it, even if she did attribute it to legend and rumor. From my experiences at the house, however, I believed at least parts of it were true.

I knew if the house stood at the edge of town, there was an off chance it would still be there. I looked at the copies Pearl had handed me. I squinted my eyes and looked close and tried to discover where it might be.

I concluded there was only one way to find out if the house still existed.

Chapter 24

I drove out to the location mentioned in the photocopied article. My excitement ramped up the closer I got. I found the approximate area and got out of the car, but it was just as I suspected.

There was no house.

I walked around a wide area. There were a few spots that

could have been a foundation, but nothing I could be certain about. There was a section of railroad track not far from the probable site. How far the track went, I don't know, but it was obvious it hadn't seen any kind of use for a very long time.

The whole area seemed to have not been frequented for a while. I chose to believe this was where the house had been. There was something, a feeling, that told me this was true. Though nothing remained of the house, there had to be a reason for the pull She had on me. But I had no idea what it could be.

Maybe there is no such thing as destiny or fate. Maybe there is. At that moment, disappointed the house was gone, I leaned more toward the belief there is no such thing.

******

"He's sick." I said to Gwendolyn. I still couldn't accept Gary's situation. We had just visited him and he wasn't having one of his good days. He looked worse. I didn't want to see it, nor did I want to accept the fact my best friend was dying.

"I know he is, but you need to know you're doing the best thing for him right now," she said.

"No, I'm not."

"Harry, you can't work miracles. He needs his friends right now and you're his best friend. Leave the miracles to the doctors and stop feeling sorry for yourself, okay?"

"You're right," I said, and she was.

I had spent too much time feeling sorry for myself and not doing much good for anyone. I certainly wasn't being a very good friend to Gary. I had never seen anyone sick like that before. It was hard to take. I was letting it get to me.

Treatments were taking a lot out of him and though they were meant to save his life, I saw the flamboyant, vibrant, wonderful man I had known and proudly called a friend disappear, and a tired, withered man take his place. The prognosis wasn't promising.

"I understand what you're going through," Gwendolyn said. "He's my friend too, so I'm with you. All we can do is be there for him and do what we can, but then, life must go on." It sounded so uncaring: especially coming from her, but it was the truth.

"I guess so," I said.

"Let's change subjects," she said. "What have you been up to?"

I smiled weakly. "Nothing. The other day, I actually took the time to visit the Historical Center."

"That's something. How was it?"

"What? You're not saying you've never been, are you?"

"That's what I'm saying. Am I missing out?"

"Boy, are you ever! It's really amazing what they have in there. All kinds of neat stuff. I wish I had gone a long time ago. I never realized Carson had such a rich, colorful history. It's full of amazing people and their likewise amazing deeds. I couldn't soak it all up in just one day."

"You're a really bad liar," she said.

"Really? I always thought it was one of my strong suits."

She shook her head. "If you have a strong suit, that isn't it."

"Seriously?"

"Nope. You have absolutely no skill when it comes to the art of deception."

"That might prove to be an advantage."

"Not today it won't," she laughed.

"Okay. You're not missing anything. It's boring and dull, just like this town. Well, save for the Sa-Tan-Ic Laxatives."

"Sa-Tan-Ic Laxatives?" She smirked, then snorted.

"Yeah, you wouldn't believe it unless you saw it yourself. There's a box of it a display case there. It must have come out of a mayor's medicine cabinet or something. It's got a big label with a depiction of His Infernal Majesty with the words 'Sa-Tan-Ic Laxa-tives' right across the top. Gives new meaning to the phrase, 'one hell of a shit.'"

"Ugh," she scowled at me. "Don't be crude."

"I'm a guy. Being crude is part of the job description."

"Whatever. You're not lying, so I may have to go see it for myself."

"As long as you're not going for the wonderful history lessons." I said, though I thought the history lesson I received was rather informative.

"You can find history anywhere, but you won't find it if you don't look," she said. "You know you can make it up, history. What were you doing there anyway?"

"Trying to find history," I answered. I wondered if I should tell her. If I did, she might think I was nuts. Not in a good way, either. We're talking straitjackets and paddy wagons. Of course, if I didn't tell her about it, then I'd just continue to feel like I was hiding something from her.

Of course, I was hiding something.

"More coffee?" I asked.

"Maybe a little. What history did you find, if you don't mind me asking?"

"Not a whole lot, but there was something. How much of it's true, I don't know. You know how it is. Things often get blown out of proportion."

Why not go ahead and risk it? What was the worst that could happen? She'd laugh and call me crazy and we'd make jokes about it. I decided I was being way too paranoid about this. I looked over the pages Pearl had given me at the center.

Though hard to make out, the newspaper story covered a murder. It claimed an intruder had broken into the home and killed the doctor. This was according to the doctor's wife, Lydia Pierce. Though both men were dead, nobody did anything to pursue it further, apparently. It wasn't a lot to go on, but with what I saw, and Pearl's story, it made a little sense.

I brought our coffee to the table.

Gwendolyn wrapped her fingers around her mug. "It's hot," she said.

"It is coffee," I said.

"Are you going to tell me about it, or are you just going to keep being evasive?"

"I didn't realize I was being evasive."

"Just a little."

"I was just curious."

"About?" she prodded.

I handed her the copied article, took a breath, and said, "I was curious because I saw this and the house and didn't know how I got there at first, but found out I could will myself there but never go back to where I started and thought I liked it, but it scares me now."

"Whoa, hold on there. You're not making any sense. Maybe if you slowed down some."

I was nervous, and rambled. I wasn't making sense, even to myself. I steadied myself and said, "I've seen the house."

"What house?"

I motioned toward the pages in her hand. "It's..." I tried to think of how I could say it before I admitted, "I don't want you to think I'm nuts."

She smiled. "I already think you're nuts."

"I'm serious."

She made a face at me. "Okay, we'll be serious then."

In it now, I thought. Let's just finish it out. "Okay. Somehow, a while back, I ended up at this house. I don't know what started it, but anyway, I was there. Inside that house." I pointed at the photocopies.

She knitted her brow as she looked at them.

"I haven't been through it all. It's kinda big, but..." I stopped.

"But what?"

"I can go back," I finished.

She studied me a moment, then said, "That's it?"

"What do you mean, that's it?" I asked. I wondered if she'd even heard what I just said, surprised she didn't get the scope of this revelation.

"Let me get this straight."

"Okay."

"You're telling me you end up at this house," she indicated the photocopies.

I nodded.

"And you can go back to it."

"Right."

She shook her head. "I'm sorry, Harry. I guess I'm not under-standing. It's not such a big deal you can go to an old house. People do it all the time."

"I'm trying to say the house doesn't exist."

"How can you go to a place that doesn't exist?"

"Well, it existed at one time, but it's gone now. One day I just ended up there, like in the past, but I have no idea how it started."

"Sorry, but I gotta say I think you're nuts."

"You're not understanding me," I mumbled. Her laughter made me uncomfortable, though it was meant without malice.

"You're right. I'm not understanding."

"I go there by will. Like...magic, for lack of a better word." I tried to gauge her reaction. She nodded for me to go on. "So, I've been going and looking around. There's been events, well, ghosts, but not really. It's like looking into the past."

"What, like a time machine?"

"Yeah. No. More like a movie. I don't understand it myself. How I can get there pretty much by wishing myself there. It scares me, in a way, but I don't think it can hurt me. At least, it hasn't yet.

I just feel like it's pulling me there all the time. Maybe there's a possibility. I hope it can't hurt me."

I finished and we stared at each other. The longer we stayed like that, the more I felt like an idiot. I was mentally preparing myself for Gwendolyn to stand up, walk out the door and never come back again.

"It does seem a little crazy," she finally said.

"It does," I agreed. I would think the same thing if our roles were reversed.

"Can anyone else go?" she asked.

"I don't know. It's funny, but Gary asked me the same thing."

"Gary knows about this?"

"Sure, he knows. He is my best friend, after all," I said, as if I needed to justify myself. "Hey, you remember when we first met?"

"Of course, I remember. You were standing there, leering at me."

"Oh, for crying out loud, I wasn't leering. I admit maybe I was staring a little, but not leering."

"Semantics, but yeah, I remember."

I felt foolish and defensive. It was too late to back out and there was no point in getting paranoid.

"I was looking, not leering, at you because you looked like..." I trailed off, unable to think of words to describe it. "I guess I'll just say the ghost. You look like a ghost I had seen at the house."

She didn't say anything straightaway, as if she wanted to be sure I wasn't just spewing bullshit. I returned to the fact I met Gwendolyn on the first day I darkened the entry of the house. It had never crossed my mind before, though maybe it should have.

Coincidence? Maybe, maybe not.

"That's a little creepy," she said. "Actually, a lot creepy."

Hell, she was going to run off now. I regretted my big mouth.

"I know." I sighed.

"Creepy, yes, but still interesting," she finished.

I hoped she wasn't able to sense my relief.

"I'm still glad you were there even if circumstances were somewhat otherworldly," she said.

"Do you think it was a coincidence I met you right after the very first time I was at the house?" I asked.

"I don't know." She looked troubled. "I've always thought there's no such thing and I still do, but I can't see the reason. Just because there isn't an obvious answer in front of you, it doesn't mean you're wrong."

"Yeah, I know. I can't think of a reason either."

"Has anyone else ever come along with you?" she asked.

"No. I don't think it would be a good idea to have anyone come along."

"Why not? Can they hurt you? You said they couldn't."

"Honestly, I don't know if they can. I wouldn't doubt it, because I can't assume anything, but being able to see you? I think they can see you and you are able to touch them, so you would think they could hurt a person."

"Maybe it would be a good idea to have more than one person along. It seems safer."

She had a point, though I could see where this was going. I didn't like it.

"Have you ever got pictures?" she asked.

"Pictures? I don't guess it ever crossed my mind to get any." I wondered why I hadn't thought of it before. If I could get pictures, would it change anything, or could I learn anything more? Could I even take a camera in, and if so, would it somehow damage the camera?

Maybe it would work.

"You should try it," she said excitedly. "If you can't get anything, there's no loss. If you can, who knows? Maybe I can go with you."

There it was.

"I'm not sure it's a good idea." I was hesitant, not for selfish reasons, but because I couldn't be sure of the dangers. I had barely considered the possible dangers to myself, but so far, so good, and I'd been able to leave as I pleased. Though I never ended up where I wanted to go, I was never returned far from home. But I didn't think I could live with myself if anything were to happen to Gwendolyn.

Gwendolyn shrugged. "That's fine, but if you decide to go, then you should at least try to get some pictures."

"I guess I could."

"Do you disappear?"

"What?"

"Disappear. Or do you just hang around like you're hypnotized? Is it something like astral projection?"

"I don't believe I've noticed one way or another." These are things I should know, but just plowing through, I never stopped to learn them. They might be important. I had some sort of an idea. "I think there must be some degree of disappearance."

"Really? How does it work?" she asked.

"You keep asking questions I don't have answers to," I said. "I don't know how it works, but whenever I leave the house..." Bloody hell, I was sounding insane. Was I really saying this shit out loud?

"C'mon, I'm a-shiver with anticipation."

"I end up somewhere else."

"Like where?"

"Downtown. In alleys. Places like that."

"Too weird."

I nodded. "I feel like a freak."

"If you're on the level, then you are a freak. Still, it's interesting."

"I guess so."

"Go get pictures."

"What, now? Are you serious?"

189

"Sure, why not?"

"You're exploiting me."

She ignored me. "Go get your camera."

"Fine, but I'm not going inside." I didn't want to cave, but that was exactly what I was doing.

"You don't want to go?"

"Not really. I'll go to get a picture. I'm not going inside the place, is all."

"Okay...?"

"It feels weird. I've always gone inside. I wonder what will happen if I don't. If I have to go inside the house to come back. I can't will myself anywhere while I'm inside the house, so I wonder if I can while I'm still outside of it."

"Life is all about discovery," she said.

"That it is."

I went to get my Polaroid and checked to make sure I had a cartridge in it with shots left. As long as I had one, it would be good enough, but I had two. Though I was nervous, I must admit I was curious and a little excited about this experiment. I should have thought of it before. I sat back in my chair with the camera draped around my neck.

"What is that thing?" Gwendolyn eyed my camera.

"It's my camera."

"They still sell film for those things?"

"Sure, why wouldn't they?"

"Just it's a little outdated. Why don't you have a digital?"

"This suits me fine. I'm not much of a picture taker and I'm much less a tech guy. Why get the newest gadgets when the ones I have now work just fine?"

"That's one of the reasons I like you," she smiled. "You're not complicated. You keep it simple and are still a fairly smart fellow."

"Fairly?"

"Yeah. I don't want you to get a big head."

"Thanks, I guess." I shifted in my chair. Relaxed, I closed my eyes.

******

"There you are," I said, as I looked at the house. She looked even more worn down and the land around Her lonelier. I was sorely tempted to go inside, but I refrained. It wouldn't be fair to Gwendolyn if I left her alone longer than necessary. Especially since I might have to walk from who knows where. I didn't want to waste any time.

The Polaroid still hung from my neck, undamaged from all appearances. At least I know the answer to that.

I framed the house in the camera's viewfinder and snapped a picture. I pulled the print out and shook it from habit. I don't think shaking it does anything to speed up the process, but habits are hard to break.

I watched as the house began to appear in the photo. It looked pretty good. Not a professional job, by any means, but it was clear and I could make out the details.

"Come in..." She said. "Stay."

She was tempting me again. I closed my eyes and tried to shut out Her voice. I pictured myself back in my chair and thought of Gwendolyn. I did my best to ignore the house.

"Come back!" She sounded angry.

I felt my body slam back and the voice faded into stillness.

******

"Damn," Gwendolyn gasped. It must have been impressive; she didn't spout out words like that on a regular basis.

My eyes were still closed, but I was back in my apartment, in my chair, just the same as when I started. If I stayed outside, I go where I started.

I still held the photograph. I opened my eyes slowly as if something would smack me across the face if I opened them too fast. Gwendolyn hadn't moved. She looked shocked.

I looked at the photograph. It was the same one I had taken, only the photo was out of focus and distorted. It was as if the house did not want to be photographed. The details were gone.

"I have a picture." I waved the photo at Gwendolyn like a cat trying to gift his human with a dead bird.

"You..." she pointed out me, her mouth open as if her jaw had quit working.

"It's not a very good picture," I plunged on. "It looked better when I took it there. It was quite good, actually. Something there..." I faded to a stop and asked, "What? What's wrong?"

"You just..." she stumbled, and I had a secret laugh because she was acting like me when I get nervous.

"I just what?"

"You left."

"No, I didn't. I'm right here." I made a show of checking my arms and legs. "Yep, I'm here, indeed."

"You disappeared. Like a magician does, only this isn't a magic show. This is real."

"Really?" I knew, but I had never actually observed my comings and goings.

"Does it hurt?" she asked. "Do you hurt?"

"No, I feel fine. Don't hurt at all." I handed her the photo again, but she only waved it away.

"I don't understand."

I shrugged. "Neither do I."

"How do you do it?"

"I'm just as clueless as you are. I ask myself the same thing, so we're both in the same boat. Look at the picture. It's why I went in the first place."

She took it and studied it for a moment. "It's not very good. Couldn't you take another? It's probably your camera. You really should think about getting something from this century."

"It is from this century. It's not that old and it's not the camera."

"Actually, it's not from this century. That thing came from the twentieth century. This is the twenty-first, in case you haven't heard yet."

"Yeah, whatever. The camera works great." I lifted up the camera and used my last exposure to snap a quick shot.

"Hey! No pictures!" She squealed and leapt toward me and grabbed for the print.

I bounded from the chair and held it out of her reach.

"Give me that picture or else!" she threatened.

"Or else what?"

"Never mind. Just give it."

"I'm just trying to show you it can't be the camera. Anyway, why shouldn't I have a picture of you?"

"Because I look horrible, that's why."

"Nah, you look great," I said, and made the mistake of taking my eyes off of her to look at the picture.

She rushed me and tackled me to the floor. She ripped the picture from my hand.

"What did you do that for?" I asked, between labored breaths.

"I warned you," she said nonchalantly, as she glanced at the picture. "Ugh. I do look horrible, but I'll admit it's not your camera. Now you can go and burn it."

"You have to get off of me first, but I'd rather you didn't," I said, and waggled my eyebrows.

"Pervert," she barked, as she pushed herself quickly to her feet.

I jumped up and snatched the photo back. "Got it!" I exclaimed. "I don't think you look horrible at all. As a matter of fact,

I think I'll keep it."

"To spite me."

"Nope. I like it. Great expression. Take it how you want."

"Fine, as long as I don't have to look at it."

"In that case, maybe I'll have it blown up."

She glared at me.

I cringed.

"Okay," I said, "but the fact is, there was something lost in the transfer. It's as if the house didn't want the picture taken, or transported to another dimension, or whatever."

"It's amazing you got anything at all. You're thinking this place is in another dimension?"

"How would you explain it?"

"You're asking me? Like I have a clue."

"I don't know how to explain it, but I feel drawn to the place."

"It's strange. Kind of scary, but exciting."

"So, you understand?" I said, with some relief.

"No. Some of it, maybe, but not all." She stood with her hands planted on her hips. "If it's possible, I want to go."

I frowned and shook my head. "No. I don't think it's a good idea. I don't know how we'd do it and I'm not sure if someone else can. Even if I did, I wouldn't want to drag you into something where you could get hurt."

"Maybe I could help you. Maybe all you need is another perspective."

"Let me guess, a woman's?"

"Of course," she said, as if it should have been obvious.

"Maybe another day," I said, defeated.

I was afraid of the idea and hoped to find a way out. A way to discourage her. I sensed impending doom. It could have just been nerves, but I couldn't help but think nerves had nothing to do with it.

Chapter 25

I decided to walk to work as the morning was cool, with a gentle breeze and fresh, clean air. I left my apartment a little early so I could casually stroll along and enjoy the weather. Nice weather is also great for thinking.

I must say my mind was put at ease since Gwendolyn learned of the unwonted affairs and didn't run off screaming I was bonkers. At least, not completely. The disappearing act did a lot to help my case, but I was troubled by her enthusiastic interest in going to the house with me. Though I hadn't run into any real trouble, it didn't mean there wouldn't be any. I would hate for something to happen to her. Though we hadn't known each other very long, I'd come to think of her as one of my best friends.

I had also fallen in love with her.

The fact caused me to panic a little. I wanted to deny it, but at the same time I couldn't and still be honest with myself. It shouldn't have been a great surprise, but it was. Scary.

I turned my thoughts to the house. Would She react differently to a female? When Pearl gave her account, she never seemed sure of its accuracy. I thought about other experiences and all the stories I'd heard about ghosts and the supernatural. Some of them seemed far-fetched when I heard them, but now, it didn't seem as improbable.

I wanted to talk to Gary about it. He would help me figure out what to do with my fears about Gwendolyn wanting to go. He'd know where I was coming from and he could help me sort things out. He had always been a great sounding board. I decided I could swing by his place after I got off work. I hoped he would be up to a visit and felt a little selfish for using a visit to benefit myself, especially since I hadn't been by in a few days.

He had closed his gallery recently. He got to where he just couldn't do it. Last time I saw him, he was a little out of it. If anything, I'd go and at least be with him. A visit would probably make him feel better if he was having one of his off days.

"Good morning," I said to Carol, as I walked into The Bookworm.

Carol looked up and smiled weakly. She was busy with a customer.

I went to the back to clock in with hopes that work might take my mind off things and allow me a bit of time to rest. It's funny how going to work can do that sometimes.

I approached the counter as Carol's customer left. She looked at me oddly and asked, "What are you doing here?"

"Um, I'm on the schedule," I answered.

"Are you feeling all right?" she asked, as I made my way behind the counter.

"Yeah, I'm feeling fine. As good as one can under the circumstances."

She nodded. "I'm sorry, Harry. Really, I am. If you'd like, I can give you some time off."

I was bewildered. "What are you talking about, Carol? Why would I want time off? You know I can't afford that. What's going on?"

"Oh, god," she moaned. She refused to look in my eyes.

"What?" I said, suddenly suspicious.

"You don't know?"

"Know what?"

"Oh Harry, I thought you already knew."

She was being evasive. I was afraid to know, but I shook my head and asked slowly, "Know what?"

Carol grasped my shoulders and took a breath. "Gary's dead, Harry."

I stumbled back a step. My voice caught in my throat. I just stared at her, and hoped this was some kind of horrible joke, but Carol wouldn't be that cruel.

"Dead?" I finally choked out. "I don't understand. He wasn't... I just saw him not that long ago. He didn't look that bad." I leaned up against the counter for support. "Dead? How? There's no way. He can't be."

"I really thought you knew, Harry. I thought maybe you heard it from someone else."

"Told me he was dead?" I laughed, short and without any humor. I felt as if an anxiety attack was coming on.

Carol looked around for any customers within earshot. She moved beside me.

"He shot himself," she said, after a long pause, her voice full of compassion.

I fell onto a nearby stool. "Shot himself? Why? I didn't even know he had a gun."

"I don't know, hon."

She wrapped her arms around me in a motherly hug. I let her do it, though I felt little comfort from it.

"They found him yesterday," she whispered, as if it would lessen the impact. It didn't.

"It's all over town," she said. "I tried calling, but all I got were busy signals. I assumed someone would have already called to tell you. That you knew."

I was reminded of what Gary said about assuming. Ass out of U and me. I wanted to laugh, cry, scream, or do something, but I couldn't. My emotions had seized up. They refused to come out.

"No, I..." I choked, cleared my throat and tried again. "I had no idea. None at all. I was going to see him after work today. Oh hell, I'm so selfish. I'm only thinking of myself."

"No, hon. You're not. Don't blame yourself."

I looked at Carol. My eyes brimmed with tears. "He didn't want to be sick," I whispered. To myself mostly.

Carol patted my shoulder. "Harry, why don't you go home. You need some time."

"No, it's okay. I can stay," I said stubbornly.

"Go on, Harry. You're not going to be any good here in this condition."

"Thanks," I tried to be sarcastic. It came out more pathetic.

"Go on. We'll be okay. It's not one of our busy days, so you go ahead."

"Okay," I said. I got up and left.

I forgot to clock out.

I forgot everything.

The walk home was slow and painful. I was glad I decided not to drive. I was like a zombie, unable to see or hear anything around me. I'm surprised I didn't get run over. Somehow, I managed to get to my apartment. I went inside without closing the door. I dropped down into my chair.

The dam finally broke.

******

Gary's memorial service was held in the chapel of the funeral home. The chapel was a good size, but it was nonetheless packed full of people. Many had to stand because they couldn't find a seat. I had not expected there to be so many people. I knew he had friends, and had met many of them, but it hadn't prepared me. I really had no idea he had affected so many people.

When he first came into town, he had a difficult time, but eventually earned the respect of everyone in town, just like Black Bart in *Blazing Saddles*. With his personality, I shouldn't have been surprised, but I was.

Gary must have planned all of this out, because the arrangements were already made and paid for. The service was a simple affair and didn't have any of the elaborations which seem so common.

I've heard it said that funerals are for the living, but I have my doubts. The ceremony, sure, that part's for the living, but its true purpose is to keep the people being memorialized in our hearts and our memories. It's a kind of immortality. It gives you something to remember the impact someone made on you and the things they contributed to your life. It could be a friend, a parent, or even a child. Life is all about relationships. When a relationship ends, you feel it, but it's not the end of your life. The departed live on in our hearts and memories. We carry a piece of them with us and give it to others. In this sense, memorials are very much for the dead.

Gary was my friend. He was my brother. All I could do was hope he knew how much I loved him. I let him go and tried to understand his reason for doing what he did. At least I thought I understood, but it was hard. I already missed him.

As soon as the service was over, Gwendolyn and I left. I wasn't up to any mingling. I was afraid I would cry again and I didn't know what to say to anyone, anyway. I let Gwendolyn drive us back and we rode in silence. The silence was more to do with not knowing what to say, rather than having nothing to say. It was a rare, awkward silence between us. I realized awkward silences can exist between two people who are comfortable enough with each other to have silent periods.

"Are you going to be okay?" Gwendolyn reached for my hand.

I nodded and continued to gaze blankly out the window.

"I'll be fine. I don't know. It's going to be so strange without him. It's like I knew him all of my life, though it's only been a few years."

"I understand," she said.

I wondered if she really did.

"I'm not angry," I said suddenly, my voice shrill. "Some people, yeah, sure maybe they're angry, but I'm not."

"It's okay if you are," said Gwendolyn.

"No. I'm not. I can't be. How could I be angry with him when I can understand and probably would have done the same thing if I were in his situation?"

"Why would you be angry?"

"About him k—" I swallowed back a sob. "You know. He knew what was going to happen. He was trying to make it easier for the rest of us. He knew he wasn't going to get any better and didn't want anyone to be burdened. He was too proud. I think he would have suffered more if someone else had to take care of him. It wouldn't have mattered to me. I would have taken care of him. Just to have him around a little longer. I guess he didn't want any more suffering and thought it wouldn't be as hard on people this way."

"He was proud," she said.

"Damn it, this is hard, too. Damn hard. I loved him."

"Yeah, me too," Gwendolyn said.

These simple words covered a multitude of things.

After a moment, she asked, "You hungry?"

"You're thinking about food?"

"Gotta eat. Are you?"

"Know a place that serves horse? I could eat one right now."

"At least you haven't lost your sense of humor, horrible as it is."

"I was under the impression I didn't possess a sense of humor."

"You do, and it is very, very bad."

"Good to know," I said, then we decided on a place to eat.

Chapter 26

Gwendolyn and I spent the evening lounging in the hammock on the roof. I had become quite proficient at getting in and out of the contraption, like an old master. It was a good night for loung-ing outside, as it was cool and the sky was clear and bright with stars. The remnant of a six pack chilled in a small cooler. I planned to finish it off, with or without Gwendolyn's help.

"Do you ever think about moving?" she asked.

"Where would I move to?"

"Another place. Away from here. Out of this old building. Maybe even out of this town."

I took a long, thoughtful sip from my bottle. "Sure, I've thought about it. Only natural to think about going somewhere else. I don't think it's something I'll do, though."

"Why not?"

"Don't know. I guess I like it here. This is home for me."

"You like it?" She didn't try to hide her astonishment. "No offense, Harry, but this place is falling apart. I'm sure you've no-ticed there's a floor missing."

"Yes, I know. It's why nobody lives there. Anyway, it's not that bad."

She laughed. "Who's to say your floor won't be next?"

"My floor's solid enough," I said.

"You're not worried?"

"Not at all. I'd notice any weakness, so before anything hap-pened, I could try to fix it. I don't keep anything really heavy, so there's not any reason to worry too much."

"I would worry about it if I lived here. I'm worried about it now," she said.

"Yeah, well...anyway, it's quiet here and there's history. She's got a unique character."

"Just like someone I know." She nudged me playfully. "So, what kind of history does *she* have?"

"It's a very long story."

"That's just a weak euphemism for 'I don't want to tell the story.' Anyway, I have plenty of time."

"So you say."

"I do. It's my time and I can choose what to do with it. Tell me this alleged long story."

"You asked for it." I finished off my beer and tossed the bottle aside. "This place was built in 1905 as the headquarters of a secret society. Small towns are perfect for that sort of thing. The society operated under the guise of a benevolent fraternal organization. Like the Elks, Moose, or any of those who name themselves after animals.

"Outside the society, people thought it was simply a group of men who got together on weekends to drink beer, play cards and trade stories. Occasionally, they'd raise money for charity or something. Members at the lower levels believed the same thing. At the higher levels, which only a few reached, it was more like a religious cult. The kind of thing Christians think Satanists and Pagans do. They held dark, mysterious rites that involved animal sacrifice. There were rumors they even held human sacrifices, using babies for their victims."

"That's horrible!" Gwendolyn gasped. "They killed babies? Little innocent babies? Here?" She looked about and shivered. "You're morbid, wanting to live here."

"I'm playing with you," I said, deadpan.

"I mean, who would..." She stopped and slugged me.

The hammock swung wildly.

I laughed and rubbed my arm. She didn't look like she could, but she was able to pack quite a punch. "That kinda hurt!"

"You're an ass! A real prick! I hate you!"

"You don't hate me," I said.

"Yes, I do! That was a mean thing to do, telling stories of butchering babies."

"You can't say I'm not able to weave a story anymore. You fell for that one. But I don't believe for a minute you hate me."

"Oh, but I do. And I'm going to hate you for a few minutes

longer. Then, I'll think about forgiving you."

"I'll allow a few minutes."

"I'll make that decision. What's the real story?"

"Nothing as exciting as secret societies butchering living beings to gain the favor of a god."

"It's not exciting. It's just sick and wrong."

"You're right," I conceded. "It was a hotel with a restaurant and bar. Nothing fancy. Prostitutes used it a lot."

"Well, that makes sense."

I smiled. "After the hotel closed, it became offices for lawyers and accountants. Charles Lewis bought the building in the sixties and converted the top three floors into apartments. He charged weekly rates and it was kind of like an extended stay hotel. She's falling apart now because she wasn't taken care of. Mr. Lewis died about twenty years ago. His wife owns it now, but she doesn't have the money to fix it up like it should be. The floor fell in because of a water leak that went undetected. Don't know how it could have been missed, but then I wasn't living here at the time. Now, I do what I can here and there and Mrs. Lewis takes it out of my rent. I'd do it for nothing, though. I love it, really I do. I'm going to buy it and fix it up the way it should be. Maybe I'll even put an elevator in."

"How do you plan on doing that?" she asked.

"I don't know. It's just one of those pipe dreams I have. I would restore it and put it back to the way it was originally if I could. Not as a hotel, but I'm not going to turn it into something modern. I'm not a big fan of modern architecture. It seems most of it is just thrown together to look like everything else. You go into one of those developments and you tour only one house because they're all exactly the same. The only way to tell it's your house is by the number."

"Maybe it's why people have those silly lawn ornaments. Gives them some kind of individuality."

"Only in trailer parks. You're not going to see pink flamingos and creepy gnomes at these houses."

"I've seen some," she said.

"Yeah? Maybe it was a redneck who lucked out and moved up from a trailer."

"Or maybe it was someone with a little individuality. But I agree, most places are mass produced. It seems there aren't many architects willing to take a risk."

"I'm sure they're out there."

"They are. At least you have a dream. Good to have goals. I guess there's been a lot of people who have come through here."

"Yeah. I've found things here and there. Mostly just papers. Letters and things. There were a couple of places that hadn't been accessed for a long time. I'm sure there's been squatters, but not since I've been here."

"Anything interesting?"

"No, not really. Wish there was," I admitted. "What about you?"

"What about me?"

"Do you have any dreams? Pipe dreams or otherwise?"

"They're stupid," she said, and blushed a little.

"I doubt it," I said. She looked beautiful with that flush.

"No, really. They're stupid. Incredibly lame."

"Tell me anyway."

"You don't let up, do you?"

"Nope."

"I dream about being in a real-life fairy tale," she said quietly.

"A fairy tale?"

"Don't laugh. I told you it was stupid."

"I'm not laughing. It's not stupid. It's just I've never thought of anyone dreaming about that kind of thing."

"Of course people do. I imagine most girls do at one time or another."

"I wouldn't know."

"No, I don't suppose you would. You are a man, after all."

"Are you saying men can't be romantic and have dreams about riding in on a white horse to save the fair damsel in distress?" I asked.

"I am saying that, yes. And you're going to tell me you've actually dreamed about that kind of thing? White horses and other fairy tale ingredients?"

"No, I don't dream of white horses."

"That's what I thought," she said smugly.

"Most of the dreams I have are more like shooting through armies of enemy soldiers with a fully automatic assault rifle to save the beautiful secret spy from the evil, mad genius bent on world domination."

"Same thing."

"It is not," I said.

"Come on, it's the exact same story, just different settings and characters."

I thought about it and said, "You're right."

"Of course I'm right."

"You want another?" I asked, as I popped the cap off another beer.

"No, I've had enough."

"More for me," I said, and took a long draw.

"You know what I'm curious about?"

"What are you curious about?" I asked and chugged my beer.

"Why haven't you tried to get me into bed?"

I choked. The beer burned as it came through my nose. Foam dribbled down my chin as she laughed. It was not a question I was prepared for.

"Why do you ask?" was all I could think to say.

"Oh, the look on your face!" She clutched her stomach and laughed until she was gasping for air.

"Glad I could entertain you," I muttered.

"I asked because I wondered. Usually, most guys want to jump right into bed with a girl. Sometimes they can't even wait for a bed. It's like it's all they're interested in."

"I think a lot of guys are only interested in that."

"Exactly. So, I wondered why you haven't tried to get into my pants."

"I haven't tried because I'm positive I couldn't fit into them, even if I wanted to. They look great on you, but they're just not my style."

"Come on, I'm being serious here."

I looked her in the eye and said, "Not all guys are like that."

She turned, mumbling, "All the guys I've dated were."

I took her chin into my hand gently and turned her face toward mine. "Hey, it's just as I said. They're not all like that. I'm not like that." I let go. "Not only am I painfully shy about it, I'm interested more in other things. People obsess over that crap way too much. They take something natural and pure and turn it into something base and dirty. People's false morality destroys nature."

"I take it you don't think it's base and dirty?"

"No," I started. "The States are pretty messed up when it comes to those things. Look at other parts of the world. Parts of Europe, for instance. They accept that part of nature. It's not treated as immoral and filthy like it is here. Something to be hidden and kept quiet. They have topless newscasters over there, and here, a woman can get hit with indecent exposure for breastfeeding her baby. I think it's why we have so many problems here. People can't, or won't, accept nature and her laws, so we have this artificial problem with pregnancy, crime and the degradation of supposed moral standards. So sex becomes pointless and stupid."

"So, what, you don't like sex?"

"I didn't say that."

"Sounded like it."

"I like it fine, I suppose. I just don't want it to be the only thing. There's so much more. If you don't obsess, then it comes naturally. I'd rather have something stable. Love and all of that."

"Oh, bullshit."

"How can you call bullshit?"

"You're a guy! There's gotta be more to it."

I was getting a little uncomfortable with the conversation. How did this get started? What could I say? Just be completely honest. "It's not bullshit. It's all true enough, but I'm also afraid it won't be any good."

She laughed, but it wasn't hateful. "Afraid it won't be good for you, or the other person?"

"Both." I felt embarrassed.

"Why?"

"You sure do ask a lot of questions."

"Am I making you uncomfortable?"

"A little, yeah."

"Okay, I'll stop. I'm sorry."

"Don't be, but really, I'm not bullshitting. I really do want something more. I don't like the idea of involving myself intimately with someone I only have a romp with. I've been burned too many times and it seems it's all they were interested in. What I could do for them in bed."

"I guess guys aren't the only ones."

"It goes both ways. A guy can want more. It's not something exclusive to one sex. It's not a bad thing. I think it can make it better."

"More, meaning love?"

"Yeah."

I had wondered many times if there was such a thing. It seemed mythical, like the fountain of youth. Something invented by philosophers and writers of romance. I thought I felt it sometimes, but in hindsight, I wasn't sure what it was. Love is elusive.

It would probably be easier to find the damn fountain.

"You have that."

She said it so softly, I almost missed it.

I wondered if I had heard her right, or if it was my imagination. Either way, I was sure "huh?" wouldn't be appropriate.

"You're being quiet," she said after a moment.

"I didn't catch what you said." I decided to err on the side of caution.

"I'm saying I love you, you big dolt." She said it loudly enough so it couldn't be mistaken.

"Oh." I felt nothing but relief.

"Is that all you're going to say? Oh?"

I faced her. "I think I loved you from the first moment I saw you."

"I should wonder if you're just saying that, but you know what?"

"What?"

"I believe you."

She leaned in close and our lips touched. I felt an unexpected shock through my body.

We separated as if for air and I pressed my lips to hers again, searching, hungry. I savored the taste of her. Her aroma was primal underneath the clean scent of her hair and it made my excitement grow all the more. Up to this moment, I had never been so joyful, excited, and afraid, all at the same time, and it was a feeling I wanted to last for eternity.

"Not so bad." Her voice was husky as she pulled away.

"No, not bad at all," I murmured and pulled her back for more.

Chapter 27

"How are you feeling, hon?" Carol asked.

"I'm super, thanks for asking," I said enthusiastically.

"I'm just asking. Let's not get sarcastic."

"Okay. I feel fine. Things could be worse."

"Isn't that the truth. I'm glad. You look good."

"Hush, Carol. I think you're trying to seduce me. I might sue for sexual harassment."

"Ha! You couldn't get that lucky. It seems you haven't lost your sense of humor."

"If people keep telling me that, I might actually believe I possess one."

"I think you have a wonderful sense of humor, Harry. You're awfully hard on yourself."

"Thanks. I'll try to be easier."

"You should."

I fiddled with the pencils by the register. "Say, Carol, I was wondering if I could have a few days off."

"Is there something the matter?" she asked.

"No, just some stuff I'd like to take care of."

She glanced at me as if she wasn't sure whether to believe me.

"Really, there's nothing wrong. The world isn't ending and I'm not planning to bury any bodies out in the woods," I assured her.

"You'd tell me if you were having a problem, wouldn't you?"

"Of course. It's just a couple of personal things. Might take me out of town for a couple of days." I hated to lie, but no reason to drag her into it. Anyway, it wasn't technically a lie.

She considered it a moment. "I don't see why not. You've gone above and beyond plenty of times. You should get a little time off. Why don't you take a week? Have a little vacation after you finish your business."

"I don't think that'll be necessary," I said. "I can't really afford to take a couple days off, much less a whole week."

"So, I'll give you a paid vacation."

"Oh, Carol. You don't need to do that. I really only need a couple days."

"Do you think you're indispensable?"

"Why, yes," I said. "Yes I do."

She rolled her eyes. "I think the store can run fine without you for a week. Now say 'Yes, Carol,' before I change my mind."

"All right. Yes, Carol. I appreciate it. Thank you."

"Don't mention it. Now don't think this gives you an excuse to slack off. I expect double the effort from you today."

"Does that mean I can't take a nap on the loveseat?"

Carol placed her hands on her hips and looked at me sternly.

"No, ma'am. No slacking and no naps. Double effort." I snapped a salute.

"Oh, get to work." She tried not to laugh.

******

I finished my workday and didn't slack off one moment. I didn't even play a single round of spider solitaire. After work, I stopped off at the grocery store and picked up a few items for Mrs. Weatherman.

She hadn't been feeling well lately. I was concerned, though I probably shouldn't have been. But, she was older. Older folks tend to have complications from illnesses younger people could sweat through and get over in a day or so.

I entered her apartment with only a courtesy knock. "Mrs. Weatherman," I called. "I got your groceries here."

"Put it on the table, dear," she sang out. "Don't come back here. I'm not decent."

"Don't tempt me," I said, and heard her girlish giggle. I started to put away the few items in their places when she came pattering in.

"What do you think you're doing, young man?" she said. She

215

tried to sound menacing, but failed miserably.

"Just being a good neighbor," I replied.

"Certainly very nice of you. All the young folks should follow your example. You're one of a kind."

"I've heard that before, but thank you."

"And polite. Why, there's just so much hatefulness and rude-ness in this dreary world these days. Back in my day, people weren't like that. There was no locking doors and we all knew our neighbors. We knew how to appreciate folks and had common decency. Not so nowadays," she lamented.

"People can seem rather rude," I agreed. It wasn't often she got into a "back in my day" speech.

"Enough of that," she said. "Would you like a cookie and a cold glass of milk?"

"No, no. I appreciate it, but I'm trying to watch my figure."

"Oh, bosh. Men don't watch their figures. You don't need to worry about that, being a man as young as you are. When you get to be my age, that's when you need to start minding the figure, but by then, you don't care anymore. You realize there are bigger things to be concerned about."

"You look great, Mrs. Weatherman," I said sincerely.

She waved off the compliment. "Save the flattery for a nice young girl. No need to waste it all on an old gal like me."

The twinkle in her eye told me she enjoyed being flattered. She couldn't hide it.

"When are you going to get around to getting yourself a girl-friend, Harry?"

"I know girls. I have friends," I said.

Mrs. Weatherman snorted. "I'm not talking about girls who are friends. You need to get out there and find yourself a pretty wife and have you some little ones. A nice boy like you doesn't need to be all alone. You're not going to find a wife staying at home, catering to an old lady."

"But I like catering to old ladies, and you, too."

"There you go again, with the flattery."

"I'm kind of seeing someone now," I said. "It's not marriage and kids, but it's something."

"Is it that nice young lady I see you running around with nowadays?"

I nodded. "Yes, that nice young lady."

"Oh, Harry. She sure is a pretty little thing. I've got a feeling about her. Reckon you should maybe hang onto that one."

"I'm not going to rush it or anything."

"Of course not. Rushing gets people hurt. I may be old, but some things never change."

"True," I agreed. "I think I'll keep her around."

"Good. It's about time you found yourself someone. A nice, pretty young *girl*, no less."

"That seems to be the sentiment going around town," I mumbled. At least she didn't come out and say she thought I was gay.

I visited a while longer. She was lonelier than she would admit. She was the type of person who would suffer long before she would ever say anything about it. Sometimes I wondered if I was the last person in the world who came around to spend time with her. I felt if I didn't, I would be guilty of neglect.

She had no other visitors. I didn't know if she had any family and I never asked. She never said anything. As much time as I had spent with her, I realized there was much about her life I didn't know.

I made her a bowl of soup. She protested, though she ate it heartily. She made me eat with her. It was part of the bargain. After we finished, I washed the bowls and spoons and put them away. I left only after I was assured she felt better and made her promise to call if there was anything else she needed.

As I walked up to my apartment, I went over my plans. Even

after the soup, I still felt hungry. I dug around my fridge and cabinets, but couldn't find anything to please my palate. Not without a lot of trouble. I thought I'd give Gwendolyn a call and see if she would be interested in going out for some Thai food. I didn't get Thai food often, so when I did, it still resembled a kind of adventure.

Adventure seemed to be the word of the day and I hoped I wasn't about to make a mistake by letting Gwendolyn get involved in the inexplicable mystery that consumed me.

Chapter 28

Gwendolyn sat comfortably in my chair while I paced the floor.

"Quit acting so nervous," she said.

"You're not?" I asked.

"Yeah, a little I guess, but you're going to make another hole if you keep it up."

"It'll be fine," I said.

"You do know it's possible nothing will happen. It's also possible there will be nothing to worry about if something does, but we won't know until we try."

I walked to the window and watched a group of birds on a power line. She was right. I was nervous. Especially since she seemed so eager. A part of me wished I had dropped the whole thing. Well, as they say, you can wish in one hand.

She was excited at the prospect. I guess I was at one time, but it faded rather quickly and turned into a compulsion. I didn't want her to be hurt, or even merely disappointed. My fear, if this worked, was I would put her in harm's way. I had this dark feeling we were planning to walk smack into danger. I did not have any real reason to feel this way. I had not run into anything I could say was dangerous. I knew I could be affected by events, but dangerous? No, not yet.

That was the key word. Yet.

I faced Gwendolyn and tried to make her forget the whole thing by telepathy, but the look in her eye said even if I tried it verbally, I'd have a hell of a time.

"This is stupid," I said. I knew it wouldn't change her mind.

"Maybe it is, but unless you go spreading the news, who's going to know?"

"No one. I'm not going to say anything. I didn't even want to tell you."

"What are you so worried about?"

"I've already told you what I'm worried about. You should be worried about it too."

"I'm sure you're just exaggerating things."

I leaned my head against the wall. "I'm not exaggerating. There's always the possibility something could go very wrong."

"It never stopped you. Anyway, we don't even know if I can go."

"No, but I don't like thinking of the risks."

"If there isn't a way, then there wouldn't be any risk."

"Why are you so insistent?" I huffed.

"Curiosity. How often does one have the chance to travel to a whole new dimension?"

I pounded my fist against the wall. "This isn't a joke!"

"I realize that. Calm down."

I tried, but was still tense. "Sorry."

"What if I'm meant to do this with you?"

I laughed. It sounded ridiculous. But something told me it wasn't.

"I thought you didn't believe in fate?"

She got up and came to me. "Sometimes I do. I don't think *everything* is fated. Maybe some things, but not all." She watched the birds with me a moment. "I get confused sometimes about it. I don't like it when people say everything was fate, or coincidence. Especially if it's something they're responsible for."

"Like the drunk who says it's God's will he's an alcoholic?"

"A little extreme, but yeah."

"I see. I'm going to hold you."

"So now you want to get romantic?" she rolled her eyes.

"I meant to go over. Don't make this into some sex thing." I wasn't in the mood to joke around. I had the feeling she was taking this too lightly. Perhaps I was being too serious, but after all, I was afraid.

"I said romantic. Nothing about sex, so whose mind is on it?"

"You know what I mean."

"Let's not argue. You're already too jumpy. I know you're wary and I should be more sensitive."

"No worries."

"Let's try," she said.

I gathered her in my arms and could feel she wanted to make some comment. Probably sarcastic, but she refrained from it. I was appreciative.

"Close your eyes."

"Do I have to? Does it work like that?"

"I don't know. Just please."

"Yes sir, Mr. Grumpy," she said, and closed her eyes.

I waited to make sure her eyes stayed shut.

"Are you checking to make sure my eyes are closed?" she asked, without opening them.

"Hush," I admonished.

She giggled.

I wasn't sure if it was something you had to do, but it seemed right. I closed my own eyes and imagined the house. I willed myself to view Her walls with Gwendolyn beside me. I felt her shift uncomfortably as I caught the scent of wildflowers, mixed with Gwendolyn's perfume. Her breathing and a soft breeze seemed to be in sync. I felt the change and chanced opening my eyes to find we were both ten yards from Her main entry. Gwendolyn still had her eyes closed. She looked as if she were asleep.

"You can open your eyes now," I said softly.

She blinked her eyes open, looked around, and whispered, "It worked."

"Yes."

"I can't believe it."

"I'm not entirely sure I do either."

"It's...I don't know what to say."

"Don't need to say anything. Come on, I don't want to waste

whatever light we have left," I said and pulled her toward the door.

"Wait!" she cried.

My hope shot up. "You just want to forget this and go back? We could if you want."

"No, I'm just a little nervous. It doesn't look very safe."

"No shit. I've been telling you that."

"Don't be rude."

"Sorry, but I have been telling you that. We should just forget it."

"No, let's go. I'll be okay."

My hopes deflated just as quickly as they had gone up. "All right."

We walked hand in hand, through the wide, rotted doorway.

"This place is a dump." She crinkled her nose as she looked around the foyer. "It smells, too."

It didn't look any worse from my point of view. More dust and debris, maybe. I understood where she was coming from, because at first, I thought the same thing, though I imagined it gave the place character. The smell of mildew hung stronger in the air, but beyond that, I couldn't sense anything much different.

The house creaked and moaned against the wind blowing from outside. I was more aware of my surroundings, having Gwendolyn there with me. I started to worry about the real possibility She could crumble on top of us and leave us with no hope of rescue. No one knew we were here. Even if I had told someone of our whereabouts, there was no way for them to get here.

"Okay, you saw it, so let's go back now."

"I've never seen anything laid out like this before," she said. She ignored me and looked about the foyer.

I mumbled agreement.

"Have you been through the whole place?"

"Downstairs, as far as I know, but not so much upstairs."

"No?"

"A lot's been going on. Let's go back," I tried again.

"No way. We managed to get here, so we're going to stay for a little while. I want to see it."

"Might as well." I sighed in resignation. I was even more nervous, whereas she showed no hint of it. I knew I felt this way because I had no knowledge of what might happen while she was here. I had no desire to stay here with her along, possibly courting danger, but she was stubborn. All I could do was make sure I didn't leave her alone.

"We can still get out before dark," she said.

"Hopefully. It's already late, so if we're going to leave before dark, we can't stay too long."

"We're going to have to, because we didn't bring any flashlights."

You would think by now I would have started carrying a little flashlight on my key chain, but I'm not that smart. Anyway, there was the unknown source of illumination I wasn't going to mention, because I wanted no excuse to stay longer.

The ignorance of where the source of light came from bothered me. I couldn't shake the feeling something bad was going to happen. I did not know what lay above us, and that didn't help.

Maybe I was just being paranoid.

Then again, maybe I wasn't.

"What's down here?" she asked.

"Right, a dining room and kitchen inside that alcove. An office, a library and stuff on that side." I pointed in the general directions.

"Why is everything closed off? Doesn't it seem strange to you?"

"Yes," I answered.

"Usually places are a little more open than this. Homes at least. It's like an antique suite of offices rather than a house."

"I thought the same thing. I think it's sort of creepy."

"Don't be silly," she chided and asked, "What's upstairs?"

"Bedrooms for sure, a water closet. I don't know about the rest. Some of the doors are locked."

"Locked? Can you pop them open?"

I patted my pocket where I kept the found keys on a flashlightless key chain. "I have keys. Maybe they'll open the doors."

"But you're not sure?"

"Can't be sure. I found keys that opened other doors. Can't see why these will be any different."

"If they don't work, you can always kick 'em down."

"I don't think it'll work that way," I said. "Anyway, I don't want to vandalize the place. You never know if someone, or something, will get upset."

"Are you afraid of spooks?"

"I don't know anymore."

A long, deep moan filled the room. We both jumped.

"What was that?" Gwendolyn gasped.

"It's just the house settling, is all." I hoped I sounded more convincing than I felt.

"Not like any settling I've ever heard before," she said. "Sounds like a wounded animal or something."

"It's an old house. You're the one who's being silly now."

"But this is an old phantom house," she said.

I couldn't argue.

"We can leave if you want. We don't have to stay if you're scared." I hoped she would choose to leave.

"No, I don't want to leave yet. We just got here."

"Okay, but let's get this over with before it gets too dark."

We went into the alcove and through the dining room door. I hoped her curiosity would be sated in a few minutes and we could get out.

"Where is the light coming from?" she asked.

The reddish glow began to appear. I should have known.

"I can't answer that. It's always been here." I wished I had an explanation for it. I said nothing about how it started out a cool blue and had gradually turned into the angry red we saw now.

"It's weird."

"Let's hope weird is all it is," I said.

The room began to flicker as if someone was playing with a light switch. For mere seconds, it was meticulously clean, and set for dinner. When it stopped, and the red glow regained its place, the room was again in shambles, worse than the way I had last seen it.

"Did you see that?" she asked.

"Yeah. It's happened before. I don't know what it is, or why it does it."

"That's super weird. It looked really nice, but now, it's like no one wanted to clean up after the party," Gwendolyn said. She reached for one of the china plates.

"Don't touch that!" I shouted. I felt a sense of danger from the seemingly mundane item.

"Why not?" she asked, as the plate turned into powder and sifted through her fingers. "What the—?"

"I don't know how safe it is, or what could happen. Maybe we shouldn't touch anything."

"I'm okay. I'm not hurt or anything."

"Still, we should be careful."

"If we were going to be careful, then we should've stayed home and watched a William Castle movie."

"I just..."

"Worry too much. Stop," she said.

I sighed. She was right and I was probably overreacting. It didn't abate the fear I felt, but I reminded myself I hadn't run into any real harm, save for a stumble or two. Only a scare now and then, and those were harmless enough. I did get knocked over by a door, but I was in the way.

Stop making excuses! I thought. Even though I hadn't been harmed directly by any apparitions, I was still affected by them.

Since we were here, I couldn't do anything, so I should relax as much as possible, I reasoned, and satisfy myself with keeping her within sight. I'd just try to get her to leave very soon.

I watched her walk with careful steps. Her eyes drank in every detail. Her deep concentration enhanced her beauty.

"You know what's weird?" she asked.

"What?"

"There aren't any bugs or anything."

"Sure there are," I said. I remembered seeing them.

"Nope. There's old food, but no bugs, mice or anything. No indication there ever was."

I scanned the table and saw she was right, never mind what I had seen before. "Maybe it's too old for even the bugs to enjoy."

"Doesn't seem right to me. Every place like this has bugs and all manner of creepy crawly things. At least a rat. "

The mention of a rat made me shudder. "I don't like rats, but I've seen them here before. Maybe they're just hiding."

She turned around and started through the swinging door. I rushed after her. I had to keep her in sight.

"Nice kitchen," she said sarcastically, as she walked along the floor littered with the wood from rotted counters and the metal of banged-up pots.

"Yeah, you hungry? I could whip us up something," I said.

She snorted. "You're funny. Did you see a ghost here?"

"Yeah. Let's get out of here. It's already dark," I said.

"In a minute. The ones killing each other?"

"Like I said, I'm not sure it was ghosts. It was like an old movie."

I noticed the look I interpreted as, *you're ready for the loony bin.*

"I'm not crazy."

"Didn't say you were. Don't get all defensive."

"Sorry, it's just...this makes me nervous."

"Shouldn't make you nervous. If you're this nervous now, how did you stand it in here by yourself?"

"It's different now."

"Because of me?"

"Yeah. I can handle just me, but I don't want anything to happen to you."

"That's sweet," she said without argument. "Can you make them come back?"

"What? I don't think I have any control. I knew nothing about them."

"You knew nothing about the house either."

"True, but no. I'm not going to try to call them forth like I'm some sort of medium. I don't think I can. They probably came on their own to tell me something. I still don't understand it."

"Just a theory."

"I'm drawing the line there. I didn't really care to see it and there's nothing to see except crazy crap. Now can we get out of here before all the light outside is gone?" I begged.

"Yeah, if it'll make you feel better and stop whining."

"I'm not whining. We can come back another time if you really want to," I said, and kicked myself mentally for saying it.

"We'll think about that later," she said.

We left the kitchen.

I hoped this excursion had been so lacking in excitement it wouldn't come up again.

A loud crash burst through the door.

"What was that?" Gwendolyn shouted.

"Sounded like the roof fell in or something," I said.

If the house was falling down, we needed to get the hell out now.

Chapter 29

I pushed through the door and looked around the foyer for the source of the crash.

"It doesn't seem the roof fell in," I said.

"Then what was that noise?"

"Holy hell," I muttered.

I ran to the entrance. The door had closed and was shut tight. I grasped the knob and pulled at it violently.

"Damn it!" I yelled.

"Harry?" Gwendolyn's voice grew thick.

"The door's locked," I said in resignation.

"But how? It was rotted off the hinges?"

"How the hell am I supposed to know?"

"Who crapped in your pancakes?"

"I'm sorry," I said. This was something new. We were both scared. "It just...defies logic. I don't know what to do. I didn't expect this to happen."

That was an understatement.

"Aren't there other ways?" she asked. "What about the windows?"

I hadn't thought of that. I went to the window, grabbed the

heavy drapes and started to pull them aside.

Stuck. It was as if they were welded to the window frames. They wouldn't give at all.

"Damn it!" I pounded on the curtain, only to find it had as much give as a steel plate.

Gwendolyn looked at me. She tried to seem brave, but she couldn't hide the fear in her eyes.

"We're stuck," I said.

"You mean we can't get out?"

"That's what being stuck means."

"What about the window?"

"Can't even get to the window." I wondered if she had been paying attention. "Give it a shot if you'd like."

She tried pulling on the curtains and got the same result, though she did try harder.

"Okay, stop before you wear yourself out," I said.

She gave up, then said, "Isn't there another door? Or window?"

I thought for a moment then remembered. "There's one in the kitchen."

We backtracked to the kitchen. We ignored the deeper red glow. It was brighter, though it didn't illuminate the place any better. Instead, it seemed to swallow everything.

We entered the kitchen and I went straight for the door. I twisted and jerked the knob, but it was as if someone had nailed it shut with spikes. I rattled the doorknob again, only to have it fall into my hand.

Dread washed over me and panic bubbled up.

"Harry?" Fear trembled in Gwendolyn's voice.

"It's locked too," I said and let the knob drop. It clattered on the floor with the sound of finality.

I tried to be brave. I wasn't. I saw the window, unadorned. It offered a dim view of the smokehouse in the shadow of darkness. I thought, unconvincingly, it might offer us an escape. I found a thick cylinder of oak, and gripped it like a baseball bat. I swung it hard against the window. The wood ricocheted off the pane and vibrated in my hands. I dropped the makeshift bat and rubbed my palms together. "It's like a friggin' brick wall."

"This is starting to scare me a little," Gwendolyn said. She sounded braver than I felt.

"Yeah?"

What else could I say? I thought maybe this might have happened even if we had tried to leave earlier. The house was just waiting for us to try to go before locking us in. What I had hoped wouldn't happen did, and all I had left was the hope we could still escape. At least hope it couldn't get worse.

Another groan emitted from the house, and I could not attribute it to the house settling. It really did sound like a wounded animal. The sky had lost all its light and the red glow seemed to have started bleeding from the walls.

"Look." I didn't bother to conceal the shake in my voice. "I'm not sure what's happening right now. Until we can find out, we should maybe stick together."

"Don't have to ask me twice," Gwendolyn said. "What are we going to do now?"

"Nothing to do but just keep trying to find a way out. Maybe we need to do something, or we have something She wants."

I motioned for her to follow me toward the library.

The house continued to utter its groans as if speaking in an unknown tongue. She seemed to be trying to speak to me, though I was unable to understand. I couldn't fathom what She could want. I was sure it leaned toward the pernicious, and I tried my best to interpret it.

"What's in there?" Gwendolyn asked as we reached the library door.

"Books," I answered.

I turned the knob and the door seemed to open under its own power.

"How's that going to help?"

"I don't know."

"What?"

"I don't know what the hell we're supposed to do!" I yelled.

"Yeah? Great! It's your fault we're stuck," she yelled back.

"Hey..." I tried to interject a defense, but she mocked me and blurred whatever I was thinking.

"All you say is, 'We're stuck. I don't know what to do.' What the fuck, Harry!"

Her language fazed me. "Hey, you're the one who kept pushing for this shit! Don't go blaming me for something you wanted. I didn't want this, if you remember!"

Her eyes burned and her lips quivered with anger. She couldn't get the words out of her mouth. I swore she was about to swing at me.

"We shouldn't be arguing like this," I said, before anything could escalate. "It's not going to help us, or get us anywhere."

Emotion rushed out of her like a hot gust of wind. "You're right. I'm just scared."

"There's nothing to be afraid of," I said, without believing it. "We'll get out of here. There's bound to be a way."

"You're not very convincing." She tried to smile.

"I know. I'm scared too, but we really are going to find a way out, okay?"

She nodded, sniffed, and hugged her arms to herself.

We ventured fully into the library. I walked to the windows to try my luck at pulling back the curtains, but like the others, they were fused together.

"Can't get to these either," I said.

She just stood there. She seemed to be studying the painting. I left her to it and walked to the shelf filled with the colorful books.

The books, bound in leather and dyed in reds, violets and blues, were shelved randomly between carved roaring lion bookends fixed to the shelves. I pulled out a volume and blindly flipped the pages. The print was small and faded; I couldn't read it in the diminished light.

"What about not touching anything?" Gwendolyn asked from behind me. "And why isn't it turning to dust?"

"I don't know. Maybe the plate was meant to scare us or something."

"I think locking us up in here did a better job of it."

I didn't answer. I just started to put the book back on the shelf. I got a mind to rearrange the books so the colored spines matched into three solid blocks.

Blue, violet, then red.

As I pushed the last book into place, the bookcase began to laboriously sink into the wall. It groaned with effort and I stepped back, just in case something jumped out and attacked.

"What's happening?" Gwendolyn moved behind me and peered over my shoulder.

"I think I might have uncovered a secret room or something," I answered, and gazed into the darkness beyond the shelves.

The house moaned. I heard a bright tinkling beneath the din. It sounded like an old-fashioned bicycle bell. The bookcase creaked to a stop, and the bell grew louder. The room brightened and dimmed as if someone were playing with a hidden dimmer switch.

A small boy rode an antique tricycle into the room. His head hunched over as he concentrated on his legs pumping the pedals. He stopped a few feet from us and raised his head.

A long, thick gash from his forehead to his nose, dripped with blood and gore. It made his wide-set eyes even wider. His face was bruised and small cuts decorated his face like macabre freckles. He looked at me briefly, then turned to Gwendolyn. His lips moved without sound as he raised his arms to her, as if reaching to be held.

Gwendolyn retched and swallowed as she slunk behind me. She gripped my arms tightly.

"What is he saying?" she whispered. "I can't hear him."

"No, you can't," I said.

I had resigned myself to the fact long ago these apparitions are unable to communicate verbally.

The boy's small, pale lips seemed to form the same word over and over again. Soon, I realized he was saying "mama." His inno-cent eyes pled, his little arms reached toward her, and he slowly melted from our view as the moaning subsided.

"What happened?" she asked quietly and released her iron grip.

"To the boy?" I asked.

"Yes, to the boy. What else would I be talking about?"

"He disappeared," I said solemnly.

"Hey!" I yelped in surprise as she pushed me forward.

"Don't get smart with me. I'm not in the mood."

"Okay, okay!" I said as I straightened and smoothed my shirt. "I don't know what happened to him, nor do I know why he showed up. It's been the same with the others. I think they're try-ing to show me something, but I've never been able to hear them. Sometimes I can make out what they're saying."

"How?"

"Reading their lips, but not often."

"Did you understand what he was trying to say?"

"I think so."

"Well?"

I sighed and put my hands into my pockets. I looked into the dark recess beyond the bookcase. I turned and looked at her. "I believe he thinks you're his mother."

"What?" she coughed. "His mother?"

"I've told you before. You kind of resemble one of the ghosts I saw. Maybe she was his mother and he thinks you're her."

"I don't like this," she said, after absorbing the information.

"Well, I'm not a huge fan, but you already knew that. As I said, there isn't much of a choice now but to deal with it."

There was something deeply unsettling about being stuck like this in the house. The idea it could happen had crossed my mind, but not really. Now, I was forced to deal with it. It was much different now there was no door to the outside, nor any window to crawl through.

We needed a way out. There had to be one, somewhere.

Any good feelings I'd had about the place were now gone. I couldn't feel good about anything that would hold me hostage, much less Gwendolyn. She didn't have anything to do with this. She was an innocent in this game.

"Maybe there's a way out behind the bookcase," I said.

"We should find out."

"Yeah, nothing to lose by trying."

She gripped me by the arm and we walked through the wall. We were immediately enveloped in complete darkness. Even the red glow that permeated the rest of the house was denied admittance here.

"I can't see anything." Gwendolyn's voice sounded far away, though she was close enough for me to feel her body heat.

"Me neither," I said.

I reached into my pocket and wrapped my fingers around the familiar shape of my Zippo. It opened with its trademark click and I spun the wheel with my thumb. The lighter came to life and lighted the immediate area. I thought, in the darkness, the lighter would have done a better job, but the dark swallowed the light like a hungry animal.

"I still can't see anything," Gwendolyn said.

"We can go back."

"No, I'll be okay."

"We'll be careful," I said as we went in deeper.

The walls, made of stone and damp, were about five feet apart and led us one way. There weren't any doors to the sides we could discern.

We moved forward. The ground started to slope down. It made me feel like we were being swallowed into the earth. Blindly, we moved ahead and I thought we would be led to a secret room that did duty as a laboratory. Or perhaps some medieval torture chamber, rather than find a way out. Maybe I've watched too many horror movies.

We kept walking, the air grew danker the deeper we went into the black tunnel. It was like walking a treadmill. We didn't seem to be going anywhere.

"I don't like this, Harry." Gwendolyn's voice shivered.

"Me neither," I said, as my lighter sputtered and blanked out. "Crap. Ran out of fluid."

"It's so dark," Gwendolyn whispered.

"Yeah. Let's go back. Are you scared?"

"Of course not. Why should I be?" She said it defiantly, but I knew better.

"Nothing wrong with it. Perfectly natural given the circum-stances."

"You might be, but I'm not."

"I can admit I am," I said.

We turned and started back.

It wasn't long before we hit the slope. It seemed strange we had come back to it so quickly. It seemed we had walked quite a long way in. We came back into the library, back into the red glow. It didn't seem as dismaying after the pitch-black we had just left.

"How did the boy get up the hill?" asked Gwendolyn.

"I don't question things like that anymore. It doesn't seem any of it's logical."

"Who was he?"

"Probably someone's kid. Someone who lived here, but

whose, I don't know. If he thought you were his mother, then we can assume the girl was his mother. He looks kind of like the boy in the portrait out there, except in the picture, his brains weren't falling out of his head."

"Ugh, don't remind me," she groaned. "Can't you close up the hole? It's creepy. I don't want anything else coming out of there."

"If there was something in there, it would have gotten us already," I reasoned.

"Don't say that! Close it!"

I didn't give any indication of how much the thought unnerved me. I went to the shelf and only had to remove a single book to start the bookcase back. It made a show as it ground back into place. I turned to Gwendolyn. "Now what?"

"We should have brought flashlights."

I laughed. I had often thought the same thing.

"What's so funny?"

"Just thinking if we did bring some, we wouldn't need them. Anyway, there's other ways to light up. We can use the lamps."

"How do you propose to light them?" she asked.

Right, my lighter's out, I thought. I just shrugged.

"Let's look at the pictures."

"Shouldn't we concentrate on getting out?"

She didn't reply, only stared at me for a moment. I thought maybe she was letting what I said sink in. Maybe she didn't realize our predicament.

Maybe she did.

She went to the door, and left me to wonder what was going through her mind.

Chapter 30

The darkness seemed to deepen when we returned to the foyer. It could have been my hypersensitive imagination. I led Gwendolyn to the portrait. She studied it for a moment, then wiped her hand against the surface.

"What are you doing?" I worried she would cause the painting to disintegrate, as if the piece had worlds of meaning for me.

"I'm just cleaning off the dust." She looked at me like I was a complete idiot. "I just wanted to get a better look. There may be some important detail underneath all of this dust."

"Yeah, they might be wearing name tags."

"It's the same boy." She ignored my joke. "Is that his sister?"

"I would assume, but can't be sure." I breathed easier after I saw the painting would remain intact.

Gwendolyn looked at the other painting without touching it. Her brow wrinkled in concentration. "She's pretty, but she looks so hard. I can't help but think she looks familiar."

"How?" I asked.

"I don't know. I can't place it, it just seems..." She didn't finish and I didn't push it.

She stood there and stared as if hypnotized. I started to worry before she finally snapped back and asked, "What now?"

I thought for a moment, then said, "Let's go upstairs. We might be able to find a way out there."

"Upstairs? I doubt it, unless you want to break something."

"You never know. Anyway, I haven't been through all of it and I've got keys that will probably fit the locked doors."

"Where did you find keys?"

"Around. I keep them in my pocket all the time, just in case I need to use them."

She looked warily at the stairs. "Is it safe?"

"As long as you're careful, but I don't assume anything here is safe. We'll be okay, I think."

"Not too sure I believe it."

I wasn't sure I believed it either, but I wasn't going to make the admission out loud.

"Come on and stay close to the edge," I said, I led us up the stairs, confident if I made it, she would too. She was much lighter than me.

As we ascended, each step creaked in protest. The railing felt loose in my hand, like it was going to fall off at any second. I tried not to favor it and hoped the steps wouldn't collapse beneath us.

We made it to the top safely and looked down to the bottom, both of us relieved.

"I don't like this," she said.

"It doesn't matter now. I wasn't fond of the idea of you coming. Frankly, I'm not really too fond of it at all anymore. The fact is, we're stuck. Somehow, She's locked us in here."

Gwendolyn walked to the broken stained-glass window and looked out, her hands in her back pockets. I could feel a breeze coming through, crisp and cool.

"We could jump out of this window."

"Yeah, but we'd probably break our legs doing it. Even if we didn't, I don't know if we could." I pointed at the jagged shards jutting out of the frame. "We probably wouldn't be able to break those off, so we'd at least lose blood. I'd rather find a surer way. One where the chances of getting killed are less."

"I'm afraid we're going to get killed anyway." Her voice was tremulous.

"Don't flake out on me now."

"I'm trying not to."

"I know." I felt the same, but knew I needed to stay strong.

I went to the window myself and looked out. I was unable to even see shadows. The breeze was like breath coming from the gaping jaw of a monster. The wind proved we had a connection to the outside, and worst-case scenario, we might have to use this as an escape.

I reached my hand to the window and pushed it outside. Something sharp bit me. I jerked my hand back. Blood welled from the tip of my finger. I instinctively put my finger in my mouth. I tasted the coppery saltiness of my own blood.

"Are you okay?" Gwendolyn pulled my hand to her. "You're bleeding."

"I'm fine," I said. I took my hand back and started up the short steps to the hallway.

"But you're bleeding," she repeated, as if I hadn't noticed.

"Really, just a scratch. No big deal."

"But you didn't even touch the glass."

"I must have." I knew full well I hadn't.

The glow gave the impression of the hallway being bathed in blood.

I wondered if any significant meaning was attached to the colors. To the changes from blue to red. Perhaps it was a warning of some sort. Blue usually represents cold, the element of water. Red, heat, the element of fire. It could mean anger, or even sexual passion. Some might see it as evil. Most people who linked the two see human nature as inherently evil. Hell is depicted in reds. Hell was once thought of as cold, so blue made sense. I wondered if the changing hues of the house's light meant something similar. If somehow, something had angered Her. The thought was in no way pleasant.

"Is this light getting dimmer?" Gwendolyn asked, as we walked farther down the hallway.

"Yeah."

"It's spooky. Why is it darker?"

"I don't know."

We reached the end of the hallway. The urn on the pedestal had fallen and lay in large pieces on the floor. Someone had to have been up here because I couldn't think of any way it could have fallen. But then, things seemed to happen in defiance of logic here. A small pile of stones stood between the pieces in such a way it couldn't have happened naturally. I knelt down to get a closer look.

"What did you find?" Gwendolyn asked.

"Stones, gemstones I think, but I can't tell in this light."

She knelt beside me and took a look herself. "I think that's tiger's eye." She pointed at a stone about the size of a pecan.

She indicated another. "That's obsidian, I think. I can't remember what the others are, for sure."

I was impressed. "How do you know what they are?"

"I used to have some stones just like those. I used to carry a tiger's eye because it's supposed to be protective and help you discern the truth. I lost it a long time ago. It just kinda disappeared like things do sometimes. I wonder if that's it."

"I'm at the point to where I wouldn't doubt anything," I said, "but I wouldn't touch them."

I thought doing so might bring trouble. It was an irrational thought, perhaps, but I couldn't be sure if it was a trick. It didn't make any sense, but then, nothing here seemed to.

Who put gemstones in an urn and for what purposes were they here now? Could some of them have been Gwendolyn's? We stood up and I tried the locked door from the last time I was here. It was still locked, so I dug the keys out of my pocket and used the first one I grasped.

"Did you hear something?" Gwendolyn whispered behind me.

"It was the keys," I said.

"No, it was something else."

I stood still. I held the key ring against my leg to keep them from jingling and listened. "I don't hear anything," I said after a minute.

"I heard something," she insisted.

"Probably just your imagination," I said, as I slid the key into the keyhole. It didn't work, so I selected another.

"I don't think it was, but okay," she said nervously.

The lock clicked open and the door creaked as it swung in. I wondered how long it had been since this door had been opened. We stepped into the room. The floorboards creaked. Some bowed noticeably as we walked on them and threatened to give way, though they didn't.

The room was different from the others. It looked like it was being lived in. It lacked the dust, broken pieces of furniture and scarred walls. The walls were covered with a subtle paisley-patterned wallpaper. The floors looked polished. A small bed was pushed into a corner and was neatly made with frilly pillows against the headboard. An armoire sat cockeyed in the corner. Shelves along the wall held dolls. The toys were situated low enough so a child could reach them easily.

Above the shelves hung a landscape painting of rolling hills, an azure sky with large puffy clouds. Horses scattered across the pasture. In the center of the room was a dollhouse atop a large, oval-shaped, woven rug.

I walked to the window and attempted to pull back the drapes, astonished when they separated. There was no view as it was too dark and I only saw my reflection looking back at me, colored by the red permeating the whole house.

"It's a little girl's room," Gwendolyn said.

"No shit?" I mocked.

"Stop it."

"Sorry. It's clean in here."

"What?" She knelt down beside the dollhouse.

"The room's cleaned up. It's like someone's living here."

"Someone did live here," she pointed out.

"Yeah, but I mean living here at the moment. Nobody lives here now. This place isn't supposed to exist anymore," I said, and I tugged on the doors of the armoire. They didn't want to give, so I pulled harder and they came open. Inside were little dresses. They were in excellent shape and I fingered the material. The dresses were real, though no less strange.

"Harry?"

"Yeah?"

"This is weird."

"Glad to know you finally realize it."

"I mean, it's really, really weird," she insisted.

It was her tone that made me pay attention. "What is?"

"This dollhouse."

I looked at the dollhouse. It was like any other you might see, though of a better quality than most. There wasn't anything particularly strange about it, save for the location, so I asked, "What's so weird about the dollhouse?"

"I've seen it before."

My insides lurched. I wanted to say it was a mere coincidence, but something told me it wasn't. I was torn. I wanted to know, but didn't.

"Where have you seen it before?"

Wanting to know won.

"It's just like my grandma's dollhouse. I'd almost swear it's

245

the exact same one. My sister and I, we'd play with it for hours. We'd make up stories together." She paused. "You don't suppose it's the same one?"

"I don't know," I said.

If things from our past can show up here, then it changed things.

"I'd recognize it anywhere. I recognize it now. It's got the same tear right here in the wall. I'm sure it's the same house, but I can't imagine how it got here. After Grandma died, Bella got the dollhouse."

"Does she still have it?" I asked.

"What?" She looked up at me and frowned. "No, not anymore. She lost it."

"How?"

"A fire. She lost everything."

"Sorry."

"No, it's not your fault. It was some years back. They lived in a trailer and you know how those things can go up. It's like they're built out of paper. Lucky to get out when she did. No one got hurt."

"That's good."

"It's uncanny, how much..." Her voice trailed off.

"What?"

"Nothing. It's nothing."

I looked at her questioningly.

"Really, it's nothing," she assured me. "I'm just thinking of past things."

"All right," I said.

I found it most curious. It wasn't just her recollection of the dollhouse, though it was, in itself, curious. It was this room. It was easy to believe the little girl who lived here would come skipping in at any minute and pick one of the dolls from off the shelf to hold in her arms. I wondered what Gwendolyn was thinking. Perhaps it was only of the dollhouse, but I couldn't help but think there were other things on her mind. This house? This room? I wouldn't press the issue. If she wanted me to know, then she would tell me.

I looked outside the window again, as if somehow it would be different, but it was the same. It looked like someone had painted it from the outside with black paint. It crossed my mind I should be more concerned with the red glow, but instead, I took solace in the fact it helped to light our way, even though the coloring made some things harder to discern.

"I wonder if I could break this window," I said.

"It wouldn't hurt to try," said Gwendolyn.

"We could tie together some of this stuff and climb out."

"We don't have anything to lose, so just try it," she encouraged.

"It probably won't work."

"And maybe it will."

"Yeah, maybe. I'm kind of worried. Nothing seems to be safe and She's locked us in here. There's a possibility She can hurt us."

"Who can?"

"The house."

"You think this place is a person? A real person?"

"Why not? There's something, or someone, here keeping us in. It seems so normal in here. I thought maybe this room hadn't been touched yet. We might be able to break out this window."

"We don't have anything to lose," she said.

There's a lot we can lose, I thought. I also knew we had a lot to lose by staying.

I scanned the room and looked for something I could use to break the window. I spotted a wooden hobby horse, half hidden in a corner. I picked it up. I felt the heft of the toy's head and struck it against my palm. I thought it would be more than sufficient to break any normal window with minimal effort. I gripped the shaft and swung the heavy head at the window with all my strength.

The wood cracked loudly as the shaft snapped in two. It didn't even scratch the window. I let what remained of the toy slide out of my hand, closed my eyes and sighed in defeat.

I wished I could learn why we were imprisoned here. Learn what She wanted from us. I thought it might be my bringing someone else in. I should have followed my instincts and dropped it long ago. Damn my curiosity. At the very least, I should have been firm and refused to let Gwendolyn come along.

"It didn't work!" Gwendolyn cried. "How are we going to get out?"

Her eyes started to well and I turned away. I felt guilty for bringing us to this. I couldn't allow her to see my own fear, couldn't let her know I still knew nothing. I had to put on my brave, fearless mask and wear it well.

"We have to keep trying. The last thing we need to do is give up. There's a way out and there's a reason for this. We just need to find it. We will get out."

"I'm not so sure."

I turned to her, placed my hands on her shoulders. "Be sure."

"Yeah." She shrugged out from under me and opened the door to leave.

I followed her out and pulled the door to. I wondered what the room's condition would be if we went back in. Thus far, it seemed the rooms changed as they willed with no logic behind it. Would the room be in shambles, with the furniture worn out and broken? The toys and clothing scattered, forgotten and unloved? The rug moth-eaten and the walls chewed up by termites and time, with dust and cobwebs thick and heavy in every corner?

Was the dollhouse the same one Gwendolyn remembered from her childhood? Did this mean she had some connection to this place? There were so many questions and it seemed anytime I got an answer to one, it only spawned more. I dismissed the idea Gwendolyn had a connection, because if it were so, then she would have been the one coming here, the one called, instead of me.

But, I thought, she was here. Right now.

There was no room for speculation. We were short on time. I pushed the questions to the back of my mind to deal with later.

"Earth to Harry," Gwendolyn called.

"I'm here."

"Maybe you are now, but you weren't for a minute there. Thought I'd lost you."

"You're not going to have an easy time losing me," I tried to be funny. I wasn't. "I was only thinking."

"You too?"

"I wonder if they're all bedrooms," I said, as we looked down the long hallway. "This one's still locked too." I jiggled the handle of the door next to the girl's room. I thought maybe this door would have become unlocked, but no such luck. I fitted a key into the slot.

"Were those stairs back there down the hall?" she asked.

"Mm-hmm," I mumbled, as I tried to get the correct key.

"Where do they go?"

"They go upstairs."

"I'm being serious," she said through gritted teeth.

"Me too. I don't know what they lead to. I assume it goes up to an attic. Don't see it being much of anything else. Can't imagine there being another floor of rooms, unless it was a hotel, which I don't believe it was."

The door finally unlocked and I pushed it open. Straightaway, the differences were obvious. Broken toys were scattered all about the floor. Blocks of wood, probably used to make a little model fort, had been knocked over and leaden toy soldiers lay around it as if killed in battle. The bed was broken. Pieces from it lay haphazardly on the floor and the shelving was loosened from the wall, the edge piercing a tin drum. The only thing intact was a rocking horse. Its teeth were bared in an evil sneer. It had eyes opened wide and wild as if it were demon possessed. Only the dust and cobwebs covering it shattered the illusion. The dust, now disturbed, brought on a fit of sneezing. I used my shirt to cover my nose and mouth.

The two rooms were similar in layout, but it was where any similarities ended. Dark blotches of what I thought was water damage, or maybe paint, covered the walls. It looked as if someone had taken dark paint and flung it about the room without a brush, in imitation of Jackson Pollock. I ran my fingers over some of the stains, but whatever it was, it had long ago dried.

"What is that?" Gwendolyn asked.

"Paint, maybe," I answered.

"Could it be...?" She didn't finish.

I had the same thought, but hoped it wasn't. "Let's go somewhere else," I said.

We turned to leave. A loud crack of thunder boomed and shook the room.

"Is it storming?" Gwendolyn asked. She looked around as if she could see the sky from inside.

I didn't have time to answer before flashes, like a hidden strobe light, brightened the room in intervals. Each pass of light brought an image, like a slide show, frame by frame.

******

The woman enters the bedroom, a heavy butcher knife hung loosely at her side. A small boy sits on the floor, cross-legged. He made half-hearted attempts at play with his toy soldiers. He hears the woman enter. He turns to her. A smile crosses his face as he sees her.

A madwoman is hiding behind a mask of love.

The boy pushes himself to his feet and raises his arms to her to be held. His lips move as he calls to her.

Her mouth goes wide and her face contorts as she screams at him. Her empty hand shoots out and slaps him across the face. His eyes water, his lips quiver, but he tries his best not to cry. Her hand returns and slaps him again. He drops to the floor, hurt and confused. The woman grabs his arm, her claw-like fingers digging into his flesh, and she jerks him to his feet. His face winces in pain as his arm is dislocated from his shoulder.

She lets the arm go. It falls limply to his side. She steps back and lifts the knife above her head.

The boy, who sees and knows, begins to shake his head back and forth, the fear flinging off of him, the smell of it so strong it pours into other dimensions.

She takes one of his little hands into hers, lovingly, one part of her contradicting the other. The knife comes down. It cracks his young skull. Blood gushes from the wound as shock overtakes the boy's face. His knees wobble. The woman releases her hand from his and she brings the knife down again. The blade sinks deeply into his shoulder. Blood spurts and flows out rapidly as he drops to his knees and falls over backward. She grabs him and lifts him into the air. She swings his limp body around and releases it. He smashes against the wall, splattering blood everywhere. She stabs him, hacking at his breathless body until it is beyond recognition.

She turns toward us. She lifts her head, her face dyed red with blood, and our eyes meet. Her eyes burn into mine as she grips the knife tightly. She glances at Gwendolyn and steps forward. A black, nefarious grin spreads across her face as a last bright strobe flash ends the nightmare.

******

I blinked my eyes rapidly and tried to shake off not only the temporary blindness caused by the last flash, but the sudden wave of fear that washed over me. She looked right at me, right at Gwendolyn. She knew we were both here. I realized then, she meant us nothing but harm and would not let us out until we were dead. I was absolutely certain of this and it only intensified my fear, though I tried to keep it under my skin for Gwendolyn's sake, as well as my own sanity. I looked at Gwendolyn. She stood there as if in a trance.

"Gwendolyn? Are you all right?" I asked.

She didn't respond, only stood there, her mouth agape as she stared blankly into space.

"Gwendolyn?" I called again. I waved my hand close to her face. I started to worry as I whistled softly, and continued to fan my hand over her eyes.

"D-did you—" she stuttered.

I sighed, glad to know she was at least still here with me, though my concern wasn't lessened. "Yeah," I said.

"It was blood," she whispered.

"Uh-huh," I croaked.

The last thing I'd wanted was for her to witness the horrible scene played out in front of us. The boy being beaten, cut up by a woman who might have been his mother. I didn't want to believe a mother would be able to do something like that to her own child. It was unimaginable to have those images flashed at us against our will and in such graphic detail. It was the most horrible thing I had ever witnessed and I only hoped I wouldn't have to experience such brutality in my life again.

"Why?" Gwendolyn cried, and then she crumbled.

I grabbed her and wrapped her in my arms. I held her close and tried to offer some semblance of comfort. She trembled under my embrace and shuddered with heavy sobs. I led her out and closed the door behind us. She tried to bury her head deeper into my chest. We stood there in the hallway. I let her vent, so she could get it all out of her system. I almost wanted to join her, but one of us had to stay strong and coherent. We couldn't both lose control. Who knew what it might lead to?

"I...I wanna go home. I don't like this. I don't like it at all." Her voice came in mewling cries, muffled by my shirt, where her head was still burrowed.

I understood how she felt. I felt the same way. I did not want to be here either, but the choice wasn't ours anymore.

I regretted bringing her along. I'd regretted the idea from the beginning, but it was worse now. It was too late. Complaining would not get us out.

"We're going to try and get home," I said to her quietly. I stroked her hair and could smell the grief and fear coming from her. I felt so helpless.

It was all my fault we were in this mess. Sure, I could go with the "I told you so's," but it wouldn't accomplish anything. As of now, time was not on our side. I should never have told her about this place. Never should have encouraged the spirits here. I should have just let Her be and, somehow, ignored the calls and the haunted dreams. I had given in during a moment of weakness and because of that weakness, we were trapped. We were her prisoners. My emotions did not matter. We did not matter. She had us and no one could help us.

My fears had been realized.

Chapter 31

We stood outside in the hallway, the door closed between us and the room. It was a poor barrier, but at least it was a barrier. I tried to comfort Gwendolyn, which helped me manage my own fear. I should be used to the sudden, macabre outbursts of the house by now, but Gwendolyn had them thrown at her without warning. Not that I could ever get used to seeing acts of violence. Especially against children.

When she calmed, we continued going through the bedroom I'd already been in. We searched more closely for any possible clues or secret passageways, but there weren't any to be found. I was disappointed, because I expected there to be something in every room. I had hoped so, anyway. At least there weren't any more scenes.

"Are you okay?" I asked Gwendolyn.

"I'm fine. Why do you keep asking me that?"

"Just want to make sure. I worry about you."

"You don't need to worry about me. I had a moment, but I'm fine now. Worry about getting out of this place."

I gave a short laugh. "I am."

Of course, I was going to keep being concerned about her. She still seemed to be shaken, though by all appearances, she handled it well. She was walking on her own and still functioned mentally. A lot of people would have just fallen apart and not been good for anything. I remembered what it was like the first time I saw something. It was horrific, but not even close to what we had just witnessed.

No other apparitions made appearances and I hoped there wouldn't be any more. Nothing I could count on, though.

"Maybe we should try the other side. There's nothing here," said Gwendolyn.

"I haven't been that way yet. Maybe we can find something there. Can't see why there wouldn't be."

I tried to sound hopeful.

The west side was laid out in much the same way. The rooms offered no information except apparently, the doctor and his wife had separate bedrooms. A small third bedroom was plain with simple furniture. I assumed it had belonged to a maid, as a guest room would presumably be more comfortable. A linen closet stood empty and smelled of mildew. A door at the very end led to a smoking room. It had a billiard table, a custom card table, and a bar lined with partially filled bottles and decanters. I had no interest in sampling them.

A few glasses remained intact, coated in a layer of dust. There were broken glasses, their pieces splintered and scattered over the bar and floor. The artwork was masculine and featured game animals and the sea. It was a room for a man to entertain friends and associates. A place where they could have cigars and brandy, play a few hands of cards and tell bawdy jokes. A couple of elk-head trophies hung on the wall, the moth-eaten fur and glass eyes dulled with time. They did not hold much attraction for me, as I'm not a fan of hunting. Like motorcycles, I must admit I'm afraid of guns. Not a big fan of hanging corpses on the wall, either.

I thought first, it would be best to leave this room and look elsewhere. There didn't seem to be a way out in here. Instead, I hung back in the room. It was more to give Gwendolyn a little time to relax and calm down as best as she could. I didn't want to be a jerk and push her. It would only lead to complications and possibly put us in more danger. I'd hate for it to all be in vain. The biggest upset thus far was not finding anything substantial, except for the dollhouse, and it seemed to appeal only to Gwendolyn's sense of nostalgia. Though it was something, I wished it could help us get out instead of merely resurrecting childhood memories.

"You ready to move on?" I asked her.

"I'm ready to get out of here. You're not angry, are you?" Guilt trimmed the edge of her voice.

"Why would I be?"

"For pushing you to let me come," she said quietly.

I shook my head and reassured her, "I couldn't be mad at you. Don't think I would be, okay?"

"Okay, I just...I'm sorry."

"Hey, we're going to get out. It's just going to take a little more time than I thought."

"I trust you, Harry. I want you to know that."

"Probably not such a great idea." I tried to smile, but the truth was, I didn't feel very trustworthy and I feared she would be disappointed in me.

"Even so, I do. Want to go up those steps?" she asked.

"The ones going up?"

"No, the ones going down," she said.

I rolled my eyes, though I was glad to see a bit of the old Gwendolyn come out. "Why not? Got nothing else to do. Want a drink first?"

"Nah, how about a hug?"

"You're weird." I gave her a quick hug and we headed down the hall to see what lay above us.

256

Chapter 32

"These stairs are awfully narrow," I observed, as we stood at the foot of the stairwell. They spiraled up and out of view.

"They are," she agreed.

"I wonder if it is an attic. How would you be able to get anything up these stairs?"

"Maybe it's where they kept their ugly, psychotic relatives."

"Don't you start being morbid. I've a mind to make you go up there by yourself, just in case."

"No, you won't. You go. You're the man," she said and prodded me in the back.

"What happened to equality and all that stuff?"

"Only for pay. We get to pick and choose."

"That's hypocritical," I said, and took the first few steps then stopped. I pressed my hands against the walls. I may not be skinny, but I'm not fat either. Even so, I couldn't help but feel like I had to squeeze through the stairwell.

"Are you going to just stand there, or are you going to move?" she asked and poked me again.

"Okay, okay!" I barked, and started up again.

"These days, the owner of this place would be sued for discriminating against fat people," observed Gwendolyn as we climbed upward.

"I think the PC term is 'nutritionally challenged.'"

She laughed. "Since when are you PC?"

"Since never, I'm just saying."

"Why do I put up with you?" she sighed.

"Because you love me?"

"Nope, that's not it. I'll give you one more guess."

"Uh..." I turned to her the best I could. "Would you give me a hint?"

"No hints."

"Okay, then." I tapped my finger on my chin and hummed under my breath. "I'll guess it's because you don't have a choice?"

"Ding, ding, ding! We have a winner!"

"What do I win?" I asked. "I hope it's a new car. I could use one of those."

She laughed and leaned up to give me a quick kiss. "That's all you get."

"That's much better than a new car. Not only is it tasty, it's tax free."

She shook her head. "You exasperate me. Let's go."

"Big word, me no understand," I said, in my best dumb jock impression.

"Just move." She prodded my back again, harder this time.

We were both faking our light-hearted mood, but it was the best we could do.

The stairwell spiraled up to a large attic. The ceiling, with exposed beams, tapered down to the floor so there were no actual walls, save for the east and west ends. There were several stacks of trunks, boxes and accumulated junk, which created individual spaces in the attic. The warm air was suffocating. There was no ventilation, and it was difficult to breathe.

"It's really stuffy up here," Gwendolyn said.

"It is." I looked around. "Guess it is an attic. Maybe the kids would come up here to play on rainy days."

"Can't see why anyone would want to spend any amount of time up here," she said.

"I would have loved an attic to play in. Playing treasure hunters, making forts out of blankets, all the fun stuff. The house I grew up in didn't have much of an attic. It wasn't even a good storage space. You couldn't even walk upright and you'd fall through the ceiling if you took a slight misstep. Nothing but beams to crawl on."

"You poor baby. You had such a deprived childhood," Gwendolyn teased. "Poor thing probably didn't have a basement either."

"Hell no, we didn't have a basement," I sniffed.

Gwendolyn patted my back while doing an imaginary cry.

"But we did have an attic fan."

"At least it's something."

"Yeah, it was. I loved the attic fan. I remember during the fall, on some nights, we'd have our windows open and with it going, the outside air would get pulled in. The noise it made was comforting. I loved lying in bed and feeling the air blow over me."

"Sounds nice. We didn't have anything like that."

"Yeah, it was. You're missing out. I shared a room with my brother and his bed was by the window. He got full advantage of the fan."

"And you wanted the spot, huh?"

"Yeah. I told him the man in the moon was going to come down and eat him if he looked out the window. It scared him enough to switch places with me."

"You're mean!"

I shrugged. "Gotta do what you gotta do. I got the breeze."

"You ought to be ashamed of yourself."

"Don't tell me you never did something to your sister to get what you wanted."

"I'll take the fifth." She blushed slightly.

"So you did!"

"I didn't say that."

"Anytime someone says they take the fifth, it means they're guilty of something."

"Not always," she argued. "Sometimes they take the fifth to make someone think they're guilty of something."

"There isn't anyone in the world who isn't."

"Maybe you're right."

"No maybe about it," I said.

"Watch out. Your pants aren't that big."

"Maybe I'll find a bigger pair in here," I said.

We rummaged through some of the boxes and trunks. We didn't find anything to help us, just a bunch of old clothing and mementos that served no purpose for us. If She was going to give up Her secrets in any tangible way, She wasn't going to make it easy.

Behind a stack of boxes, I saw a sliver of glass, so I began to move boxes aside to open up the space.

"Is that a window?" Gwendolyn asked.

"Looks that way," I said, as I tugged the last box out of the way and.

"I'm going to try to open it," she said, as she squatted in front of it and pulled up as hard as she could, grunting with the effort.

"Let me give it a try," I said.

"It's stuck," she replied.

"Maybe not."

"What, because I'm a woman, I can't open it?"

"No, I didn't say that." I scanned the window for any signs of tampering, such as someone nailing or painting it shut. There was nothing I could see, so I pulled up on the window with a quick, hard jerk and it gave a little.

"You got it!" Gwendolyn shouted happily.

"Don't get too excited. It's stuck again." I pulled at the window, straining until my head hurt, to no avail.

The window had only moved up a few inches, which wasn't enough for anyone to crawl through, but it did allow a welcome breeze to bring some cool relief. I took the fresh air into my lungs, and feeling renewed, I gave it another try, only to struggle without success.

It wasn't as if the window would be a good escape route, even if we did get it open. It was three stories up, so we would surely hurt ourselves severely, if not kill ourselves, trying to jump out. I wondered if jumping out would transport us back somewhere else and not cause any damage. That's the way it worked when I walked outside the front door. I couldn't say with assurance whether I would wind up on the ground or fall three stories, if I tried. I decided I wasn't desperate enough to try it. Not yet.

"Let's see if there's anything we can use to pry the window open some more," I said.

We scrounged around and Gwendolyn came up with an iron pipe, about a yard long. "Will this work?" she asked, handing it to me.

"Maybe." I took it and checked the weight of it in my hand. I thought it just might provide enough leverage.

I placed the rod through the gap in the window and pushed downward. I felt the window give slightly and was about to express my joy at this bit of success when the window slammed shut of its own accord and snapped the iron pipe in two, one piece tumbling outside as I held the other in my hand.

The red glow deepened and began to throb. A deep guttural groaning shook the floor,. The stacks rattled and some fell and spilled their contents.

"I think we just pissed it off," I whispered.

"Pissed what off?" She looked around the room for an angry entity.

"The house," I answered.

"That's impossible."

"Unlike everything else that's happened tonight?" I gestured around the room. "The sourceless light, the noises and little boys riding around with their fucking heads split open!"

"Cut it out!" Gwendolyn snapped.

I turned and threw the piece of iron as hard as I could at the window.

It bounced off the glass like it was a rubber ball on concrete.

"Oh hell, I can't do this. We're not getting out. I can't even break a goddamn window and jump three stories." I pushed my hands through my hair. I was at my wit's end.

"Don't talk like that. We can find a way out. We can do it together. Nothing's impossible if we work together." She massaged my shoulders and spoke to me in her soothing voice. My muscles relaxed and I calmed down a bit.

"You're remarkably optimistic," I said.

"Someone's gotta be."

"Are you really, though?" I asked. "I didn't mean to blow up. I'm just totally frustrated. I came here afraid something like this was going to happen. You don't think I caused this, do you?"

"No, you didn't make this happen. We're not going to find our way out if we spend all our time snapping at each other and blaming ourselves. I'm just as guilty."

"Maybe it's what She wants us to do," I said.

"If it is, then it's not going to get any satisfaction."

"Like Mick Jagger," I said, with a forced chuckle.

"Yeah, just like Jagger," she agreed.

The room began to shake. It groaned heavily, loudly. The tremor was strong enough to topple me. I hit the floor and a sharp pain shot up my arm as I landed on my elbow. I grimaced as I moved it, thankful it wasn't broken. It had knocked Gwendolyn down, and I rushed to check on her.

"Are you okay?" I had to shout over the din.

The groans sounded like words in a forgotten, ancient tongue. They grew in volume and intensity. The room gave another shake. It lasted longer than the last by half a minute.

"What's going on? Is it an earthquake?" Gwendolyn asked, her voice almost overwhelmed by the house's language.

"No, I don't think it's an earthquake," I shouted. "Like I said, I think the house is angry."

"But why?" she cried.

Before I could answer, a portal began to open. A dark, swirling mist emerged, spinning like a hypnotic wheel. It began to suck in everything around it. I wrapped my arms around a support beam. The portal grew more powerful.

"Hang on!" I screamed at Gwendolyn. I hoped she could hear me.

She was already hanging onto me as tightly as she could. I closed my eyes. My muscles strained. The pain shot through my body, hot and intense.

A shrill cry sounded. It grated against my eardrums and into my brain. It tempted me to release my grip and plug my ears. I bore it and resisted the urge. I knew if I let go, not only would the portal suck me in, it would also take Gwendolyn. I gritted my teeth as Gwendolyn crushed her body against me. Her fingernails dug painfully into my sides. The force coming from within the portal was so strong it lifted both of our bodies off the floor and gave us the appearance of floating on the air as it tried to suck us into what I was sure was oblivion.

"Don't let go!" I screamed, not sure if it was for my benefit or hers.

I could feel my arms start to slip from the beam. I pulled myself toward it while I tried to avoid trunks and smaller items flying at me on their way to feed the portal. I ignored the throbbing pain in my muscles and though Gwendolyn's hold was strong, I could feel it weaken.

I didn't know if the house was trying to kill us, scare us, or if this was an extreme way of telling us something. The portal created such a racket I wasn't able to hear anything else. If Gwendolyn tried to get my attention, she wouldn't be able to. I could hardly hear my own thoughts, much less my voice.

Suddenly, the portal's vortex vanished, and our bodies slammed back to the floor.

"What the hell was that?" Gwendolyn's voice rasped in the abrupt silence.

I caught my breath and rubbed my arms. I knew my muscles were going to be sore later.

"No idea," I finally answered. "I can only guess She isn't happy."

"You think?"

"That's what I think." I ignored the sarcasm.

"You told me nothing was going to hurt us! I don't know if you noticed, but that hurt!" she yelled.

"What I said was it hadn't hurt me yet. Never said it wouldn't. I think I remember saying there was a damn good possibility. Don't put words into my mouth, okay?"

"Whatever." She turned away from me.

"Don't do this," I said. "At least we're okay. Are you?"

"I'm fine. Just nerves. That thing was trying to eat us, Harry!" she suddenly exclaimed. "And what was all that noise?"

"I don't think it was just noise. I think She might have been trying to talk to us."

"Talk? Well, I didn't understand a word. How does a house talk?"

I threw my hands up in resignation. "I don't doubt anything here anymore. It just seemed talking made sense. I just don't know what it was trying to say."

"You think another language?"

I only nodded.

"If it was talking in another language, then it's some sort of demon tongue."

"It would be a great explanation if you were some sort of re-ligious fanatic."

"It's not a religious thing, Harry. How else can we explain it? It's an explanation, which we don't have now."

"It seems to defy explanation. We've run smack into a wall of otherworldly."

"No, we may not be able to understand it, but there it is."

"I don't care. I just want to get the hell out of here."

We found our way to the stairs and went back down to the second floor. We wandered around and figured if we couldn't get out, then all we could do was keep looking and hope we stumbled on something that would open a door for us. It was a long shot, but it was all we had.

Chapter 33

We scoured the second floor again and avoided the bedroom on the east side. We hoped it would keep us from having to deal with another show like we had witnessed in the boy's room. Anyway, I was sure we had exhausted all of the possibilities on that side of the house.

We explored the west side again, but found nothing to give us hope. The rooms were almost bare, so searching them took a very short time.

"There really isn't a way out," I said sadly.

"Don't say that," Gwendolyn scolded. "We have to keep trying."

"We have tried. I don't think we missed anything. What other options do we have?"

"Let's try the billiard room on the end again."

"Yeah, and we're not going to get out from that room either."

"Stop being so negative."

"Oh, we'll definitely find an exit in there!" I said, with as much fake enthusiasm as I could muster.

She frowned at me. "Don't be sarcastic, either."

"How else am I supposed to be? I'm scared." I felt ashamed in admitting it, but there it was.

"I am too, but it'll be okay."

"I'm supposed to be fearless."

"Whatever. Let's go, Braveheart."

We went into the room and immediately noticed it had deteriorated further. A thick moldy smell hung in the air, stronger than in the other areas.

"It stinks in here," said Gwendolyn.

"Yeah, but this is our last hope." It sounded so final. "Let's just move everything and check every corner and floorboard."

We spent at least an hour scouring every inch of the room. We moved the paintings, furniture, and anything else not anchored down. No luck. Gwendolyn took a stool at the bar and sat down. I moved behind the bar, grabbed a glass, and said, "Would the lady care for a drink?"

"Stop playing around," she sighed. "I'm tired."

"Who says I'm playing? If you don't want one, I'll make a drink for myself."

I couldn't say if it was a good idea, drinking what was on those shelves, but I scanned them and found half a dozen bottles. They had a fair amount of liquor left in them. I figured they would either be ruined, or stronger. I chose the bottle with the most in it and started to pull it off the shelf. It wouldn't come off the shelf, but leaned forward as if hinged in place.

The wall began to shift.

"Shit!" I gasped. "Look!"

Gwendolyn got up from the stool and came behind the bar.

"It's a secret passage," I said.

"No, really?"

I didn't acknowledge her snark. "Yeah, let's go in."

"I don't know."

"We can't afford not to." I was frustrated with her hesitation. "What if it leads out?" I grabbed her hand and pulled her in behind me. "It's all we've got right now."

The wall was much like the one in the library, except when we went in, it wasn't a hallway and the glow, the dark red of congealed blood, lighted the room dimly. As we stood in the doorway, I felt disappointment.

It was only a small room, bare except for an old brass bed frame with a thin mattress on top of it. The mattress was blotched with stains in all hues. I wouldn't want to guess the source of those stains.

Iron shackles hung from the corners of each post. A tart smell left a bad taste in my mouth. The smell was mingled with the rank stench of fresh excrement. I suppressed the gorge rising up in my throat and covered my nose and mouth.

Gwendolyn retched as her hands flew to her face. "It smells like crap! Literal crap."

"No denying that." My voice was muffled behind my hand.

"Where is it coming from?"

I looked over the room for the source, but unable to discover it, deduced it was either from the mattress, or under the bed. It was a safe bet I wasn't going to be looking beneath the bed. "No way to know where it's coming from, but it definitely smells fresh."

"This room is so small," Gwendolyn said.

"Yeah, it looks like a place people might use to mete out punishment or something."

"What?"

"What else could it be for?" I asked. "It's a bed with shackles attached to it. Otherwise, the room is empty. It makes perfect sense to me. Well, I guess it might have been some sort of kinky thing that went on here."

"In a room that smells like shit? That's sick! Why do you have to be so disgusting?"

"I'm just making observations," I reasoned. "It could be something a lot worse than a fetishist playroom."

"I think it's gross," she insisted.

Indeed, I thought.

The wall slammed shut behind us. It startled me, and I almost fell as I turned briskly.

"No, no, no!" I banged my fist against the wall we had just come through. "Son of a bitch!" I cursed as I struggled to pry the wall back to no avail.

"Oh, please don't tell me!" Gwendolyn cried.

"Our fucking exit's blocked." I gave voice to our fear.

"We're stuck? Again? In here?" I heard the tears in her voice as they formed in her eyes.

"Don't give up too fast. There has to be a way out of this." I sounded more optimistic than I felt.

"Are you kidding me?" Gwendolyn shouted. "There's only one way out of here and it's closed off! We're not only stuck in a whole house, but a room! A little stuffy room that smells like an outhouse!"

"Let's not lose hope here," I said, though I wasn't feeling very hopeful myself.

"Yeah? You want to be the optimist now? Well, I think it's a little too late," Gwendolyn said, as she pounded her fists weakly against my chest.

"Yeah."

I was giving up.

Gwendolyn looked around the room, presumably for a place to sit down, but there was no place to do so, save for the bed. I didn't think even a rat would venture onto it, and rats will venture onto just about anything.

I searched the room as Gwendolyn stood there, wrapped in her own arms as if she were trying to hold herself together. I ran my hands and fingers along the walls and ignored the sticky, grimy feel of them as I searched for a knob, switch, button, or anything to open the wall from this side. I checked everywhere, from floor to ceiling as high as I could reach. An intense feeling of claustrophobia panicked me.

I stopped a moment to catch my breath and ignored the stench. I turned to check on Gwendolyn. She was on the other side of the room, also looking for something along the walls.

I kept telling myself we'd be all right, though it seemed like a lie. I began to wonder if there might be a trap door or something under the bed. I shuddered at the thought of touching the filthy mattress. Then I heard Gwendolyn scream.

"Harry!" she cried out. "Help me!"

I spun around to see Gwendolyn being lifted off her feet by some invisible force. She kicked her legs wildly and fought against an unseen enemy, who slammed her down on the polluted mattress.

The force of the impact caused the foul odors to renew with a mad intensity. Gwendolyn struggled against the force. She swung her arms blindly to no effect.

Full of rage, I sprang to free her from the invisible attacker, but when I got within arm's reach, something pummeled my solar plexus. It knocked me against the wall, and expelled the wind out of me. In the minutes it took me to recover, I had to watch Gwendolyn struggle, alone, with whatever held her. Finally, I pushed off the wall and went to her rescue again.

Electricity shot through me like I had grabbed a high voltage fence as I careened into an invisible barrier that blocked me from Gwendolyn. I tried again, and again. Every attempt I made was unsuccessful. I couldn't tell if the liquid streaming down my face was sweat or tears.

"Gwendolyn!" I screamed, but she did not seem to hear me. Whatever had her ignored me, although I thought I heard a guttural laugh.

"Let her go! It's me you want! Let her go and take me!" I challenged the invisible monster, but received no response.

There was nothing, it seemed, I could do, but it didn't stop me from trying.

Gwendolyn's arm slammed against the post as the iron shackle snaked up toward her wrist. She clawed at the restraint with her other hand, her face wet with tears of fury, but she was unable to pull it away as it closed tightly around her wrist with a loud clack. The process repeated. I rushed again, bracing myself for another shock, when something like a hammer slammed into my abdomen. I doubled over and vomited, unable to catch my breath.

Whatever it was, it would not let me get near as the final restraint closed around her ankle.

I realized I could not save her.

"Let her go, let her go!" I cried out repeatedly.

The bloody glow pulsed in time with a deep, throbbing bass sound, like someone was twanging a large rubber band. Gwendolyn kept fighting in vain. She screamed and cursed at the force holding her. Her eyes were wide in fear as she implored my help. I kept trying to fight through the invisible wall between us.

Though I realized it was a losing battle, I refused to surrender.

A dark shadow enveloped her, slowly inching its way from her toes to her head and wrapped her in a shroud of evil. It was more sinister than a shadow, thicker and darker, like the blackest fog. I kept trying to break through the barrier, then suddenly realized Gwendolyn was silent. The dark fog hid the entire bed and encased my Gwendolyn in a malevolent cocoon. The deep rhythmic noise groaned a word I could plainly understand.

"No! Never!" I shrieked at it. "You can't have her!" I was delirious. I didn't want to understand it. I did not want to hear it.

The voice spoke again, loud and clear.

It said, "Mine."

Chapter 34

The dark shroud hung over the bed for what seemed an eternity before it rolled back and revealed an empty mattress.

"What did you do with her?" My voice shrilled as I dropped to the floor and screamed at the emptiness.

The room was unnaturally quiet, punctuated only by my angry sobs. I heard the grinding sound of something being pushed across the floor and in the deep background, once again, the evil, mocking laughter. I got back on my feet and glared around the room with my fists clenched until the knuckles turned white.

The entrance to the room was open again. It allowed a chance for escape, but only able to think of one thing, I ignored it.

"What did you do with her? Where is she, damn it?" I bellowed.

I was answered only with a torturous silence that penetrated like a dagger.

I stepped back, eyes riveted on the empty, soiled mattress. I hoped she would appear. My hands shook with rage and fear as I tried to find some clue to tell me what happened. My heart was in turmoil, and I feared I had lost Gwendolyn forever. But no, I refused to accept it.

I vowed I wouldn't rest until I found the girl who had roared into my life and stolen my heart. I felt we were fated to be together, though she would probably laugh at the idea. I wasn't sure what I could trust anymore as my established beliefs were challenged to the limit.

I even found myself briefly wishing I believed in a god. Any god would have suited me. I wanted something I could implore, something I could pray to and be relieved of this experience.

"Don't be ridiculous," I said.

I was letting these things get to me. I was letting this house and everything in it drive me crazy. I couldn't afford to let it happen. It was, I realized, up to me alone to find Gwendolyn and get out of this predicament.

I jogged through the house and didn't pay attention to the creaking floor, or the occasional bowing of weak flooring that threatened to give in from room to room. I tried every switch, book and wall panel throughout the second story. I called Gwendolyn's name as I searched.

I went to the other end of the house, and saw the stones on the floor. I thought of Gwendolyn and the one she used to carry with her. Without hesitation, I grabbed the tiger's eye from the pile and put it in my pocket. I thought maybe it would offer some protection, and perhaps even lead me to what I needed to know. At this point, I would try anything.

I found all the draperies could be moved to expose the dark night outside, so I looked behind those as well as under the beds, while I pushed aside any fears of rabid rats that might be hiding beneath. The longer I searched, the crazier I got. I peered into improbably tiny crevices and tried to discover where she had been taken.

The idea she might not be alive tried to sneak into my mind, but I knew it wasn't true. I had no doubt she was alive. Something profound, deep inside my heart, assured me it was true. It was how long she would remain so that concerned me. It pushed me ever onward in a race against unknown time. Adrenaline rushed through my veins and wouldn't allow me a chance to get tired. My worry for Gwendolyn energized me, as if I had slammed down a dozen energy drinks and a handful of caffeine pills.

After I exhausted every possible choice upstairs, I went to the main staircase. I pushed away the fear I wouldn't find her, that she was somewhere being put through horrendous torture before her final breath. Physically, I knew I was tiring. My throat was parched and my muscles cramped. I vanquished the thought, for it would only make things worse.

I made my way down the stairs, mentally going over my next move. I knew my options were becoming increasingly limited. As I neared the bottom, I felt a draft push its way across my skin, cool and mysterious. I looked up to see the front door was open. This made me immediately wary. Even if I weren't being deceived and the way out was open, there was no way I was going to leave this place without Gwendolyn. I would die before I would take that route.

I couldn't imagine my life without her, or living with the guilt of not being able to save her. I had brought her here and I was going to get her out. It was my responsibility and I wasn't going to shirk it.

The house was rapidly filling with palpable waves of jealousy and rage. Why did She offer me an escape now, rather than earlier, when escape would have been welcomed? She wanted me to abandon Gwendolyn, I was sure, but it wasn't going to happen. I wasn't about to give in to the temptation of the open door. No way in hell. I knew Gwendolyn was somewhere in this house, and I was going to find her.

Chapter 35

In the parlor, I started my search much like I had before. Everything that could be moved, I moved. I even got down on my hands and knees and sifted through the cold ashes of the fireplace, with the thought there might have been a trap door hidden underneath, but had no luck. I pushed and pulled on every brick. I even risked standing on a chair to reach the ones near the ceiling. I pecked at the piano keys, in the hope something might be triggered, but all it did was tell me the piano was out of tune. After a thorough search, I learned there was nothing to be found. I moved from the parlor to the library and tore at everything in the room. I constantly called Gwendolyn's name until my throat was raw. I hoped she would somehow hear me and answer back, but was only answered with unbearable silence.

After I moved the tables and chairs, I rolled up the tattered rugs to look underneath them, but only exposed a bare floor. I considered the bookcase hiding the long, dark, narrow passage. The thought I would find her in there crossed my mind, but I wasn't sure. I thought I would exhaust every other option before I entered the dark tunnel again.

I went back to the foyer. The wind blew into the house and

cooled it considerably. The temptation to walk through the door came upon me as I shivered with the cold.

"No," I answered the solicitation, and turned away from the door. I went to the other side of the house toward the study.

An angry flash of heat swept through the foyer then abruptly disappeared and intensified the cold as I entered the study. I pulled the drawers out of the desk, overturned the bookcases, threw books and journals aside. I ripped them out without regard to the thought they might have information I would have previously welcomed. I no longer cared if they were rare, or even if they contained the secrets of alchemy. The only information I was interested in was Gwendolyn's whereabouts.

She was all that mattered.

The house held Gwendolyn hostage, and by doing so, had declared war. Though I knew not how, I was going to fight to my last breath. All evidence to the contrary, I still had hope it was just a terrible dream. I would awaken in my apartment. Gwendolyn would be there, Gary would still be alive, and this house would have never existed outside the dream world.

I knew better, and She knew it.

I left the study looking like a hurricane had blown through and noticed the desk sitting flush against the wall. I realized it looked out of place there, so I pulled it away and shoved it across the floor. It was heavy, but I didn't care about the weight. There wasn't anything in the space behind the desk and my anger grew. I pushed at the grandfather clock standing next to it. The large clock rocked back as I shoved. The glass shattered as it crashed to the ground.

I briefly felt guilty for destroying the beautiful clock just before I saw it had hidden a small door in the space behind it. A surge of hope filled me as I pulled at the door, which opened easily.

The room behind the door was narrow, deep and empty. I took several steps into it and had to crouch as the ceiling slanted with the stairs above. Out of the darkness appeared a figure crouched on its haunches, dressed in a dirty smock. Its hair was frizzled and pointed in all directions. It was chewing on something. I moved closer, then realized it was feasting on a human arm. It was small, like a child's, so I knew it hadn't belonged to Gwendolyn and felt a morbid sense of relief.

She threw her head up and her eyes, glowing evilly, bore into me. She bared her teeth as a growl rumbled from her like a lion about to attack.

I jumped up and slammed my head against the stairs above me. Stars flashed in my eyes and I wobbled, on the verge of passing out, but managed to stay upright. I stumbled backward toward the door. The woman dropped the bloody, mangled arm and sprang toward me just as I found the door and fell out of it. I slammed it shut and quickly pushed the shattered clock in front of it, irrationally thinking it would offer sufficient protection from the thing hiding under the stairs.

I stood and leaned against the wall. My hand felt the knot forming on the back of my head. It was painful to the touch and I felt light-headed. I hoped I hadn't managed to give myself a concussion.

"Gwendolyn!" I screamed and ignored the pain that rocked me between the ears.

I heard the taunting laughter of the house and it made me angry. My rage rose. It felt like it had been building up for days instead of the hours since we came into this house together.

The house continued Her laughter and uttered untranslatable things. I knew, despite not understanding, Her words weren't meant to help me.

My bones began to ache with the chill and my throat was rough from shouting and from thirst. I ignored it and continued into the dining room.

The room was unrecognizable from the last time I had been

280

there. The table lay in a broken pile with the china cabinets toppled and the artwork torn and askew on the wall. There wasn't much to look for here and after I finished, I rested my head against the jamb to the swinging door. I felt weary, but told myself I would only al-low myself a few moments' rest. I kept telling myself not to lose hope, but it was becoming increasingly difficult.

I remembered as a child, my mother would always tell me to have faith. Whenever something went wrong, or things weren't going my way, she would say, "have faith." She was big on believ-ing for the best. Of course, when she spoke of faith, she was speaking of her religious faith. Faith in God, that he would see you through. God would look out for those who placed their faith in him. I had not believed in the god my mother so loved since I was a child, but I think I understand what she meant.

Faith doesn't belong to any one person or a particular reli-gion; it is universal. It is for all. I had to take hold of faith. The faith I had in myself, in Gwendolyn, in our humanity. I had to have faith I could follow through and find her. It was all I had left. The belief in myself, in us. I thought of my mother and how her faith had seen her through her own struggles. It was the thought that gave me the strength to carry through, that told me I could do it.

Though things looked bleak right now, I had faith.

Chapter 36

I felt a renewal of strength and pushed through the swinging door. I paused, surprised at the condition the kitchen was in. It was neat and tidy, like someone had come in and cleaned up all the dust and debris so they could prepare a meal. The menacing red light which had been predominant throughout the house was absent. Instead, a soft, blue glow suffused the room. The sinister sounds and head-pounding drones seemed to be unwelcome here. It was peaceful and I knew this was more like the way it was in Her better days. I looked toward the door and wondered if Gwendolyn might be in one of the outbuildings and considered going to check, but feared I might end up somewhere else, like back in town, and lose completely.

Then I saw there was someone here. She stood at the sink, her back toward me. My heart quickened, because my first thought was it was Gwendolyn, but it wasn't.

I watched her and it was like she didn't notice I had come into the room. I went further inside, but she didn't flinch. I held my breath and thought I ought to be afraid, but strangely, I wasn't.

"Who are you?" I broke the silence.

She didn't answer straightaway, but turned to face me. She

had a peaceful countenance and a slight smile on her lips. She was the same girl I had encountered here what seemed like ages ago, but this time she didn't exhibit the same misery. I saw she was beautiful and the room was lighted by her presence.

"Who are you?" I asked again. I couldn't take my eyes off of her.

"My name is Amelia, but that isn't of any importance. Not anymore."

It was strange. At first, her lips had moved without me being able to hear her speak, but this time, it was the opposite. I could hear her voice, a soft voice, gentle and sweet, without movement of her lips.

"What is important?" I asked. It took a moment, but I realized she was communicating with me telepathically. "Why am I here? Why did you bring me?"

"I did not bring you here," she said.

"Then who did?"

"You'll find out in time," she answered.

"I don't want to find out in time. I want to know right now." I was frustrated. I knew there were answers and she was the only link I had to finding them. But it seemed she wasn't going to make it easy.

"I know where you can find her." Her eyes never left mine. There was an honesty in those eyes and I knew she didn't have the ability, or the heart, to deceive anyone. She wasn't going to lie to me. The aura surrounding her was the opposite of the one belonging to the house. I found comfort in her still, small voice.

I maintained eye contact and told myself that no matter how I felt about her now, I had to be wary. Good as she seemed, I understood I still needed to proceed with caution. If I had learned anything from all of this, it was that not everything is what it seems. Evil can come in all manner of pleasant disguises.

"Find who?" I asked, though I already knew the answer. I

desperately wanted to believe her.

"The one you love."

"Gwendolyn?" My voice caught as I said her name.

She didn't answer in words, only smiled as she inclined her head in affirmation.

"Where? Where is she?" I asked. "Tell me!" I began to raise my voice when she didn't answer straightaway.

I must have seemed overexcited and in truth, I was. She chose not to reply immediately, only looked at me with those soulful, patient eyes. I felt guilty and tried to hide my impatience though I knew I couldn't hide such things from her.

I took a deep breath and counted, before I asked again in a calm and reasoned voice. "Where is she?"

"The labyrinth," she answered.

The labyrinth? I thought. Oh, bloody hell, I suppose David Bowie is going to be there prancing about, telling me I remind him of the babe with the power of hoodoo.

Amelia laughed. It sounded like small, tinkling bells. Her face glowed as if the laughter infused her with light. "I assure you I speak the truth, though you might find it ridiculous."

"Okay, so she's in a labyrinth," I said, after telling myself I needed to listen to her, no matter how stupid it might sound. "Where would it be?"

"Patience," she said. "First, you must prepare."

"Listen," I said, my impatience was beginning to creep back and expose itself. "I don't have a lot of time here. Gwendolyn could be in trouble and I don't want to dance around, preparing for hell knows what, when I could be there right now, getting her out and going home. That's all I want to do. I want to go home, but I'll be damned if I'm going without her. Do you understand? I don't have time to waste on this crap."

"And what is time?" she asked in her quiet voice.

I sighed in annoyance and thought, we have ourselves a

philosopher here.

"Time you have, Harry, and it shan't be wasted if only you allow me to help you. Only you can make that decision."

"You know my name?" I wondered how she knew it without being told.

"Of course I know your name." She said it as if I shouldn't have been at all surprised. "I know a lot of things about you."

"What do you know about me?" I was skeptical.

She shook her head. "Not now. You say you do not want to waste any time and discussing it would do nothing but waste the time so precious to you."

"All right," I acquiesced. "How are you going to help me?"

"I can help by telling you how to get her back."

I did not answer straightaway. Though I was skeptical, I was willing to try anything to get Gwendolyn back. Everything that happened had broken through the wall of skepticism which normally surrounded me. I looked at Amelia and wondered if I was right to trust her. It seemed outrageous, but she knew things. It helped to put things into perspective because I was talking to, for all intents and purposes, a ghost.

"I cannot help unless you allow me to," she said.

"Okay, I'm listening." Why not give her a chance? I had nothing to lose except my life. If I didn't get Gwendolyn back, I didn't see much use for it. Amelia didn't seem to be against me, and that helped.

"She is of my blood, and the woman wants her destroyed," she said simply.

"Hold on there," I said. "You're talking blood and destruction. That doesn't sound good. Who is this woman?"

"The woman is Lydia, my mother. She wants to destroy Gwendolyn because she is pure and has remained so."

"Whoa, what does she have to do with anything? She has nothing to do with this."

"She is my relation," Amelia said calmly.

"I don't understand."

"By virtue of staying pure, Gwendolyn has the opportunity to break the curse which has plagued my family, also her family, for a long time."

"A curse? Family? What is this about her breaking a curse? What curse?" I fired the questions at her.

"Slow down, Harry. Remember, though it is short, you do have time. There is no need to rush things. Rushing will only bring you danger."

That sounded familiar. "Hell, I..." I stopped and took a breath. "Okay, so what kind of curse are you talking about and what do I have to do with it?"

Amelia smiled. It struck me then how very similar her face and expressions were to Gwendolyn's.

"Many years ago," she started, "a curse was placed on those descended from the woman, Lydia."

"I thought she was your mother?" I interrupted.

"I am her daughter, yes, but I do not wish to acknowledge her as such. As far as I'm concerned, my mother died and something else entered her." She waited for me to either ask another question, or be quiet.

"I'm sorry for interrupting."

"I can forgive you," she said and waited a beat before she continued. "It was foretold by Lydia that all females descended from her line, all those who were of her blood, would never find happiness and love. They would only know pain and suffering, and bring it to all unfortunate enough to get involved with them. Lydia was the one who created this curse, because she could not bear to see anyone happy and free. She wanted everyone to be as miserable as she was. She was very jealous of the happiness of others. Her curse would have died with my daughter, had she not survived."

"Survived? What are you talking about?" I asked, then I realized where it was going. "You don't mean?"

"Yes, Harry, but I shall get there in time."

I was starting to get fed up with this time issue. I felt by standing here and talking curses and history, it was not going to get me any closer to rescuing Gwendolyn. I wanted to see it through, however, because I realized I needed all the help I could get. And I wanted to believe Amelia could help me reach her. I replied, simply, "Okay."

"My father was a doctor who took care of the town. He worked here, sometimes, but usually he was at his office there. Lydia would often have breakdowns. My father thought it was her mind, but really, she was a heavy user of opium and absinthe. She thought no one knew, but I did. It made her crazy. My father would pore over all his books and try to learn what he could, so he could help her. Psychoanalysis was getting quite a bit of attention in some circles and he would spend hours, days, in research. He never got the breakthrough. It was all for his wife, whom he loved with his whole heart, but he never knew, or suspected, the truth.

"There were days when she seemed fine, but other days, her delusions would make her destructive. The minister said it was Satan who was getting into her. Demons. My father did not accept it, and thought he was the only one who could help her. He tried, but her violence only grew more toward everyone, but especially men. Mixed with the poison, she got an insatiable desire for..." She paused, trying to find proper words and I thought I could detect a slight blush. "The physical act," she finished.

"Sex," I offered.

"If you must be crass, yes." She gave me a look of repugnance that could only be a product of her time. It was slight, but I caught it.

"Oh, my father may have suspected these things were going on, but he never tried to prove it. I don't believe he wanted to know.

He did love her, so he allowed himself to be deceived. I believe he knew about her smoking and drinking, but treated it the same way. Self-denial is a potent disease of its own.

"It happened that he came home early, before dinner. This was quite unusual. I was in the kitchen, helping cook dinner when he came home. He caught her with a man, and was forced to acknowledge what was happening. He had let it boil inside of him for a long time. He killed the man here." She nodded toward the floor by my feet. I remembered it well and was curious if she saw me that day.

"It was then she lost her senses completely. She killed my father. He was only the first. Afterward, she would take in her paramours and kill them, too. She used various means, mostly poisons, or she would set up accidents. She not only killed them, but me and my son as well. The only one to survive was my daughter, and that was a miracle."

"Your daughter? You had children?" I shouldn't have been surprised, but I had assumed the children belonged to the woman, Lydia.

She laughed, saying, "Why do you look as if you had never heard of such a thing?"

"I don't..." Words didn't want to come out. "Who was their father?"

"My husband was their father, of course," she said.

I could tell I offended her. "I'm sorry, I didn't mean to upset you."

"No, I am not upset. Shortly after my daughter, Madeline, was born, my husband was killed. He was on the Maine when it exploded."

"The battleship?" I asked. "He was in the Navy?"

"Yes," she answered, and I could detect a little pride in her voice.

"Oh, I'm sorry." I felt I'd been insensitive to her loss.

She gave me a reassuring smile. "If I may continue?"

"Yes, please."

"Lydia tried to kill Madeline, she did. Tried to drown her upstairs in the tub. She was close to killing her and would have been successful if it weren't for my son walking in during the act. Lydia thought Madeline was already dead, so she turned attentions to him. She went to his room and William got the worst of it. After she killed him, she went into a kind of swoon. It must have been too much for her, and she fainted. I got there too late for poor, sweet William, but found Madeline. She was trying to catch her breath as she hung on the side of the tub. Knowing there wasn't much time, I bundled her up and gave her instructions to run as fast as she could to my uncle and his wife who lived about a mile away. He was my father's brother and I knew if Madeline could make it there, she would be safe.

"I told her, 'Run. Don't look back. Keep running until you get there.' I sent her with only her coat, and stayed behind to try to keep Lydia from following her. Thank goodness Madeline got there safely." She looked sad as she spoke of her daughter. Her eyes were focused on the floor where her father had died. She looked up at me and I thought I could see a tear forming in her eye.

"So, Gwendolyn is..." I didn't finish, not sure of the answer.

Amelia nodded. "My great-great granddaughter."

"I think I'm starting to understand," I said, then asked, "Were you ever able to find your daughter afterward?"

"Lydia attacked me shortly after I sent Madeline away. She demanded to know where she was, but I refused to tell her. I did not want to lose another child at the hands of that woman—that monster. She was certainly no longer my mother. She grabbed me by the neck and vowed that all of us, her female descendants, would be miserable and lead unfortunate lives. She knew not where Madeline went, only she survived. And it is why she cursed us. Then she..." Amelia undid the buttons of her dress and showed me her wounds without embarrassment. Dozens of stab wounds and gashes were scattered across her chest and abdomen. They looked fresh.

I swallowed back a lump and turned away from her. I didn't want to see it.

"Lydia finalized her curse by spilling her own blood."

"She killed herself?"

Amelia nodded. "The curse can only be broken by two with pure hearts. Gwendolyn is the first in our line to have attained that heart and it's possible she will be the last for a very long time, if ever. You, Harry, you are the key to break the curse which keeps my family in misery."

"Me?" I asked in astonishment. "No way. I'm not the one. I'm far from being pure. I like to smoke and drink. I curse, have violent thoughts, sometimes lustful thoughts. I'm a glutton. I could keep going on, but the list is endless." I laughed. "You've definitely got the wrong guy."

"You're human, Harry," she answered. "Your heart, your intentions. Those are pure. That's what matters. There is nothing impure about being human. Only what you choose to do with your humanity. That is the crux of the matter."

"I don't know." I wasn't sure what to believe. Purity and all. None of it was important. The only thing important was to find Gwendolyn. Find her safe and take her home.

"Do you love her?" Amelia asked.

"Yes, of course I love her," I said without hesitation.

"Can't you see? You did not have to think about an answer. It came to you right away. When you were given an easy way out, love kept you from taking it."

I gaped at her. I realized what she meant. "You closed and opened the door?"

"No, it wasn't I who did it. It was Lydia. She was tempting you in hopes you would give up and walk away."

I thought about what she said and asked, "What would have happened if I had walked away?" I didn't harbor any thoughts of doing it, but I was curious. "Nothing?"

"Yes, nothing. You would continue in your life and never return here."

"What about Gwendolyn? What would happen to her?"

"It would not be your concern."

"What do you mean, 'not my concern?' She is my concern and don't you get any ideas otherwise." My temper flared.

Amelia only smiled as I felt my face grow hot. "You see? You are exhibiting true love."

"Sure," I scoffed. "What's true love?"

"When you would do anything for someone, anything they need, to the point of giving your own life."

"That doesn't sound like anything I believe," I said.

"But you do, deep inside. It's why you didn't leave when given the opportunity. Emotions do not always seem rational. Sometimes we are tested as to our true feelings. This is your test."

"I don't like it, but you're right. I would do anything for her." I shuddered at the possibilities. I did not want to imagine my days without her. Life would always seem empty, topped with the fact I couldn't forgive myself for bringing her into this house and for whatever she might be suffering at the hands of that monstrous woman. Her death was a very real possibility, which would leave her blood on my hands. Amelia did say Lydia wanted her destroyed. There's nothing else it could mean.

"What do I need to do?" I asked.

"In the library, a book will open the door."

So, that was the way, I thought. "So, the long tunnel leads to the labyrinth?"

"Yes, that is the way, but before you go in, you need the book. It holds a map and things which will help you. The map will lead you to the center of the labyrinth, where Lydia is holding your love. She is hoping you go after her. She will try to destroy you also."

"Wow, that sucks. What about you?" I asked with concern.

"No need to worry about me," she said.

"But I do. I feel responsible."

"She doesn't know I am helping you. It wouldn't matter if she did. I am already in another existence."

"But why are you helping me?"

"Because if you succeed, then I can finally go to my rest. I will no longer be bound to this earth. By helping you, I help myself."

"I can live with that," I said, but realized too late it was a bad choice of words. "I didn't mean it."

"No, of course you didn't," she smiled.

"So, I need to go through the tunnel. How long is it? We were in it once, but it went on forever."

"It is not so very long. You needed to go in at the proper time. It wasn't time then."

"I can't see in there and I don't have a flashlight, or anything."

"Everything you will need is in the book. Keep going forward until you find the door. It opens to the labyrinth."

"Okay, so how do I defeat Lydia? I don't have any weapons, but I get the feeling they wouldn't do me any good if I did."

"No, conventional weapons wouldn't. You would defeat her and break the curse the same way you came here. Also, there is something you can use in the book."

"What are you saying? I just will the curse to break?" I couldn't believe it. Maybe the rest of it, but not this.

"It's not that easy."

"So, what do I do, exactly?"

"You have the power in you, Harry. Use your energy. Your energy will open the portal, into which she must go. When she goes through the portal, back to where she came from, the curse will be broken, but only if that happens."

"This is sounding stunningly like bullshit." I wasn't able to completely hide my skepticism, or the sneer that crept into my voice. "You've got to tell me, am I dreaming this?"

Amelia's face flared. "You are not dreaming and I can assure you, this is very real. It may be something you don't want to believe, but what you want and believe is beside the point. The point is, she believes it. Lydia believes and it is her belief which has kept this curse hanging over generations. It is a truth that if you believe something strongly enough, it can come into existence. The only way to defeat Lydia is to use her belief against her.

"She has been using you, Harry. To bring Gwendolyn to her so she can destroy the only way her curse can be broken. If that happens, no one can know how long it will take to have another chance."

"Using me?" I held my head in my hands and moaned. I wished this had never happened. I wished I had never continued. That I had not been a party to Gwendolyn's demise by bringing her to this house. I brought her here to face a terrible fate. "It's all my fault," I cried through my fingers.

"No, Harry. Remember, this can be turned for good. You can defeat Lydia and give the one you love a freedom she might never be able to enjoy otherwise. Not only will she enjoy the peace and comfort love and all good things bring, all of her people, now and generations after, will enjoy the same.

"It had to happen this way, don't you see? You are the only one who can defeat her. The only other option is to fail. There is no way to know how many more generations will suffer if you do."

"You're putting a whole lot on my shoulders right now, you realize." I hoped I was up to the task. I could only trust Amelia's faith in me was not in vain.

"Yes, I understand. It is why I am helping you. I believe you will be successful. I believe this because your love is pure and it is also strong, just as Gwendolyn's is. But neither of you can succeed alone. You must have each other. Lydia must see the love. Seeing the love you share will be enough to weaken her to the point where it will be possible to finish it and push her through the portal."

"You make it sound easy," I said.

"No, it won't be easy. Nothing worthwhile is ever easy," she answered.

"So, what? I just go and shove her through some portal and everything will be hunky dory?" I asked. "Sounds easy to me."

"Don't deceive yourself. She will fight you. She has the ability to hurt, and even kill you. It is important you understand this. You must protect yourself."

"How do I do that?" I asked.

"Your energy will protect and defend you. Use your mind and what is made available to you. Use your mind, for it is strong. Strong enough to create the energy you will need, but use it wisely."

"Okay." I sensed this was everything she needed to tell me.

"Harry, my rest and your lives are in your hands. Godspeed."

I watched her as she faded from view. I stood alone in the kitchen. There was a battle ahead of me I still did not understand. All I understood was I was frightened and there was a force that could do horrible things, even go so far as to cancel the Harry show forever. I wasn't looking forward to this, but I knew it had to be done. I didn't want to put Gwendolyn in any more danger than she was already in. I didn't want to get hurt. Maybe frightened wasn't such a good word.

I was scared shitless.

Chapter 37

I knew I had to follow through for Gwendolyn and myself. I had to fight this battle based on the beliefs of some woman who had lived over a century ago, and I wished there was another way to do this. I was alone and there was no help left.

The path I was about to walk would be both a blessing and a curse for me. I had to do my best to demolish the curse, so all that would be left was the blessing.

The responsibility lay heavy on my back. I wondered if I was truly up to the task, as Amelia believed. I hoped so.

I now knew the general direction I needed to go and a basic idea of what to do when I got there. I remembered there was a compass in the parlor and thought it could come in handy, so I went there to retrieve it. When I went in, I noticed the room was darker than before, more tattered. The piano was crooked on the floor with a leg broken off and some of the keys missing. It looked like a decaying mouth. The bookcase still stood, though the porcelain figures were smashed and the lenses of the binoculars were cracked. I found the compass, and it seemed to be in working order, so I put it in my pocket and ran to the library.

I burst in and went straight for the bookcases. I skimmed the shelves for something that stood out. The shelves were lined up just as I had left them. My eyes sped over each of the books until I saw one in a lighter shade of red than the others, a slight discoloration would have been easy to miss if I hadn't been looking for it. I pulled the book off the shelf and opened it. It wasn't a book at all, but a leather-covered wooden box. The outside edges were painted to resemble pages. If I had seen it in someone else's hand, I would not have doubted it was a book.

The inside of the box contained several pieces of yellowed parchment. I pulled them out cautiously, so as not to tear them, and carefully unfolded the pages. They contained information on portals and several spells, which I read through and considered. The last parchment was an intricately drawn map of the labyrinth. It looked complex, but with the map, it shouldn't be too hard to follow. The box also contained a small wand, only a few inches long. It was carved of wood and topped with a pointed quartz crystal. It matched the description I found in the parchments and I wondered why the doctor, who seemed to be the type to keep himself grounded in science, would have such things in his house. He certainly didn't seem to be one who would give in to flights of fancy or occult matters.

I picked up the wand and thought I felt something coming from it. A tingling sensation tickled the palm of my hand. I felt a little ridiculous, like I was playing some childhood game, but I reminded myself I was doing it to find Gwendolyn and save our lives. No matter how stupid I might feel, I would probably forget the hard parts and silly feelings when it was all over. If I survived. The thought sobered me enough to continue on.

"Lydia," I said to myself. I finally understood. She believed this kind of thing, so it seemed only natural these would have belonged to her and she had them hidden from her husband. I was sure her dabbling in matters she didn't fully understand had led to her final condition. She was seeking power she couldn't handle and got in too deep.

I read over the parchments again, particularly the incantations, and found the one to repeat over the small wand. I held it in my left hand and brought the parchment closer to my eyes. I pushed away all the feelings of ridiculousness and took a deep breath. I told myself this was necessary. No one was going to hear it and it would help me rescue Gwendolyn from whatever was holding her. All I knew for certain was her captor was no longer human.

I cleared my throat and read the incantation over the wand. The crystal began to glow and pulse like a heartbeat. I could feel the power and energy move up the polished shaft and into my arm, and fill my body with its energy. I no longer felt silly or stupid, and said the rest of the incantations, then folded them and put them in the pocket opposite the one holding the map. I slid the empty box back on the shelf and arranged the books to open up the hidden door. I waited until the door opened fully and stopped with a thud.

As I entered the opening, the wand began to glow brighter and broke through the blood-red glow that hung like a thick fog. A deep, horrible pulsing sound encircled me. It seemed to come from all directions. It was speaking, but it was impossible for me to understand it all. I thought I could make out a single word—"Leave."

I tried my best to ignore the sounds and kept my mind on the end result. It would have been easier to ignore if it hadn't been broken up by intervals of dead silence. I had a feeling of dread that only grew the further I traveled into the tunnel. Time seemed to have no meaning here. A minute seemed a year, and a year, a century. I could have been walking on a treadmill, and wouldn't have known it.

I heard a small squeak and felt the weight of a rat on my shoe as it brushed against my shin. Naturally, I screamed and started to run back the way I came. I stopped myself, and leaned my head against the damp, rough wall and grasped the wand as it hung at my side.

"Just a little rat," I said to myself. "Don't do this to yourself. You can't go back. Gwendolyn." I turned around and penetrated deeper into the tunnel. The wand's crystal lighted a small path in front of me.

To my immense relief, a heavy wooden door eventually appeared a few feet in front of me and I found the knob. It was small, dwarfed by the massive door, and seemed out of place. I turned the knob and pushed. I grunted with effort. It felt like the door had welded itself shut and stood gathering rust for a thousand years.

I felt it give a little and the more I pushed, the easier it opened. After the gap was wide enough for me to squeeze through, I stepped outside and was surrounded by the sounds of the night. A full moon hung high above me, thin clouds scudding across its surface. The wand's glow had dimmed, but the moon lighted my surroundings. I took the fresh air into my lungs and felt at least partly rejuvenated.

"You can't relax for a moment," I said. I had much to do and no idea of what lay ahead. Though the air perked me up some, I still felt tired, but I managed to convince myself I had plenty of energy and did not need a rest.

I was on a stone patio with tall, green shrubs surrounding me. They blocked the view of whatever else might lie beyond. An opening was ahead, about twenty yards. A large mosaic, depicting a compass rose, was embedded in the patio. The North point was directed at the opening in the shrubbery. I assumed this was the starting point of the labyrinth.

I took the compass out of my pocket and studied it against the mosaic. It matched. I pulled out the map and looked it over. I tried to memorize as much as I could. After I felt confident as to where to go, I folded it and put it back in my pocket.

I stood at the entrance and realized once inside, there would be no turning back. Though there were no doors out here to close me in, I knew barricades did not always have to be made of wood or impenetrable glass. I entered without any reluctance, for I knew ultimately, I would find Gwendolyn alive, and waiting for me.

Chapter 38

The labyrinth was wholly made of thick, well-trimmed shrubbery and stood at least eight feet tall. The stone floor was pitted and worn by long years of exposure to the elements, although it was swept clear of any loose leaves and twigs. I wondered who had been taking care of it, as nobody lived here except the spirits of the dead.

I stopped suddenly. I heard the sound of rustling leaves. I stood still and held my breath as I listened. Something was nearby. As it came closer, I heard more distinctly the sound of footfalls and ragged breathing.

It did not sound pleasant.

In an attempt to conceal myself, I slid into the shrubbery, only to realize too late the branches were covered with thick, sharp thorns. Nonetheless, I weaseled my way in and bit my lip to keep from crying out. I could taste the coppery tang of my own blood and only hoped whatever was approaching wouldn't be able to see, hear, or smell me.

As I stood, hidden, it stalked by. I saw its nose first, attached to a long snout. When it came into view, I saw it was the biggest rat I had ever seen. It was easily four feet in length, not counting the tail. I gasped and backed further into the shrubs. The thorns bit further into me. The giant rat turned, stood on its haunches and stared me in the eye.

The rat hissed; its whiskers twitched furiously as a defeated moan escaped my lips. It opened its mouth and exposed rows of sharp, yellowed teeth I was sure could cut through me like razors. My legs trembled and I feared they would give out. I raised my wand. The thorns tore my skin as I brought the wand down on the rat's nose. Its eyes registered surprise as its head was knocked back, like I had hit it with a brick. I came out of the shrubs and slapped it across the face with the wand.

The rat snarled in angry pain and snapped at me. It grabbed a piece of my shirt as I tried to jump out of its way. Its eyes were wild as and it reared back to strike again. I swiped the wand at the creature. A streak of bright light burst from the crystal tip and struck the rat. It tumbled back a couple yards. It took both the rat and myself a moment to recover.

The rat shook itself and crouched to jump again. I stepped back, pointed the wand. It fired again and hit the rat between the eyes. It screamed as it melted away.

I began to breathe, not realizing I had been holding my breath. I held the wand up in front of me and stared at it. Despite its size, it was evidently a formidable weapon. One I would need, for if there were one giant rat, there surely would be more. I was glad I hadn't disregarded the wand, for if I had, I wouldn't have a chance.

After the adrenaline wore off, I felt the sting of the scrapes on my face and arms, inflicted by the thorns. I looked over the wounds and saw they were superficial. It was obvious one could not cheat the labyrinth by going through the shrubs. They were too thick and the thorns too plentiful and sharp. It would take more time to try and cut through them than to go through the thing properly. The idea of taking a shortcut was out.

After the run-in with the giant rat, I knew I was ill-prepared for what could be just around the corner. My only focus was to find Gwendolyn and get out of this place. It was this desire that gave me the determination to face anything I might meet. Will got me here, and will would get me out. I knew there would be more of those creatures stalking the labyrinth, but I couldn't forget there might be other things as well. I hoped I could make it. These things fed off of fear, so I had to keep my own at bay. If telling myself there was nothing real to fear would alleviate it, then I'd tell myself this constantly, whether I believed it or not.

I checked the map and compass again to make sure I was on the right path. It looked like I was probably a little under a quarter of the way to my goal. I stowed the map and started again. I had been moving through without incident, I turned a corner and as I moved down the path, I realized I had taken a wrong turn somewhere. I was at a dead end. I cursed myself silently for not paying attention and started for my pocket when an enormous creature materialized from the thorny shrubs in front of me. I managed to stumble back a few paces before I froze in place.

The creature approached. It had a single bloodshot, jaundiced eye in the center of its head. It was bigger than the rat I had encountered and looked similar to a wolf. Only twice as big as a regular wolf. Its body was slightly transparent with a bloody, otherworldly glow. Its large yellowed fangs seemed sharp and real enough. I watched as it stalked toward me. Its head swung low, left and right. It seemed to be searching more with its nose than its eye. A rumbling growl emanated from its massive frame.

I gathered my wits and backed away from the wolf-creature. It raised its head, it snarled, crouched low and sprang toward me. I slung myself against the green wall. The thorns bit into my flesh again. The creature stumbled as it landed. It turned around and faced me again. Its eye glowed with rage. Its mouth drooled hungrily as if it planned on having me for dinner. It crouched again to pounce. I pointed the wand and let the energy shoot from it. The burst hit the creature in the chest as it leapt.

"Shit!" I yelled and spun out of its way. I realized my attack had only made it angry. The wand did not seem to faze it in the least. I didn't want to take a chance, so I slammed the wand down and let the energy shoot out. It was weaker this time. It hit the creature on the nose, but didn't cause any real damage. I realized I had to wait for the wand to recharge before I used it again. Perhaps magical weapons weren't auto-fire.

The creature stalked around me. Neither of us took our eyes off the other. I knew it was about to attack me again and I held my breath. I hoped my little weapon would follow through.

The creature lunged toward me a few times, but appeared to be weaker, and I was able to avoid its advances. I hoped the wand had enough time to recharge and fired it. It hit the creature in the middle of the chest. It yelped and dissolved into mist and drifted into the air.

"How many of these things are here?" I asked. I knew I should expect many more and prepare for it. It was obvious that though the wand was powerful, I would have to rely on my own power to fully succeed in my quest.

My body stung with the scratches from the thorns, many of them one on top of the other. I ignored the pain as much as I could and looked over the map. I found where I had missed the turn and went back.

Not only did my body hurt, my will was weakening the longer I trudged through the labyrinth. I knew I had to push myself further and keep focused on my reason for going on.

The air grew thicker the further I went in. Several times, gathering clouds, dark and pendulous, swarmed through the sky. They blocked the moonlight and cast the path into darkness. During the moments the path grew too dark to see, the crystal would glow and lend enough light to make my way.

As I walked, I heard the eerie sounds of a dark forest, an owl hooting, crickets chirping. Giant creatures smelling my blood and stalking in for the kill. I stopped often to check the map. I didn't want to make another wrong turn and lose more time.

The farther I went in, the more effort it required to move, as if my feet were bogged down in mire. Something was trying to weaken me and keep me from accomplishing my goal. Just ahead in the periodic darkness, I saw the red glow of two eyes, and I heard something slither and hiss. The eyes grew bigger. I braced myself for another fight.

The creature advanced to within a few feet, and the face of another giant rat came into view. It grinned evilly with its sharp, yellowed teeth. I backed up, only to have my foot catch on some-thing behind me. I went down on my rump and heard a loud hiss in my ear. I turned my head slightly and came eye to eye with a large snake. A forked tongue darted from its angled head inches from my nose. Instinct took over and I grabbed the snake behind its head and rolled just as the rat attacked. It sank its teeth into the snake's midsection.

The snake flailed its whole body in pain. It twisted and pulled against my fingers. I rolled and jumped to my feet, still holding onto the snake, whose life was fast draining away. My feet felt as if they were stuck in glue and the rat seemed to know I was in trou-ble.

I threw what was left of the snake at it as a distraction while I used my wand to fire energy at it. It dodged the bolt, as if it ex-pected my move. I thought I could hear it laughing at me. I moved as best as I could and we went in circles, both waiting for an op-portunity to strike. The rat grew impatient, reared up and threw itself forward.

A claw caught my arm as I tried to turn away.

I cursed loudly, but saw it had landed in the mire and had the same trouble with moving as I did. I took the chance and brought my elbow down on its neck and shoved the wand into it. The crystal's sharp point sliced through the matted fur and into its flesh. The rat squealed, loud and shrill, as its eyes went wide. I felt energy rush into the rat and it exploded. Pieces of rat guts flew everywhere, including on me.

"Son of a bitch!" I screamed in disgust. I didn't bother to suppress the gorge coming up from my stomach.

I tried to clean myself off the best I could, which wasn't much at all. I managed to clear most of it from my face and hands with some of the leaves from the shrubs.

"That really sucked. Hope I won't have to do that again," I said. I still felt queasy.

I trudged down the mucky path and found more solid ground at another turn. I stopped and allowed myself to rest a moment and check the map. The sky stayed mostly clear, and according to the map I was more than halfway there. I wondered how much longer this would take and how many more obstacles would be thrown at me. I tried not to think too much about it and took my time to make sure I went the right way. If I just stayed calm and focused, I would finish and be able to take Gwendolyn home.

I heard them before I saw them.

They growled loudly, menacingly. When I rounded the corner, they were standing there. Three of the huge, one-eyed, long-fanged wolf monsters drooled and snarled at me. They eyed me, their heads low and ready to pounce, eyes full of sadistic glee. They bared their fangs and foaming saliva dripped from the pointed tips, their lips pulled back in evil smiles. They methodically encircled me, so I couldn't escape. Their measured movements prepared them to pounce at the opportune time.

I stepped back. I didn't take my eyes off them and went over my options. I discovered, without surprise, I didn't have any, save to fight.

"Shit, what do I do?" I muttered. All three eyes laughed at me.

I couldn't run, for surely they were faster. I couldn't hide, for there wasn't any place where they couldn't see my movements, and I wasn't about to jump back into the shrubs only to tear myself up and grow weaker. I didn't even have a stick to beat them off with. Well, I had the wand, but what good was it against three of them?

"Your energy will protect and defend you," I heard Amelia's voice come back to me. I felt the wand, still gripped tightly in my hand. Of course, I had to work with what I had. Not trying would do nothing but get me killed and would be the end of everything. I just had to remember patience and timing.

I focused my mind and stared down the wolves and tried to hide as much of my fear as I could. I jumped toward them and re-leased a very loud, very bad war cry. I swung the wand in an arc, as if I were sweeping a sword across my enemies. A bow of energy came from the wand in a steady stream. It hit all three creatures. They stumbled backward, head over tail, releasing a chaotic cho-rus of yelps. I looked at the wand and back at the wolves in awe. I don't know what I had expected, but certainly not that.

The creatures rolled over, shook their heads and crouched in attack positions. To state the obvious, they were very, very pissed.

I focused again. I did not have time to reflect. The confidence I had in myself and the small weapon I held in my hand rose.

The creature in front leapt at me, his fangs bared. I attempted to attack with the wand again, but it was too soon and the energy was faint. It didn't seem to faze the creature and I juked to one side, able to dodge it. The other two attacked immediately behind the first. My body twisted. I tried to avoid them, but wasn't able to dodge both. One gashed my arm from inside the elbow to a few inches above my wrist. I felt the blood soak into my shirt. It hurt like hell, but I didn't have time to concern myself with my injuries. I had to allow time for the wand to recharge. It felt like an impos-sible situation.

The monsters uttered throaty chuckles as they encircled me again on the narrow pathway. I was at a disadvantage. We watched each other, both sides waiting for the other to make a mistake. I began breathing in a rhythm. I could smell their unpleasant musky scent as I inhaled through my nose. I realized some of it was coming from me. It was a fetid smell of wet, dirty dog and rat parts. It made me angry.

I could feel the energy build up. It moved through my arms, my fingers, and into the wand. I glared at the creatures and released a loud bark as I swung the wand again, willing its energy toward them. The bolt shot from the wand brightly and cut through all three creatures and blinded me for a moment.

They yipped and yelped. One dissolved into the air, leaving two of them. One was weakened considerably, but I couldn't gauge the other's condition. I knew I would have to focus more on the one, as I didn't feel as much of a threat coming from the weaker wolf.

The weaker came at me, jaws open wide, and it was hard to tell if it was yawning, or preparing to bite down on my flesh. I dodged and swung my fist as I turned. I connected to the side of its face. It appeared stunned, but not without a price. I felt like I had hurt my hand more than I hurt its jaw.

The other came at me directly from behind and I threw my foot out. It landed in the middle of its chest. The creature crumpled, the wind knocked out of it.

I couldn't feel the blood running over my arm from the wound anymore, so I figured it wasn't as bad as I had thought. It was a good thing. Too much soda, coffee and fatty foods may spell clogged arteries and heart attacks later in life, but at this point, it was possible it kept me from bleeding to death.

Both creatures struggled as they got back on their feet. They did not look as confident. I had enough time to build up energy and used it against the weaker one. It melted into the air and left me with only the one to contend with. The last creature leaped and growled a lot. It was quite a show and since it was much easier to avoid at this point, I let it do its deeds.

I didn't want to play with it for too long, lest it be able to build up more strength. I slapped at it, punched it a few times as I let the wand's energy replenish. The creature circled and started to run and jumped at me once more. I fired at it and it evaporated without so much as its breath on my skin.

I dropped to the ground, exhausted. I rested a couple of minutes and used the time to check my map again. There wasn't much farther to go, so I rested a bit more and hoped there weren't any more of those creatures to gang up on me. I wasn't sure I had the stamina for more; but then, I had no choice, if I was going to see this through. I needed to find Lydia and open the portal to send her off to wherever it was malevolent spirits went. I knew if I found her, I would find Gwendolyn.

My muscles ached and my wounds burned as salty sweat seeped into them. I couldn't focus on that. I had to move and get to Gwendolyn before it was too late.

The sky grew cloudier with large, grey layers blocking the moonlight at longer intervals. They allowed the moon to peek out for only seconds at a time. There was a distant rumble that sounded like thunder. As the path had darkened considerably, I used the wand to read over the map one last time. The wind battered the page so it was difficult to hold onto. An unpleasant smell hit me as the wind blew past. Though I could not discern what the scent was, I knew I must be close to my goal.

I made my way to the center of the labyrinth without further incident. I got caught a few times in the shrubbery. I ignored the pain and pushed onward until I saw a glow emitting from an opening. It cast a red hue, as if it were a gaping wound. A deep bass sound, prophesying impending doom, whispered beneath like a motion picture score.

This was it. I could feel it, a mixture of excitement and terror as I approached the opening, where the glow was strongest. I edged my way to the corner and peeked around while I tried to remain invisible. I didn't see anything ready to jump out at me, so I went in.

The inner circle of the labyrinth was large. Weeds fought their way up through cracks in the mosaic floor. At the far end of the enclosure, a lion's head fountain gushed clear water from its mouth. In the center stood a rim of stones surrounding a pit.

I knew Gwendolyn was there. I could feel her.

Chapter 39

I started toward the well. I almost got close enough to peek inside when she materialized from out of the tall hedges. She levitated about two feet off the ground. Lydia's movements were smooth as she glided toward me. Not wasting any time, she shot at me, a bright orange orb that looked like a ball of fire. I ducked away from it just in time as it whizzed past my ear, missing me by no more than an inch. The ball exploded as it hit the hedge and the leaves began to smolder. There was no doubt left in my mind Lydia was able to hurt me, for I could smell my own singed hair.

Lydia shrieked loudly, angry she had missed, and shot another ball at me. This one was much weaker.

Good—she, too, needed time to recharge. I quickly calculated the best plan to take advantage of this new information.

I moved around the circular arena, spotted an opportune moment and fired my wand at her. It impacted her arm and she let out a hiss.

"You will die!" she seethed.

I smirked at her in challenge. She would definitely follow through on her threat. I tried to suppress my fear.

"Where's the girl?" I demanded.

"Dead! The girl is dead!"

"You lie!"

Lydia flew at me and fired another ball without taking enough recharge time. Her shot went wild and missed me completely. She didn't wait long enough between attacks to sufficiently build up her energy.

"You will never get her! She belongs to me!"

"She belongs to no one but herself," I said. "If she decides to come with me, or stay here, it's her decision. Not yours."

Lydia snarled as she floated around the pit. I watched her and waited for an opening. She looked more ghoulish than she had appeared before. Her clothing draped off her in tattered rags and her face was sunken, which showed the contours of her skull. This was not the handsome woman I had seen inside the house. Lydia's features expressed raging anger, intensifying as she swooped toward me.

She's quick, I thought. I raised my arm as a last-resort defense. She cut through me, felling my body with a chill so strong I gasped and shivered. I raised myself and gathered all my strength as I shot her with the wand. I hit her in the abdomen and she screamed shrilly, as she fired at me again. The ball hit me in the shoulder like a searing flame. I twisted with the impact and suppressed a cry as I fell to the ground.

I gritted my teeth, tried to ignore the burning pain and not show that she had hurt me, though it was an intensity I had never experienced before. Dread threatened to freeze my will, fear she was too strong, and this would end in disaster. I had to rally.

"You will give me the girl," I demanded, in as commanding a voice as I could muster.

Lydia only laughed. It was a loud, grating sound. It rattled my nerves. I refused to let it get to me, and hid my emotions from her, though I felt she could see right through me. I knew I would have to open the portal, and soon. I realized with horror I didn't have any idea how I would do it. I frantically scoured my mind for the formula I thought I had memorized.

She seemed to intuit my predicament, but I was able to turn it to my advantage and provoked her to attack again. I knew her attacks would grow weaker if I could make her continually fire at me. It was a risky move, but I had no other options.

Lydia must have caught on to my plan. She held her fire. We launched into a battle of wills. I resorted to taunting her and tried to rile her up enough to attack without weighing the consequences. I refused to strike first. I knew I needed all my energy to open the portal. My life, and Gwendolyn's, depended on my success.

Without warning, she hurtled herself at me. I threw myself to the ground. The wand flew out of my hand as I slammed onto the stone floor. I frantically scrambled to reach the wand before she could attack again. My fingers felt the smooth wood and I tried to grasp it as her fireball struck my arm. White hot pain shot through my entire body. She cackled with glee.

My arm was blistering horribly, but I ignored it. I grabbed the wand and fired as soon as my fingers closed around it. A strong bolt of bright, white light flew out and hit Lydia in the chest. It propelled her forcefully into the hedge and she screamed.

Her eyes narrowed. She fired again. The ball was weak and wobbly, easy to avoid. As I leapt aside, I felt a sliver of hope. I suddenly heard my own voice reciting the incantation inside my head. I began to shout out the words. Lydia's eyes grew wild as she realized what I was doing, and she threw another attack at me. I dodged it without losing the rhythm of the incantation. As she launched another haphazard attack, a portal began to open. It grew larger as I willed it into existence, visualizing Lydia being sucked into its depths.

The portal grew so powerful it started to pull me in. I grabbed onto a protruding rock and clung to it with all my strength. Lydia screamed in surprise. She hissed and fought against the portal's force. I fought like mad to keep the portal open and myself out of it. I expended tremendous amounts of energy and it weakened my will.

The portal began to shrink.

Lydia regained her power as I was losing mine. Her pale lips formed a wicked grin as the portal weakened and the odds tilted in her favor.

I fought against resignation as the portal grew smaller, but feared it was too late.

"I'm sorry, Gwendolyn," I whispered. "I can't do this." The effort I exerted was taking its toll.

Lydia grinned at me diabolically and laughed. "You are both mine!"

"Harry!" I heard my name cried out. It was close, but sounded far away.

"Gwendolyn?" I gathered enough energy to call her name.

"Harry!" she cried again.

I felt a new strength surge through me. I channeled the energy back into the portal. It grew quickly in size and strength.

Caught off guard, Lydia took her focus off me for a moment. Able now to stand the force of the portal, I stood and glared at her as I raised the wand. I concentrated all my strength and shot a mighty bolt of energy at Lydia. It hit her full force. The impact catapulted her into the depths of the portal. It closed behind her with a greedy, sucking noise. To be on the safe side, I recited the incantation to close the portal, although it seemed to have determined on its own its work was done.

The spirit of the evil woman was annihilated.

I called Gwendolyn's name as I went to the edge of the pit and looked down.

"Gwendolyn," I said with relief.

"Harry, get me out of here," she cried when she saw me.

"How do I do that?"

"Like I'm supposed to know?" She glared up at me.

The pit looked to be somewhere between ten and fifteen feet deep, with mostly smooth walls. It would have been difficult, maybe impossible to climb out, and it was too wide to crawl out using both back and legs.

"Is there a way to climb out?" I asked, but I already knew.

"No," she answered. "I think I sprained my ankle. Is there a rope, or something?"

"Here?" I looked around, but didn't see anything that would make a good rope. The shrubbery was too thorny and stout to just pull off a branch.

"Well?" she asked impatiently.

"I'm thinking," I said, as I pondered the situation.

I hit upon an idea and only hoped it would work. I stripped out of my clothes, down to my boxers and tied my shirt to the leg of my jeans.

"Take off your clothes," I yelled down at her.

"Are you crazy?" she shot back. "This is not the time to be getting naked."

"It is if you want to get out of this thing."

"I'm not taking off my clothes, Harry." She crossed her arms and looked away.

"Come on, Gwendolyn. I'm not trying to get kinky or any-thing. There's no one else around, so you don't have to worry about any peepers."

"How do you know?" she questioned, still in her defensive stance.

"I just want to tie them together to make a rope," I explained. "It's the only thing I can think of. Maybe you can come up with something better."

She didn't say anything, but I could tell she was thinking.

"Do you think I enjoy this?" I asked, as I dropped my

makeshift rope down the shaft. It wasn't long enough.

"Yeah, I think you're enjoying this immensely," she said.

"Well, I'm not. I just want to get us out of here."

"Fine," she said, and started to undress, though it seemed she was taking her sweet time with it.

"Throw them up, and I'll make sure they hold." I looked down at her, using all my strength to not give a teasing whistle. It just wasn't the time for it.

"Stop looking at me," she demanded.

"I can't help it."

"You better start helping it, or you'll regret it."

"Okay, okay. I'll stop." I pulled my clothes out and turned until she was finished.

"Done," she said, as her clothing landed next to the pit.

I tied them together firmly, and tested each knot. I was glad she wasn't wearing a skirt, or something that would have made the whole rope-of-clothing operation pointless. The fact she was wearing a light jacket was an added bonus. The T-shirt had some give, but I thought it would hold well enough to do the job. I was certain Gwendolyn didn't weigh enough to tear it apart, but I still needed to be careful.

I let the rope down and breathed a sigh of relief when it proved to be long enough for her to get a good grip on it.

"Use your feet to climb a little," I said.

"My ankle hurts," she complained.

"Try, could you?"

"Okay, I'll try."

I began to pull on the makeshift rope and I heard her suck in air as she put pressure on her ankle. I pulled as hard as I could. I could feel the burn in my muscles as the rope inched its way up.

"Are you okay?" I asked.

"I'm fine," she answered, but I could tell she was in pain.

I reeled in the rope and felt it give a little. Gwendolyn cried out, but it still held.

"Are you okay?" I asked again.

"I said, I'm fine!" she yelled. "You better hurry, because I'm not sure if this thing is going to hold much longer."

I wrapped the leg of my jeans in my hand and moved carefully to the rim of the pit. I leaned over and tried to look into it. I could see her, a little more than halfway up. I pulled up some more and heard a rip.

"It's tearing," I said.

"No shit? I think maybe I can reach. Give me your hand."

I wrapped the slack around my waist, pulled some more, and reached for her with my free hand as I strained to hold onto the rope with the other. I grabbed her hand and released the rope. She tried to use her feet to climb and I pulled. I ignored the pain, though it intensified the longer I held on. Finally, Gwendolyn threw herself over the rim of the pit.

I reached my hands underneath her arms and pulled her the rest of the way up. I fell over backward as she was freed and tumbled on top of me.

"Are you okay?" I asked.

"You keep asking that, but I think so. You really stink."

"I know."

"Are you okay?"

"I'm super." I lied, but I was happy to see her again.

"I don't believe you," she said.

"Why not?"

"Because I can tell when you're lying."

"So, you're saying it's impossible for me to lie to you?"

She smiled. "That's what I'm saying, so don't start now."

"I'll be okay, but if we stay like this, I'm afraid that..."

"Pervert," she huffed as she rolled off of me. "You seriously need to get a bath. You're all smelly and slimy."

"Yeah, I had a little run-in with something."

I went to the fountain and tried to wash as much of the gunk off of me as I could and tried to take it easy around my wounds. It wasn't a real shower, but it was better than nothing.

After my quasi-bath, I went back to Gwendolyn. "Let me look at your ankle."

"What are you, some kind of foot fetishist?" She waggled her eyebrows at me, but I could tell she was channeling her immense relief at being rescued into a lame attempt at humor.

"Let's be serious a moment, okay?" I squatted down and started to untie her shoe. She sucked in her breath as I pulled the shoe off her foot. "Okay?" I hesitated.

"No, but you go right ahead, smelly boy," she said, through gritted teeth.

After my brief examination, I said, "It doesn't look great, but I don't think you'll die from it. Just a sprain."

"Thanks, Doc. I feel so much better now."

I ignored her sarcasm. "We'll have to wait until we get back to have this attended to properly."

"Are we going to get back?" she asked, her voice suddenly small.

I looked at her and saw doubt in her eyes. "Yeah," I said. "We're going to get back."

"How?" she asked, and I knew she was still afraid. I didn't want to have her hurt anymore. I hoped this experience would be something she could get over, but I knew a part of her would never forget.

I was relieved to see her mostly unharmed as we sat there in the middle of the labyrinth in nothing but our underwear. The moon broke through the dissipating clouds and shed its pale light once again as the stars lit the sky around it like a million candles.

After a moment, I looked over at her and commented on her pink, lace-trimmed bra by saying, "Cute."

"Shut up," she snapped.

Chapter 40

"So, what happened to you?" I asked. Curiosity got the best of me as I stood with my back to her so she could finish dressing.

"What do you mean, what happened?"

"When you disappeared. What I saw was you getting thrown around and some shadow thing came along and ate you. That's what it looked like. You were just gone after."

"Honestly, I don't remember," she said, as she examined her clothing. "Oh darn, my shirt's all stretched out."

I watched as she fiddled with her shirt, which had stretched out so the collar hung off her shoulder. "I think it's a good look for you, but I'll buy you a new one."

"You don't have to."

"I'm going to do it anyway. You don't remember anything?" I felt relieved she seemed to have blanked out most of it.

"No. I only remember the very beginning. I guess I must have passed out or something, because all I really remember is waking up in that hole."

"You're lucky then."

"How am I lucky? I don't feel very lucky."

"All sorts of craziness went on," I said quietly.

"I'll just take your word for it. What do we do now?"

"I guess we go back."

"Home?"

"Let's hope."

"I don't want to hope, I just want to go home."

"Me too. We'll get there," I assured her. "Can you walk if I let you lean on my shoulder?"

"But you stink."

"Yeah, I know, but I've done all I could about it for now. With your ankle, you probably should just bear it. My stink, I mean, not your weight on your foot."

"Okay." She rested her arm on my good shoulder. We took a few test steps, which she handled without complaint.

We walked through the labyrinth slowly, Gwendolyn limped along and used my shoulder for balance. I was wary and kept my eyes and ears open for those creatures to pounce out again. The farther we went back toward the house, the more I felt assured they had disappeared with Lydia, though I still held some suspicion.

It remained quiet, save for the occasional hoot of an owl, which was much less ominous this time around.

"Not to sound weird or anything, but this is nice," Gwendolyn said.

"What, this labyrinth?"

"Yeah. I wouldn't mind having one someday. Have a place with enough land to build a decent sized one. Not as scary, though."

"It's better now than it was on the way in."

"That bad?"

I nodded. "You don't want to know."

We managed to make it through without incident to the big, heavy door. I looked back and felt another chapter close. "Lean on the wall while I open the door," I said.

"Where did you find this?"

"It was what was at the end of the tunnel in the library."

"Oh."

We went into the passageway, which was dark. I expected the wand to light the way, but it no longer worked.

"Do you have anything for light?" she asked.

"No, I guess not. Why, are you afraid of the dark?"

"Not anymore," she answered. "Not as long as you're with me." She hugged my arm and I could feel her smile. I blushed, thankful for the darkness that hid it.

We reached the end of the passage and went back into the library. I put the parchments and the wand back into the box disguised as a book and then replaced everything so the bookcase would slide back and close the passageway, putting an end to that part of the nightmare.

"Wow," Gwendolyn said quietly.

I turned to see what she was 'wowing' about. The library was lighted by lamps and a warm fire blazed in the fireplace. The floor was covered with lush, decorative rugs and the room was inviting, with the furnishings looking as if they were all new and well cared for. There was no dust, nor any cobwebs. Nothing to tarnish the allure of the place.

"This is what it must have been like before," I said.

"It's beautiful."

"That it is," I agreed. "I should go put this back where I found it." I fingered the compass in my palm. I silently thanked it for leading me the right way.

We left the library and went into the foyer. The area was bright, the stained-glass window intact. Shades of blue and green surrounded a sun, colored with reds, oranges and yellows. The staircase was even more majestic than I had imagined it to be.

"Do you suppose we went back in time?" Gwendolyn asked.

"Maybe. I don't know," I said, but I thought it was a good

possibility.

We went into the parlor and I made Gwendolyn sit down in one of the chairs. She sighed contentedly and allowed herself to sink into the comfortable cushions in front of the warm fireplace.

I placed the compass back on the shelf, and ran my hand over the smooth wood. It no longer coated my fingers with dust. "Are you ready?" I asked Gwendolyn.

"I guess."

I helped her to her feet and we returned to the foyer. The portraits hung in their places on the wall, untouched by age and dust. I looked at the portrait of Lydia. She was the same woman who was so intent on destroying Gwendolyn and me, but I found I held no grudge. I was ready to just put it all behind me.

"I think I could live here," Gwendolyn said.

I smiled. I remembered I had felt the same thing before.

"I couldn't." I said it with the knowledge it was the truth. I had imagined myself living within Her walls, what seemed to be ages ago, but with everything I had gone through and witnessed, I realized She was better off left in the past. It was better for Her only to be visited sometimes in dreams.

She was indeed beautiful, but I knew I could never live here. I would rather be back home. Back to my simple life where all I had to worry about was the occasional annoying customer instead of phantoms, strange creatures and houses that came from nowhere. Back to my life without curses and horror.

I heard the door open and I turned to see Amelia come in from the dining room. The boy appeared from behind her with his little hand clasped around Amelia's fingers. He was unmarked and had a bright smile. Amelia looked beautiful, despite being pale, but it was to be expected.

"Hi," I said.

"Hello, Harry."

"This is Gwendolyn," I introduced her.

"Yes, I know." She smiled and looked at the little boy beside her, her face full of love. "This is my son, William."

"Hi, William," I said, and waved at him.

"Hi," he shyly replied, then hid himself behind the folds of Amelia's dress.

"How do you know me?" Gwendolyn asked. "Who are you?"

"This is Amelia," I answered. "She's the reason we met. You're related to her."

"I am?"

Amelia didn't say anything, only smiled at her. I wondered if Gwendolyn noticed how similar they were, but maybe she didn't. Sometimes you're too close to something to really see it.

"Thank you," Amelia said to me. "Thank you for everything. I can now go to my rest." She turned to Gwendolyn and said, "And you, you are free now."

"Free from what?" Gwendolyn asked.

"The things that have haunted you. You no longer need to fear."

"I don't understand."

"You will."

"I should thank you, too," I said.

"No, there is no need. It was meant to be. Some things we are destined for and it is up to us whether we follow. Remember, in the end, there is no such thing."

"No such thing as what?" Gwendolyn asked.

I laughed at the confused expression on her face and took her into my arms. "No such thing as coincidence," I said. I held her close as Amelia, William and the house began to fade away. I closed my eyes and said, "Let's go home."

Epilogue

Gwendolyn and I ended up back in my apartment, instead of some strange locale in Carson. It was a nice feeling, not to be lost; to be safe at home. I know I made good on my promise, the one I made to Amelia, so long ago. The promise I would help.

In turn, she has helped me in ways I couldn't have imagined. It's because of her I am able to hold the girl of my dreams in my arms. I will offer my thanks to her every day for the rest of my life. I hope Amelia is truly at peace now. She deserves it, especially after all this time.

Gwendolyn and I are together, but it is more serious than you might think. We're planning on getting married in a few months. I still wake up some mornings and think this is all a dream. We're going to have our ceremony outdoors, with my brother, Jim, as best man and Mrs. Weatherman as matron of honor. It's going to be as perfect as we can make it. (Belinda and Mark are not on the guest list.)

After we're married, we're going to stay here in Carson. Sure, there are many other places better, but this is home for us. We've grown attached to it. We'll make our home right here, in my apartment building. You may think I'm talking crazy. Gwendolyn wouldn't let me make our home in a place where the floors are missing and everything, and you'd be right. Don't worry. I'm not crazy. I'm buying the building and having it restored.

How can I afford it on my bookstore salary, you ask? I'll put your mind at ease. I haven't turned to drug dealing or anything. It's legitimate.

A few days after the horrific events, I received a phone call from some big lawyer from the city who said he was handling Gary's estate. I never imagined Gary with an estate, so I thought the guy was nuts. When I think estate, I think of a huge mansion with guest houses, servants and big fancy gardens.

It took the guy a while to convince me, but it appears Gary had made out a will not too long after his diagnosis and left almost everything to me. He also left a good chunk of change to a gay rights organization.

I would expect that from Gary. He was a guy who had a big heart and a deep concern for people. He was a staunch believer in freedom and equal rights for all people. I can't remember him ever turning away anyone who asked him for help.

Besides the LGBTQ Coalition, I was the only one named in his will. Something to the tune of four million dollars. I had no idea Gary was worth that much. His financial affairs, and his personal ones, I never meddled in. Money wasn't something he spoke of, so I was touched by his final gesture of friendship. I still get sad thinking of him. He was my best friend and I'll never forget him, nor will I forget his big heart and how good he always was to me, even after his passing.

Gwendolyn got a letter from her sister. It had been several years since she'd heard from Bella. She always worried about her. Now they talk all the time on the phone. Women and phones; how did they ever survive before they were invented? It's nice to see them close again. It seems Bella fell in love, gave up drinking, and got her life together. Everyone's happy. I'll get to finally meet Bella at our wedding.

I bought my brother a houseboat. He was ecstatic. Got all teary-eyed and mushy on me. Not the alpha male behavior I would normally expect from my brother, but it was nice to see he was touched. He demanded we immediately spend a weekend on it, drinking beer and fishing.

The house? I never saw Her again. Once or twice in my dreams, but it was fleeting, more like a memory than a calling. Nothing more.

There was a reason for all of it. Though there was pain involved, I was grateful. They say if you go through hell to get something, it makes you appreciate it all the more, and it seems to be true. Needless to say, I'm not going to shed any tears or lose sleep over the loss. She's at rest now, and those who once occupied Her are at peace. I am at peace.

Maybe I did struggle for it. Maybe I did suffer, but in the end, it was without a doubt worth it. Now I have everything a man could ever want. I have a wonderful girl who is not only beautiful, but fantastic in every way. I love her and for some reason I can't fathom, she loves me back. I have a place to call home. I have great friends who are caring and supportive. I am happy about the choices I've made in life.

Fate? Destiny? Do I believe in those things? Maybe I do believe in fate. Maybe discovering the house was my destiny; it led me to now. I made the choices that got me here. I have love, happiness, and freedom. All of it is mine.

It may be my destiny, but none of it is a coincidence.

AE
AAA

Acknowledgments

Beethoven said, "Art demands of us that we don't stand still." An artist creates, but to share his creation with the world, he must rely on a number of people doing all the heavy lifting while the artist gets to sit back and revel in the glory. I'd like to rectify this here. Call it, "writer's guilt."

For this second printing, my deepest thanks to the following:

Anyone who picked up the first edition and actually enjoyed it, and then shared it!

Everyone from Winding Hall Publishers who first believed in this story. Sarah and Linda for editing and designing the book. You gave it original life.

Everyone at AZ Literary Press for resurrecting the book.

The people who read through my initial drafts and offered criticisms and suggestions: Jimmy, Vinny and Larry. (Sound like a bunch of old gangsters, don't they?)

My fellow Astro Zombies..."We don't care!"

My family and friends who gave me their support and resources. Thank you for believing in me.

Most of all, I want to thank you for picking up a copy of this second edition. I sincerely hope you enjoy reading it as much as I enjoyed creating (and recreating) it for you.

About the Author

Richard Leighland is an old curmudgeon who lives a reclusive life deep in the woods of Minnesota. *House of Fate* is his first published novel.

www.ingramcontent.com/pod-product-compliance
Lightning Source LLC
Chambersburg PA
CBHW011507170626
46812CB00009B/3010